THE ANGELS BRIDGE

WRITTEN BY:
JEANIE ANGELINA STRATTON-REESE

PublishAmerica
Baltimore

© 2011 by Jeanie Stratton-Reese
All rights reserved. No part of this book may be reproduced, stored in a retrieval system or transmitted in any form or by any means without the prior written permission of the publishers, except by a reviewer who may quote brief passages in a review to be printed in a newspaper, magazine or journal.

First printing

This is a work of fiction. Names, characters, places, and incidents either are the product of the author's imagination or are used fictitiously. Any resemblance to actual persons, living or dead, events, or locales is entirely coincidental.

PublishAmerica has allowed this work to remain exactly as the author intended, verbatim, without editorial input.

Hardcover 978-1-4560-5311-6
Softcover 978-1-4560-5310-9
PUBLISHED BY PUBLISHAMERICA, LLLP
www.publishamerica.com
Baltimore

Printed in the United States of America

Acknowledgements

My husband: Willie A. Reese, daughter: Tiffany M. Stratton, grandchildren:

Courtney, Jibe, Caitlin and Cassidy and my mother Mrs. Mary Carrasco

My very good friends: Joy Shagena, and Dustin Johnson for the long hours of dedication in helping proof read the final draft of this book for the publishers and Joy, without your prodding I probably would have never finished this work. A special thank you to Kim Caserta Panter for her hours of work in editing this Novel.

In Memory of

My Son

Derrel Scott Stratton

February 07, 1966 – February 17, 2009

Table of Contents

Chapter 1
KIDDNAPPED 9

Chapter 2
LUTHER 33

Chapter 3
THE PRISON 57

Chapter 4
THE BRIDGE 78

Chapter 5
THE PARK 100

Chapter 6
THREE DAYS OF DARKNESS 118

Chapter 7
NIGHTMARE 138

Chapter 8
DECEPTION 151

Chapter 9
PRISONER 166

Chapter 10
DEATH 182

Chapter 11
ARMAGEDDON 196

Chapter 12
GOODBYE 216
Chapter 13
THE LETTER 241

Chapter 1
KIDDNAPPED

I was awakened by a shrill scream coming from my throat. The reoccurring nightmare was back, haunting me again for the third time this week. I had beads of sweat dripping from my forehead and I was shaking uncontrollably. I tried to recall why this bizarre dream frightened me so badly, and then I remembered, in the dream I was running always running! Climbing the walls, and hiding in the attics of churches and gothic buildings. Running to escape the enemy, even though I didn't know who or what it was. I remember crawling up the wall into a niche where a life size replica of La Pieta statue was housed. It was inside a 16th century European cathedral. There were candles glowing ominously around the huge white marble altar. I slid behind La Pieta statue trying to hide, not be noticed, and yet I knew that I had been.

Somehow, I pulled myself out of the niche and climbed further up the wall until the ornate ceiling was within my reach, and then in the next moment, the ceiling opened and I was in a musty dark, attic, running once again terrified, my heart pounding so hard that I could hear the sound of it beat in my ears. Every hair on the back of my neck stood on end as I felt the swift air of a hand that barely missed me.

I could never see what was chasing me, zapping every bit of breath from me, making me feel like my heart would surely explode from my chest. I only knew that I had to keep running and climbing, trying to get away from what I knew had to be some kind of evil entity that was pursuing me night after night in this bizarre dream.

I looked at the clock on the dresser. It was already 5:00am, and I was tired from being unable to sleep most of the night. I quickly shed my damp silk nightgown and ran the water in the shower until it was nice and warm. I felt a little more refreshed after I had finished bathing. I put on my white terry robe and wrapped my hair in a large Turkish towel and padded barefoot back into the bedroom stopping in front of my large walk-in closet.

My Siamese cat, Boots, lay on the end of the bed watching me curiously as I got dressed for work. I suddenly felt guilty for leaving my kitty alone so much.

"Good morning, Mr. Boots! I'll try to be home early today so that I can keep you company." I ran my hand over his smooth, silky coat with a loving pat before I left the room. As I closed the door behind me, I gave a little sigh of relief to have something to concentrate on rather than that awful dream.

I hailed a checkered cab to Vatican City, where I have been working for the past few months for the Vatican Newspaper, L'Osservatore Vaticano, as the senior reporter of paranormal events that took place in the Vatican City. The job is grueling; because there are so many kooks making claims of seeing demons, serpents, or whatever else their imaginations can conjure with regard to their ideas of good vs. evil. No wonder I have such vivid nightmares I thought to myself.

I softly swore under my breath, "Damn I wish I had worn a light jacket or raincoat." It was cool for this time of year, and was beginning to drizzle a light mist. I seldom remembered that the weather was not anything like Arizona where I was used to going without a jacket. So as usual, I didn't have one with me today. Maybe when I get tired of coming to work with my hair wet and plastered against my head on rainy days, I may be embarrassed enough to at least remember an umbrella. However, knowing me, I doubt it.

The cab driver dropped me off at the gate to the guardhouse, the entrance for the one hundred and ten acre City. I had to show my passport to the guard at the entrance because I haven't been issued a Vatican ID card as of yet and the rules in this little city are so strict that if you don't have a valid ID, you had better show your passport or you would never be allowed to enter the City. The guard nodded me through the gates with a salute, and I quickly ran to the newspaper building trying not to get to wet. I glanced up at the sky and was happy to see signs of the sun peeking through the clouds.

The office was pretty quiet for this time of the morning and the only other person in the building was Heidi Morans, the Administrative Secretary to the Editor-In-Chief.

"Hi Rebecca, you're here bright and early this morning." She greeted me with a warm smile. It didn't make any difference how early anyone got to the office; Heidi was there before them and always had a smile for everyone.

"Hi, I don't look too drowned do I?" I sure didn't want our boss Mr. Bellini getting upset with me for looking unprofessional while at the Vatican.

"You look terrific as usual, but you really should start carrying an umbrella with you. I know you haven't been here very long, but in September we never know whether we are going to have rain or sunshine and sometimes the temperatures can be pretty cool."

"I look that bad, huh?" I said, wrinkling my nose.

"Oh no!" She blushed. "I only meant you could catch you death if you don't start keeping yourself warm in this damp weather."

"It's okay Heidi, I was just teasing you. Besides, I can see myself in the mirror. I am pretty wet. Is there any coffee made yet?" I don't know why I asked; I knew she would have already made a pot. Before she had time to answer, I headed straight for the employees lounge to get a fresh cup."

"Would you like a cup of coffee Heidi?" I asked, I noticed she already had her nose back in her work, wearing a worried frown on her face.

"No thanks! I don't drink coffee. I just make it every morning because I know everyone else gets pretty crabby if they can't start their day with a cup."

The aroma of the coffee coming from the lounge was so inviting that I quickly forgot about the worried frown on Heidi's face as I poured myself a large cup, stirring in the cream and artificial sweetener, until it tasted just the way I liked it

"Thanks for doing this everyday," I said in real appreciation of her steadfast loyalty to all of us at the office. I carried my cup straight back to my desk, sat down, and between gulps of coffee, soon became absorbed in my own work. I was so preoccupied with all the different stories I received in my mail that I didn't even notice when the office became a place of busy typing and chatter.

"Becca!" A male voice called out to me, it had to be Mr. Bellini because he was the only one who remembered that I preferred to be called by my nickname, Becca, instead of my given name Rebecca, which just sounded too formal for me.

"I'm happy to see you are busy, but I need you in my office for a minute," he said.

I hadn't even noticed that the Editor-in-Chief had called out to me three times before I looked up at him with questioning eyes. I put the last article I was reading into my "to do" folder, so that I could take up where I left off. As I stood I laid the folder on the right side of my desk and quickly followed him into his office.

"I just wanted to inform you that we are having a private meeting with the Security Commander in charge of the Swiss Guard tomorrow morning. Something has come up in regards threats to the Holy Father. I was wondering if you have had any communications or leads that might motivate us to get involved?"

"Why would we get involved sir? So far everything I have read has just been the typical sort of communications we always get. Someone saw the devil at the end of his or her bed or someone thinks they are experiencing a vision, or some other nonsense. What would it have to do with us? They don't think anyone here is responsible do they?"

He rolled his eyes and said, "You're the typical reporter, aren't you? Trying to find the answers before I even get a chance to explain what's going on.' He shook his head in disbelief. "Evidently the Pope has been getting letters and phone calls talking about his demise through some supernatural means. I was just wondering if you have had any letters that hinted to any of this. I'm pretty sure that is what the Director wants to know. It's the only reason I can think of that he asked for you in particular to accompany me. "

I was busy thinking how important this could be, and he was patiently waiting for me to say something.

"I'll keep my eyes open of course, but we usually don't get anything that exciting. Is there a story in this for me?" I quickly asked, getting a little excited about the whole idea.

He tapped his pencil against his desk, and seemed to be thinking about this. "I don't know but we will pay close attention tomorrow and if you and I become interested in anything we might publish, we will make sure to jump right on it, won't we?"

"Yes Sir!"

"Okay, than meet me here at 6:30 tomorrow morning and we'll go together to the Security Office to meet Mr. Ferrachi. He has to meet with us early because he has such a busy schedule."

"Alright Sir. You can depend on me. I'll see you bright and early in the morning."

He looked at me respectably, telling me to close the office door behind me. I pulled the frosted glass door shut and walked back to my desk, all the while wondering what this threat could possibly entail. I started paying closer attention to the rest of my mail to keen to anything that might even hint at some kind of threat. I didn't notice a single item throughout the rest of the day, so I concentrated on writing an article that I thought might be interesting to our readers.

My alarm clock started ringing at 4:30 the next morning, and I jumped right out of bed. No bad dreams to keep me awake all night certainly made for a nice refreshing start to the day. After my shower, I dressed in the off-white silk suit I had laid out the night before.

Slipping into my beige high-heeled shoes, I went back into the dressing room to smooth my long jet-black hair, carefully making sure that every hair was in place. I noticed that my green eyes didn't look tired for a change. I leaned forward towards the mirror and carefully applied mascara to my long eyelashes and curled them. All I needed was a little blush and a touch of lip-gloss and along with my umbrella, and I was on my way.

I arrived at the office before Mr. Bellini, and surprisingly before Heidi. I went to the lounge and made the coffee and had just poured myself a cup when Heidi came breezing through the door.

"Oh, thanks Rebecca. Mr. Bellini said you would be in early this morning, but I never expected you here before me. What a nice surprise."

"Are you ready?"

The sound came from behind us. We both turned to see our Editor-in-Chief dressed in a nice dark brown suit, beckoning me towards the door. I put my cup down and followed him to the elevator and waved goodbye to Heidi.

We grabbed one of the cabs that were always waiting outside the office and rode the short distance to the Vatican Guard Headquarters, chatting about the cool weather, which was nice and sunny for a change.

Everything was so formal here. The guard upon having our papers inspected saluted us, and then again when we entered the Papal Palace. Then we were saluted a third time at the end of the long corridor that led in one direction to the Administrators office and the other to the Papal Apartments. It was there that four Swiss Guard snapped to attention two of them crossing their swords in front of them to keep us from going in the direction of the Papal Apartments. The other two led us to Mr. Ferrachi's office. We were asked to wait outside while one of the guards went through the massive, ornately carved doors to announce us. I looked around thinking to myself how I had always wanted to see the Vatican, but never in my wildest dreams did I ever think I would see it from the inside. It was absolutely beautiful. The antique art was so amazing, more than anything we could do today, especially when you thought about what the artists from centuries past had to work with. I was looking around, absolutely mesmerized by the beauty, when the door opened and we were asked to enter.

A young priest led us to a sitting room where we were offered tea, and a large tray of various pastries. Before either of us even had a chance to sit down, the young priest said:

"Mr. Ferrachi is running about a half hour late. Please enjoy yourselves until his arrival. There are some Vatican picture albums on the side table that you might enjoy looking through."

We must have waited for forty-five minutes or longer before Mr. Bellini began pacing the floor. He wasn't very good at waiting patiently when people were late for scheduled meetings. Before very long he pulled a white hankie out of his pocket and began to wipe his brow. I noticed that his balding head was beginning to take on sheen from the light perspiration that was gathering there.

"Mr. B, please sit down, you're making me nervous with your pacing back and forth. I'm already starting to shake my leg back and forth and I don't usually do that unless I'm really freaked out. Before Mr. Ferrachi gets here we are going to both be nervous wrecks and he night think we are crazy."

"Well you think he would realize other people have work to do besides him. This is damned rude of him!" He grumbled.

"Do you want me to reschedule our meeting?" I asked. I could tell he was beginning to get angry and he didn't use very nice language when he got angry. I didn't want him to do anything to embarrass the newspaper.

"No! We will give him ten more minutes and if he's not here we will leave and he will have one hell of a time getting an appointment with me again. "

"All right let's lea…" I started to say. Before I had a chance to get the words out of my mouth, the door opened and the most handsome man I had ever seen in my life walked into the room. His large beautiful eyes were a deep cobalt blue with a violet cast. His hair was brownish blonde, not dish water brown but a real golden brownish blonde, and it had a soft natural curl to it. His skin was fair with almost an ivory tone. His strong features made him look like he had been chiseled out of marble like one of the Greek God Statues that grace the Vatican grounds. He had an angelic look about him, yet I sensed that he was someone that you wouldn't want to reckon with. If there was such a thing as love at first sight then I was experiencing it.

"Hello." He reached his hand out to shake Mr. Bellini's' hand. "Mr. Bellini," he said, bowing his head in greeting, and then he extended his hands to me, and as he took both of my hands into his large hands, smiling down at me I felt a strange electrical tingle go through my body. It took me by surprise and I quickly pulled my hands away from his. I couldn't remember anyone who had touched me ever having that effect on me before. I blushed and lowered my eyes in embarrassment. Suddenly I felt like a fool! How would he know what kind of an effect his handshake had on me?

"Miss Malone I believe. Rebecca Malone?" He seemed to ignore the rude reaction of my pulling away from him.

I stared into his smoldering eyes and I wondered if he could see the confusion in mine. I could only think that now he even made my name sound like music coming from his lips.

Gathering my thoughts together, I said: "Becca," while still staring at him. I suddenly wished I had just kept my mouth shut as I noticed a twinge of amusement in his beautiful cobalt blue eyes.

"Becca it is than! My name is David Rafe, "Rafe" to my friends. I'm sorry Mr. Ferrachi may not be able to attend this meeting. He has been called to an emergency situation at St. Peters Basilica. Since I will be working with the two of you on the matter we are about to discuss, he sent me ahead of him so that you wouldn't have to wait any longer. He asked me to give you both his apologies, and said he hoped he could return before you left. Shall we go into the inner office?" Once inside he quickly pulled out a chair for me to sit in.

I said, "Thank You," still not looking into his eyes

Mr. Bellini looked at him anxiously. "I trust that whatever has happened at St. Peters isn't serious" It was more of a question than a statement, and I'm sure this was purposely done in hopes that Mr. Rafe would fill us in.

"Oh surely it is something he can handle." Mr. Rafe said, brushing off the question. "I'm sure both of you are wondering what this supernatural threat could have to do with your newspaper, so I will explain it as best as I can. Did either one of you know that the Popes sister is a nun here at the Vatican?"

Mr. Bellini and I both shook our heads and said "No" in unison.

"She is the Senior Cook for the Papal household and cooks all of her brothers meals herself." He must have realized that I was about to ask what that had to do with anything, because he held his hand up to stop me before I spoke.

"You'll understand all of this shortly, please let me continue."

I nodded in agreement and leaned back in my chair feeling stupid for not letting him tell his whole story before I interrupted him. His eyes locked with mine for a brief moment and then looking over at Mr. Bellini he continued; "Yesterday after morning mass one of the younger nuns came up to the Holy Father and handed him a note that stated that his sister was very ill, and that none of the nuns could talk her into seeing the Vatican Doctor. The nuns were sure that if the Pope would come and see her, he might be able to talk her into seeing the doctor. The Pope repeated the contents of the note to his secretary in Italian, telling him that he would be right back after he went and spoke to his sister. His young assistant knew that there were Security Guard all over the Papal Palace and so he wasn't worried about the Pope going by himself. However after a couple of hours passed without the Holy Fathers return, he became anxious and hurried to the kitchen to find out what was taking so long. He knew the Pope would not go anywhere without letting him know, because he usually went everywhere with his Holiness. When the assistant walked into the kitchen the Holy Father was not there. His sister however, was at the stove singing in Italian while she prepared her brothers lunch. He asked her where the Holy Father was and she didn't know what he was talking about. When he told her what had taken place she looked at him in wide-eyed shock. She hadn't been sick and she wanted to know which nun had come to the Papal apartments with the message. When he looked around the kitchen he didn't see anyone that resembled the young nun. He immediately went to the Swiss Guard. He returned a little later with two Swiss Guard and Mr. Ferrachi. They called all the nuns together who were in the Papal household for the Popes Assistant to pick out the one who was with the Pope. The Assistant couldn't identify the girl out of all the nuns there. He said she was dressed the same, but that it was none of these girls. Obviously the girl was an imposter."

'THE POPE HAS BEEN KIDNAPPED?' It was Mr. Bellini that interrupted this time, and it made me feel a little better when Mr. Rafe raised his hand again, but this time it was to quiet Mr. Bellini.

"Let me finish, and then we'll discuss it." He glanced at me again as if to see if I was going to say anything, but I quickly looked down at my hands, not wanting our eyes to lock again.

"At about 11:00 am, a few minutes before Monsignor Bante, the Popes Personal Secretary, was getting ready to see if the Holy Father was ready to take his mid morning walk in the Vatican gardens, a courier delivered a large envelope addressed to Monsignor Bante. Since he was in charge of all the Popes mail, he found nothing odd about this until he opened the envelope and inside was a picture of the Holy Father, gagged and bound sitting on the floor in some dingy room that appeared to be a basement somewhere. The Monsignor thought it was a joke, as he didn't know that the Pope was missing yet. There was one small paper that had some printing, in what looked like red crayon scrawled across it, making it almost illegible. But the letters were large enough that he could tell that it said, MORT, which translated to English means DEAD.

The only other information on the note was that more details would be sent through the Vatican Newspaper L'Osservatore Vaticano. It was merely signed ABADDON which translated means the destroyer, destruction, and is another name some have for Satan. Of course Monsignor Bante immediately took the picture and the note to Mr. Ferrachis office, and was at once told about the mornings events. This is all that we know at the present time, of course we have patrols looking everywhere for the Pope, but we are trying to keep it low profile as long as we can."

"So we don't know whether the Pope is dead, or going to be murdered, or where he is, or who the kidnappers are?" I said.

Mr. Bellini who was wide eyed at this point looked at us and said, "Mort means already dead, you don't suppose…"

Mr. Rafe did not let him get in the last words. "Let's hope not, but we really don't know anything, if it is just a kidnapping, they wouldn't want him dead, but if it is a threat against the Vatican and the Catholic Church, well, who knows! All we can do is wait for their next move, while we are looking for his Holiness. Becca, that's where you job is going to come in, checking out anything that comes across your desk that might give us any clue. Do you think you want to take this job? It might become pretty time consuming?"

He was doing it again, his eyes locked with mine once more, and it was almost as if he could read my thoughts. I couldn't tear my gaze away from his and it took what seemed like an eternity before I answered him.

"Mr. Rafe, it is my job. It's what I do. I have all the time in the world to be consumed by it."

Mr. Bellini looked at Mr. Rafe and said, "What exactly is your job? Are you going to be working with Mr. Ferrachi the Administrator of Security, or with us?"

Mr. Rafe looked at him and said, "let's just say that my job title is a little different, I am called the Leading Prosecutor by my superiors, and I will be working with Security and with both of you, so we should all get to know each other pretty well during the course of our work."

Mr. Bellini and I looked at each other. Obviously he wasn't going to give us any more information about what his job entailed.

The next few days passed with nothing new coming across my desk, and according to Mr. Bellini, there was no news on the Pope's location. He went over to the Administrators' office almost every day on his lunch hour to give a report and to get any updates on their end. So far we had been lucky enough to keep the kidnapping out of the media, but we knew we wouldn't be able to keep up the farce much longer, as the Vatican Prelates would be demanding an audience with the Pope sooner or later.

Monsignor Bante, the Popes Personal Secretary left for his home in France, and the rest of the staff was told that his Holiness had left on an emergency visit to Bosnia. With both men gone, it was possible that we could buy a little more time.

I found myself daydreaming a lot lately and it made me angry because my daydreams were always fixed on David Rafe. I still wondered why he left such an indelible impression on me, and how he could manage to lock his gorgeous eyes with mine like he was trying to read my mind. I wondered if it was all a figment of my imagination.

I crumbled up the story I was writing and tossed it in the trashcan, I had to stop this nonsense. It was ridiculous! Damn! I had only met the man once, and probably would never see him again as Mr. Bellini made the daily trip to the Security Office. My thoughts were interrupted when Mike Warner, a nice looking young man with sandy blonde hair and brown eyes, a year around tan, and only a few years younger than me, also an American, stopped by my desk.

"Say, good looking." He said. "Are you having troubles keeping your thoughts gathered the last few days? I notice you've been tossing a lot of your print. That's not like you."

He pulled out the chair next to me and looked around to make sure no one was listening and said, "You're falling in love with me aren't you? That's why you can't work!" He started laughing because he had been trying to entice me to go out with him ever since I had come to work here without much success, I might add.

I stuck my tongue out at him, and started laughing as well because he sounded so sincere.

"Really Rebecca, is there something wrong? I keep seeing you frown, and I'm not used to that lovely forehead of yours being furrowed up like that. I just wanted you to know that if you need help with anything, and I do mean anything, or if you just need a good listener, I'm here for you. I'd much rather have an intimate relationship with you, but I will settle with just being friends if that's what you want."

"Mike, I'm just fine really! Your offer of friendship means more to me than you know because I know it's probably a hard thing to offer. Please don't waste your time on me. Go Out! Find yourself a nice young girl to love you. You are such a sweetheart and have so much to offer the right person."

He was absentmindedly twirling a paperclip on my desk, but when he finally looked up he said, "I thought I had found the right girl, but she doesn't want me. I can't even get her to go out to dinner with me as a friend!" He pouted, pushing out his lower lip.

"All right Mike, enough already. If you don't have any plans for lunch tomorrow I'll go to lunch with you, but I have a date with Mr. Boots my cat, tomorrow night!"

He jumped up from the chair beaming, and his voice rang with excitement, but he tried to act nonchalant, as he said, "Atta Girl," and headed back to his desk, but not before he gave me a quick wink.

After work that evening I went home to my flat and fixed myself a small chef salad and a glass of wine, fed Mr. Boots, washed my dishes and settled in on my large overstuffed sofa with my cat in my lap and a stack of editorials to look at. When I was finally tired, I picked up Boots and went to bed. It wasn't long before I could hear Boots steady breathing and I knew he was asleep, but every time I closed my eyes all I could see were intense cobalt blue eyes staring into mine. When I did finally fall asleep I had the nightmare again, but this time while running away, David Rafe was always extending his hand out to me saying. "Becca, grab my hand!" but when I would go to reach for his hand it would disappear. This just added to the confusion of this awful nightmare, and I tossed and turned all night.

I must have slept through the alarm, because when I woke it was already six thirty. Which meant I had to hurry if I wanted to get to work on time. I took a quick shower, washed my hair and pulled it back into a braid. When I was dressed I hailed a cab and got to work with just ten minutes to spare.

Mike had a big smile for me, and I didn't even smile back. I hadn't had my coffee yet.

I stayed awake half the night tossing and turning, and I just wasn't in a very friendly mood this morning. I walked over to my desk, sat down and got right to work without looking at anyone. I didn't even look up when Mr. Bellini came into the office. About 10:00 am Heidi came over to my desk and said:

"Come on Rebecca, let's go have a cup of coffee."

It startled me not only was I deep in thought, but also because I knew she didn't drink coffee, and I had never seen her take a break before.

It didn't take me long to say okay when I saw the concerned look on her face. She closed the door behind us as soon as we went into the employees lounge and pulled the blinds closed. I poured myself a cup of coffee, and of course she said no when I offered her a cup.

I asked, "Is something wrong Heidi? I noticed you closed the blinds."

She quickly went back to the door, opened it and taped a piece of paper on it, closed the door and turned and looked at me.

"I also put a note on the door saying we were having a private meeting."

"Heidi, for goodness sakes, what's wrong?"

"Rebecca, I could get fired over what I'm about to tell you, but I don't know what else to do. I'm afraid that Mr. Bellini and Security might do something that just might get the Pope killed."

I stared at her in disbelief. I didn't even know that she knew anything that was going on and here she seemed to know more than I did!

"What on earth are you talking about Heidi, doesn't Mr. Bellini know that you are talking with me?"

"No! He's gone over to security already this morning, that's why I can talk to you now! He tried to sneak out without you seeing him because he didn't want you to suspect anything with him leaving early."

"For Gods sake Heidi! What is going on? Quit beating around the bush and tell me!"

She was beginning to make me angry at all this enigmatic talk.

"There is no way I can tell you this without Mr. B knowing that I told you, but I don't know what else to do." She said.

"You already said that Heidi. Evidently you think it is something that I should know, so just tell me. We'll worry about Mr. B when I know what's going on," I stated.

She pulled a chair out from the table and sat down across from me. Her hands were shaking.

"Yesterday morning Mr. Bellini got a call from someone named Mr. Baragio. He wouldn't tell me what his business was so Mr. Bellini refused to talk to him. Mr. Baragio finally said it was concerning Pope Pius XIII! And that is all he would tell me. So of course Mr. Bellini took the call. Well Mr. Baragio wanted the Popes Secretary to go to the Papal apartment and bring him the letters about Fatima written by that nun."

"Sister Lucia!" I said.

"Right. That's her. He said the secretary would have a key to get into the box where they were kept in the Popes bedroom."

"The Popes secretary is in France." I said.

"That's what Mr. B. said. So Mr. Baragio called back a few minutes later and said the Pope had a key on him that they wanted you to come and get. You and no one else."

"Okay, so why wasn't I told about it?"

" Mr. B wanted to talk to Mr. Ferrachi about it before they told you! To make a long story short Mr. Ferrachi met with a David Rafe, whoever he is, and they decided it was to dangerous for you to go, so I think Mr. Bellini plans on going himself, and I'm afraid that they will get the Pope killed if it's not done the way Mr. Baragio wants it done. He sounds like someone that no one should tangle with. So you see, I felt like I had to let you know. Since security will be going through me to Mr. Bellini, he felt like I should know everything that was going on with the Pope. The only people in this office that know any of this are Mr. Bellini, you and me."

By the time Heidi was finished telling me I was so angry I was shaking.

"Don't worry Heidi, you won't get fired. You did the right thing telling me! I am going over to Mr. Ferrachi's office right now and talk to them about this. I think you're right. The plans that they have will endanger the Pope. When is this all supposed to take place?" I asked.

"I don't know, Mr. B never discussed that part with me."

I stood up quickly. "Call me a cab. I hope they have not already left to get the key." I walked to my desk and grabbed my bag and ran for the elevator, not stopping to talk to anyone on my way out.

The guards informed me that Mr. Ferrachi was not in his office, and that they weren't sure where he was. They thought that Mr. Bellini was with him. Since it was too early for lunch there was probably only one other place they could be.

"Could you please take me to Mr. Rafe's office I asked.

The taller guard looked at me and said.
"Signore?"
Acting like he didn't know whom I was talking about.
"Look " I said. "I'm talking about Mr. David Rafe and since you were here last week the same time I was, I'm assuming that you are giving me the run around and I don't care whose guard you are, if you don't take me to Mr. Rafes' office right now, I'm going to make a scene like you have never seen in this Palace before and you won't soon forget it."

Their faces both went ashen and they looked at each other, realizing that I was about to make a big scene. Before either of them had a chance to answer me, the door across the hall opened and David Rafe, with an amused look on his face said,

"Let her in my office gentlemen, before she throws a tantrum right here in the corridor."

I gave both guards a smug look and walked past them into Mr. Rafe's office.

"They would have thrown you out, you know," he said as he closed the door, behind me.

"They're only doing their job." He spoke to me in such a calm voice, and I was further infuriated.

"I figured they would, but I would have put up a fight you can bet on that."

His demeanor remained calm, and ignoring my last remark, he said,

"Please Becca, may I call you Becca? Please sit down. It must be something very important to bring you here by yourself this morning, and considering how angry you seem to be."

"Mr. Rafe…"

He interrupted me, leaning across his large ornate desk and looking softly into my eyes, he said, "Rafe, just plain Rafe, if you remember. I said my friends call me Rafe and I certainly hope we will become friends since we will be spending so much time together until this whole ordeal is over. Now please calm yourself and tell me what is going on."

Oh Drat! I thought. That thing he did with his eyes, I could feel my temper beginning to subside just from him looking at me. "Rafe then.

It's been brought to my attention that I am being left out of some very important decisions that are being made here. Since I thought I was a part of finding his Holiness I want to know am I on this job or not?"

His eyes never left my face. "May I ask who brought this to your attention Becca?"

"No! You many not! It isn't important."

"Alright then!" He said, in an amused tone. "You are a most important part of this investigation, of course. But it is my duty to make sure that no harm comes to any of my staff. I assume you know what Mr. Barragio has asked then."

"I do! And I don't understand how the three of you could consider leaving the Pope open to harm or the possibility of being killed. I am not an idiot; I am capable of taking orders. If these people were brave enough to come in here and kidnap the Pope, I am sure we don't want to anger them any further by not doing what they ask. Now may I go and pick up the Key?" My expression was indignant as I looked into those gorgeous eyes, but I was far too angry again to become mesmerized by him.

Rafe stood up from behind his desk, still calm, but his voice was commanding.

"No, absolutely not! It is out of the question, there will be no more discussion on the subject. I am not going to endanger your life."

I interrupted him before he had a chance to say anything else; I stood up from my chair. We were both standing now staring at each other, neither one of us giving in one inch.

"Is that your final decision, or don't we all get to vote on it?"

"No!" He said. "The decision is mine and mine alone. My mind has been made up. I will not jeopardize any of my employees, especially not you."

I looked at him wide eyed. I could not believe he was actually telling me no. I opened my mouth and said,

"But…"

He looked at me hard now and I saw golden flecks starting to mingle with the blue in his eyes.

"But nothing!"

I knew in an instant that I was wasting my time.

"No!" He said once again to make sure that I understood perfectly.

I picked up my purse and as I walked toward the door I said, "Than we have nothing further to discuss here today. I'll let you know if I get any correspondence concerning the Pope," I opened the door, but before I could get it all the way open, he was behind me slamming the door shut, pinning me against it. I could feel his warm breath on my neck, and his hypnotic smell was intoxicating me. I was going to turn around to face him, not knowing what I would say because his lovely aroma had completely unnerved me, when he pulled both of his hands way from the door and stepped back. I turned and looked up into black cobalt eyes staring into mine. It took what felt like several minutes before he tore his gaze from mine and said in such a low voice that I almost asked him to repeat himself.

"Becca, please don't be angry with me. I had no intention of our starting off on the wrong foot. I just don't want to see you hurt by anyone. Please understand my position."

If it hadn't of been such an unimaginable possibility, it sounded like he was pleading with me. I had no idea what to say to him. I was still shaky from the nearness of him so I just nodded and before he had a chance to say anything else, I quickly walked out the door.

While I waited for the cab outside the Papal Palace, I leaned back against the cold stonewall, wondering what had just happened in there. He had said no, that did infuriate me, but now I was lost in the confusion of my own thoughts. Confused because never in my twenty-eight years could I ever remember anyone having such a profound affect on me. I remember thinking the same thing the day I had first met him. But now he actually made me feel like I was a tongue-tied teenager that couldn't even respond to him. I didn't want to be very far from him, and yet his magnetism frightened me to the point that I was afraid to be near him. I had no idea how I would react. I had always been in control with men, always able to somehow convince them around to my way of thinking. And yet here he was, not only disagreeing with me, but turning me into a junior high girl who could neither think nor speak in his presence. I vowed I would not be angry the next time that

I met with him. I wanted to get to know this man who had unraveled my logical thinking and had made me smolder inside.

I returned to the office at almost one o'clock, and Mike was just getting off of the elevator as I was entering.

"Oh, Rebecca, you're back. I didn't think you'd be here so I was going to lunch. Are we still on or do we need to reschedule?"

I could see the hope in his eyes and I hated to put him off.

"Mike, let me run up and see if there is anything that can't wait until after lunch. I haven't eaten yet either and I'm starving."

Mike caught the elevator back up to the third floor with me and when I checked my agenda, Heidi had left open a large slot for me, so I had plenty of time for lunch. We left together and Mike hailed a cab.

"So Mike, have you decided where we are going to eat?"

He had a huge grin on his face.

"But of course, my darling. I made reservations at the Taverna Angelica, a nice little restaurant right outside of St Peters' Square, that way we have plenty of time to eat and chat before we have to go back to work."

The restaurant was a tiny place set back in a cubbyhole that appeared to be subterranean. I'm sure I would have never found it on my own. It was quaint and impeccably clean, inside and the food was absolutely delicious. Mike had the lentil soup with pigeon breast and I had the breast of duck in balsamic reduction. I didn't really have the appetite as I first thought and barely picked at my food. Mike chattered away about all the things going on in the office and his trip to some of the museums over the weekend. He was totally oblivious to the fact that I really wasn't paying much attention to anything he had to say and was just happy to be in my company. It made me feel quite guilty when I thought about it so I tried extra hard to listen to everything he said, but my mind kept going back to this morning. Over and over the part where Rafe stood behind me, pinning me against the door and all the feelings that were going on inside of me. I wondered how he felt, did he feel anything? Or was he just trying to calm me down so I wouldn't leave in such a snit.

I had to know what was going on inside his mind. Did he feel any of the emotions that I was?

"Well did your...?"

Rebecca? Where are you?"

As soon as he said my name I realized that I hadn't been listening at all.

"I'm sorry Mike, what did you ask me? I'm just a little preoccupied today. I guess I didn't get enough sleep last night."

"That's okay. I just asked you if you had met the guy they brought in to work in the Swiss Guard headquarters that is supposed to be the highest investigator in the Church? I hear he is here in Rome and we are all wondering why."

I looked at him a little shocked. I really didn't know what Rafes official job was.

"Oh Do you mean David Rafe? I've met him, but I don't know what his title is or whether he is from here or where he is from."

Mike looked at me for a minute. After he wiped his hands with his napkin, he shrugged his shoulders and said, "I don't really know what his name is I just thought maybe you did. Do you want any desert? Otherwise I will ask for the check."

I shook my head no and excused myself to go to the ladies room and washed my hands. When I came out Mike was waiting for me at the cash register.

When we got into the cab outside the restaurant, he slid next to me and pecked me on the cheek and promptly moved back to his side of the seat, and said,

"That was fun, promise we'll do it again."

I looked at him shaking my head, "You never give up do you Mike? Thanks for the lovely lunch and yes; we'll do it again. But remember, friends, okay?"

He just laughed and patted my hand.

When we walked into the office, Heidi motioned me over to her desk

"Rebecca, I finally got to meet David Rafe. Isn't he gorgeous? I wonder if he is married? I didn't see a wedding ring!" She bubbled over with excitement!

I looked at her in surprise.

"Really! What did he want?"

"He actually came to ask you out to lunch! I told him you already had a lunch date with one of our writers, and he said to tell you he was sorry he missed you."

"Thanks Heidi" I tried to act as nonchalant as I could, as I walked away from her desk..

"Wait! Is he married? I'm dying to know!" She said

"I don't think so." Funny I had never even considered him being married to someone and never noticed whether he wore a wedding ring or not. "You know Heidi, I'm not sure. Why don't you ask Mr. Bellini and then let me know too. Just out of curiosity."

"Okay! I'll ask him just…"She stopped talking, looked down at her typewriter, quickly put a piece of paper in it and started typing, and then I saw why. Mr. Bellini had come walking through the door from lunch.

"Miss Malone, may I see you in my office please. Now!"

OH, OH, Mr. B never called me Miss Malone unless he was angry with me. I wondered if he already knew about my visit to the Papal Palace this morning.

"Yes, Sir!"

I winked at a wide-eyed Heidi as I walked past her desk to follow behind him.

"Close the door behind you, and sit down." He motioned to the chair across from his desk. "I want you to tell me just who it was that told you that Mr. Baragio called I know the answer, but I want to hear it from you."

I wished I were still at Taverna Angelica with Mike; at least his lively chatter had made me forget just how angry I was this morning. Now I could feel my temper coming back with a vengeance.

"A very dear friend of mine filled me in, not only for the Holy Fathers protection but for your protection as well, and that's all I have to say about it."

"No" he said. "I want to hear a name! You know what is going to happen to her don't you? She will lose her job over this. Don't sit there looking at me so innocently, when you know how I feel about any conversation from my office being carried to other employees. I don't care what the reason is!"

"You can't do anything without a name from me. Someone overheard you talking to another employee, and than they came and told me." I wasn't good at lying. I hoped the expression in my eyes didn't give me away, but I was not going to let Heidi get fired over this. "So can we please just drop it and let me go back to work? Mr. Rafe refused to let me pick up the key, so what difference does it make how I found out? It doesn't change anything. Unless you want to fire me for not divulging my source to you, I'm done!"

He stared across his desk at me, but I could tell by his softened expression that I had won the battle.

"Go back to work." He said.

"Nothing like this had better happen in this office again. And come and talk to me before you go running over to the investigators. Am I making myself clear?"

"Definitely! I gave a sigh under my breath. "Can I go now?'

He merely nodded at me, so I quickly got up and left his office smiling at Heidi as I walked past her desk.

Mike looked at me with a curious look as I walked past him, but I just shrugged my shoulders and kept walking.

When Mr. Bellini left before the rest of us, I asked Heidi to put Mr. Baragio's call through to me if he happened to call. I was working on a story about one of the saints who was about to be beatified when Heidi buzzed me on my phone.

"It's him!"

She said as she put the call on hold. 'I'm not leaving this office until you tell me what he has to say."

"Paranormal Events, Miss Malone speaking."

A deep male voice on the line said, "Miss Malone, this is Nicholas Baragio, I'm sure that by now you know who I am."

"What can I do for you Mr. Baragio?" I hoped that Rafe or Mr. Ferrachi hadn't said anything about their change in plans, because obviously I couldn't deal with that on my own.

"I would like for you to come and pick up the key from the Pope this evening if it's at all possible. You need to make sure that you come alone though. I am giving the directions to you and you alone. So if anyone comes with you or after you either, I will know that you gave him or her the address and this would not be a good thing for either the Pope or for you. Do you understand?"

I decided to tell him about the change in plans and then decided against it I knew it would cause problems for me if I didn't tell him. But at least the problems would only involve me and not the Pope.

"Yes Mr. Baragio, I understand you perfectly clear. But since I have to come alone and you don't want me to tell anyone, I would feel a whole lot safer if you allowed me to do it during daylight hours. I don't know my way around Rome that well and I really don't relish looking for the address after dark."

There was a long pause on the other end of the line. I heard some muffled voices.

Perhaps he had covered the phone, because I got the distinct feeling that he was conferring with someone else and didn't want me to hear. "Mr. Baragio, are you there?"

"Can you be here at 9:00 am tomorrow morning? That is the only concession we can make."

"I'll be there!" He gave me directions and I wrote them down on my message pad, ripped the paper from the pad and stuffed it into my purse.

"Don't worry, I'll be there on time."

"You do that and make sure no one else gets those directions!" That was the last thing he had to say, and then the phone went dead.

I sat at my desk drumming my fingernails on the enameled desktop trying to decide whether I wanted Heidi to know anything or not. I didn't want her to get into any trouble

The less people who knew, the better. What if something happened though? I had to tell someone. I thought about it for a while and decided not to tell anyone. If something happened they would find me eventually, either alive or dead. I just couldn't risk anyone else getting involved or getting hurt. I looked own at the pad I had written the directions on and ripped off the next two blank pages just to make sure that nothing had left an imprint through the paper.

I straightened out my desk, picked up my purse and on the way out the door I told Heidi that Mr. Baragio would call back tomorrow sometime to talk to Mr. Bellini. I don't think she believed me but she just sighed and said, "Okay Rebecca, I'll see you in the morning.

Chapter 2
LUTHER

The morning started out well enough. The sky was a brilliant blue and I could feel the warm glow from the sun, even though it was fairly early in the day. I caught a cab and gave the driver the address Mr. Barachi had given me. He gave me a strange look. "Are you sure you want to go there Lady? That's a pretty remote and seedy area of Rome."

My heart started to pound a little bit. I was pleased that I had decided to leave a note explaining my whereabouts and the address on my dining room table just on the chance I didn't return.

The cab driver was looking in the rear view mirror waiting for me to answer.

"Lady?"

"Yes take me there. I'll be fine."

I gave my bravest smile to him, but in my mind I couldn't help wonder what I had gotten myself into. Maybe Rafe had been right when he told me that it wasn't safe.

I couldn't think about that right now. I had to focus on my reason for going to pick up the key and that was it. Maybe if I was lucky I would be able to get an update on the Pope. Hopefully he was still alive. I had made up my mind that I would insist on seeing him before I left the premises.

As we drove, my mind wandered both to the office and to Heidi. She had sounded so surprised when I called this morning and told her I wouldn't be in for the day. I explained I had some important personal business to attend to and that if I happened to finish early enough, I would be in. I wished I had asked her not to tell Mr. Bellini that Mr. Baragio called yesterday evening, but I decided that if I had she might get suspicious of what I was up to. I didn't want to even begin to imagine how he would react to the whole situation. I especially didn't want to even fathom about how David Rafe would take it.

"Here we are, lady! This is the address. Make sure you guard your purse as pick pocketers and thieves are prevalent in this part of town."

"Thanks for the advice," I said as I paid him. "I'll keep my eyes open."

I closed the cab door and stepped up on the curb. It was on a corner and the lot was vacant. What should I do now, I wondered. I shouldn't have let the cab driver leave, because I had absolutely no idea how I was going to find out where I was supposed to be going. There was not a soul on the streets that I could ask. I was trying to consider which direction I wanted to go when a black limousine pulled up next to me and the passenger side window rolled down, out of the tinted window, a greasy haired man with a dark complexion and sunglasses on his head looked at me, and in a heavy Italian accent said. "You are Rebecca Malone, I presume?"

He looked me up and down in a way that made me involuntarily cringe with disgust.

"Yes, and who are you?"

"I am Nicholas, Nicholas Baragio."

He slid over to the far side of the seat so that I could get in next to him.

As I got into the car my heart began to pound wildly. First of all, Mr. Baragio didn't sound Italian to me over the phone and secondly, I had never thought I would be going anywhere other than the address that he had given me on the phone. Now how would anyone find me if something went awry. We rode in silence until we came to an old house that looked like it had been abandoned for years. The driver parked the car in the driveway. I looked out the window at the weeds that were growing up so high that you couldn't see in any of the windows. There was trash littered everywhere.

Nicholas Baragio got out of the car and began walking up the steps that led to the porch without even looking behind him to see if I had gotten out. I had to run to catch up to him. When we reached the top of the steps we went in through a side door that led down into an old kitchen that smelled of rancid grease and mold.

"Wait here," He commanded. "I'll be right back."

He walked through French doors that led to another room as I waited in the Kitchen. I took the opportunity to look around. Though the kitchen needed a desperate cleaning, it was decorated with marble floors and Spanish tile on the walls. The cabinets were made of a heavy wood, I couldn't place what kind, but it was ornately carved with a beautiful relief carving of vines cascading down the sides and around the edges of each cabinet door. No expense had been spared in the house. The ceiling was done in a beautiful carved plaster that was intricately designed with different floral motifs and the same vine pattern that ran down the cabinets graced the beams surrounding the ceiling. One thing that was odd and stood out to me was that all the walls were painted black, which only added to the

Overall dinginess of the room. There were no windows at all to let in any natural light. As I was puzzling over this, the French doors opened and Mr. Baragio motioned me into the next room. It was as elaborately decorated as the kitchen, even more ornate. The Italian furniture was decorated in stunning brocades. The carpet was black with a green vine design running through it. Velvet pillows were strewn around the floor. Strange, the walls in this room were also painted black, and lit black candles graced the tables and fireplace mantle. I noticed another man relaxing on a pile of pillows on the floor and a young girl, who I presumed to be between sixteen and seventeen feeding him grapes. He also had a dark complexion and large brown eyes. He looked at me curiously, but never acknowledged my presence aloud.

In one corner of the room, I saw the pope gagged and tied to a chair. His clothes had been ripped, and he appeared as though he had been beaten. He was very dirty and I wondered why he had been treated so cruelly. I rushed toward him to comfort him, but a strong arm reached out and blocked my way, yanking me back so hard that I could feel the welts rising before I even had a chance to pull away.

"I only want to make sure His Holiness is not badly harmed. Let me go," I yelled at Mr. Baragio.

I felt myself being grabbed by the back of my hair an thrown viciously to the floor. My forehead bumped against a chair leg as I slid into it, and I could feel a lump quickly raising over my eye..

"Don't you dare speak or move until you are spoken to, or you will wish you never had." He yelled at me.

I stubbornly rose to my feet and glared at Mr. Baragio.

"You son of a bitch! Don't you ever lay a hand on me again."

He moved toward me with lightening speed, and slapped me hard across the face, I could feel the blood dripping from my nose and the side of my lip.

"You might as well kill me here and now, because I won't take this treatment from you or anyone else!" I screamed as I raised my hand with my fist clenched to hit him. The other man who was lounging on the pillow spoke up.

"Leave her alone Nicholas, we don't want to send her back to the Vatican all beaten up. They will never let her bring us the information we need. From what I can see she is a little spitfire and you might get hurt in the process."

He began laughing with those last words as he rose to his feet and began walking toward me.

Nicholas Baragio looked at him as he backed away from me, though he looked like he would have taken great delight in killing me.

He looked back over at the man who was standing next to me now and said:

"Come on Luther just let me teach her a less…"

"Silence!" Nicholas immediately shut his mouth and just stared at this man he called Luther.

"My name is Luther Ammadon, Miss Malone." He took a hankie out of his breast pocket and started gently dabbing at the blood coming from my nose and the corner of my mouth.

"I'm sorry that Nicholas has treated you like this. Sometimes he is a little too anxious for people to obey him. You are such a beautiful woman, and obviously you are not quite as delicate as you look. A little advice though that temper may get you hurt very badly. You are no match for a man. You are far to feminine to be engaging in arguments with men. Would you like a little glass of wine to calm you down now?"

"No, thank you I'm fine."

He ignored me.

"Nicholas, go and get Miss Malone and myself a glass of wine."

He motioned me to sit on one of the large sofas in the room.

"Sit down and let's have a civil conversation. I should have never let Nicholas take control of this situation, and I do apologize to you. I hope you accept my apology." He said as he smiled a wide grin.

Luther was rather good looking, and appeared to be a gentleman, but there was something about him that made me feel very uncomfortable in his presence. I felt that he was trying to manipulate me with the hope that I wouldn't notice. His eyes were soft and warm, inviting me to trust him, and it was hard to look away from him.

I knew I definitely wanted to get the key from the Pope and get out of this house as fast as I could. I didn't feel safe around either of these men. Mr. Amaddon hadn't mistreated me. In fact if it wasn't for him I would probably be dead by now. The fact that he was involved

"Miss Malone?" He interrupted my thoughts. "It would be easier if you called me Luther since my last name is hard to remember, and if you don't mind I'll call you Becca. I promise that you will be safe here as long as you follow directions. I would rather you didn't talk to the Pope, but we will remove his gag in case there is any information he would like for you to give to his staff, with our approval of course.

A million questions ran through my mind. I found it strange that he knew to call me by my nickname since we hadn't met. How did he know what I was thinking, I thought to myself. How does he know my wish to see the pope? Is he reading my mind? He answered all the questions I was considering. I needed to find out as much about him as I could while I was here, so I decided to try and act at ease in his company.

"Thank You, Luther." His name sounded eerie to me, but I went on. "Do you mind if I ask where you are from? I don't think I have ever encountered a name like Amaddon before?"

"Oh," He said. "I travel so much that I would say I'm from everywhere. There isn't a corner of the earth I haven't been to. You

Becca aren't from here, you are from Arizona in the United States I believe, and you are what, 28 years old? That is such a good age to enjoy life and have fun."

No way Luther, I thought to myself. I am not showing any surprise at your knowledge of me.

"Yes Luther, it is a good age to enjoy life, and I am having fun."

Why would he possibly need any information about me? I was of no importance, and really not even significant to this whole ordeal. Now I was beginning to wonder how I ever got myself involved. Maybe I could get a good story out of it.

Nicholas came back into the room with glasses of white wine and a dish of strawberries and as he sat them on the table in front of us he glared at me. Luther immediately noticed the look he was giving me and said to both of us.

"Lets enjoy the wine and get on with our business. I don't want to keep Miss Malone occupied all day, and I'm sure she is more than ready to leave after the welcome you showed her, Nicholas. Go and call a cab for her and I will take her myself back to the address where you picked her up."

Nicholas grumbled under his breath, but left the room to do what he was told.

"I'll find a time and place to get even with you Miss Malone." He said.

After he left the room, Luther reached into his pocket and pulled out a large golden skeleton key and handed it to me.

"This is the key to the box with the Fatima letters in it. I will have Nicholas call later with instructions where we should meet and when you need to bring back the letters."

He then rose from the sofa, walked to the back of the room, as he reached the Pope he very gently removed the rags that covered his mouth. He began to stroke the Popes head, but His Holiness jerked his head over to the side to keep Luther from touching him. In perfect Latin, Luther asked the Pope if there was any message he wanted me to take back to the Vatican, but the Pope just ignored him and in perfect English said to me.

"Go in peace, my dear child and do not come back to this place, I warn you."

Luther didn't give him another chance to say anything; he just tied the gag back over his mouth and said:

"You had your chance to have a word!" Looking at me but talking to the Pope he said: "If she doesn't come back, the next time they see you, it will be to pick up your corpse."

Those were the cruelest words that I had heard come from Luther's mouth since he had first spoken to me. It was obvious that both of these men knew and loathed each other.

There were so many things I wanted to ask like: Why are you doing this, whom are you working for? Why have you and your friend Nicholas been so mean to this gentle man?

But the only words that came out of my mouth were: "Is there anything else I need to know before I leave?" I couldn't believe it. I was actually help to the Vatican Authorities. So I took a deep breath and said: "Who do you work for Luther?"

He looked at me in silence, his eyes grew cold and then soft again, and all he said was, "All in good time my dear, all in good time. I think we have had a long enough visit today. I will take you to your cab now. And with those final words he opened the front door and walked me to the limousine, lightly holding my elbow as we walked. It was obvious that he knew how to treat a woman. I tried to find a landmark or something that would be familiar to report back to the Vatican, but when we got into the car. Luther blindfolded me and said;

"This is for your own protection, Rebecca."

We rode silently, and when the limousine stopped and he removed my blindfold, I was back in the spot where Nicholas picked me up, and the cab was there waiting for me.

Luther took my hand in his and kissed it, saying:

"We'll meet again soon dear. Please don't make me send Nicholas after you."

When I got in the cab, I gave a big sigh of relief. Was I ever glad that was over. I instinctively took a hankie out of my purse and wiped my hand because it felt damp and slimy where he kissed it. I shivered at the thought.

When we arrived at the Vatican, I asked the cab driver to drop me off at St. Peters Square. That would give me time as I walked to decide whether to go to the office first and turn the key over to Mr. Bellini, or to go ahead and get my scolding over with first and go to the Swiss Guard headquarters and face Rafe. It would probably be safer to hand it over to Mr. Bellini and let him take it to Mr. Ferrachi and Rafe, then I would have a little time before I had to face the music. I knew one thing for sure. I needed to find a ladies room so I could comb my hair and wash my face. I hadn't even looked at myself in a mirror since Nicholas Baragio had attacked me. Just as I was about to climb the steps outside the newspaper office, a Swiss guard limousine pulled up next to me and stopped. The driver got out and opened the door and said: "Miss Malone, would you please accompany me to the Papal Palace?"

I quickly realized that this was not where I wanted to go first. I didn't want anyone to see me the way I looked right now, most of all, Rafe. "I really need to go to my office right now, could you please inform Mr. Ferrichi or Mr. Rafe that I will be there first thing in the morning?"

I quickly turned away from the driver before he had a chance to say anything more, and as I started up the steps I heard the door of the limousine slam, and I assumed that the driver had gotten back in the car to leave, when suddenly someone took hold of my arm to stop me. I turned to see Rafe standing next to me, I know my face must have gone crimson, first of all because my arm was in pain from Nicholas Baragio, and secondly, I looked a mess. Rafe quickly released my arm and I noticed the pained expression on his face as he looked down at me.

"What on earth has happened to you?"

"Rafe, could we please have this conversation tomorrow? I'm in a bit of a hurry." I turned my face away from him hoping that he hadn't noticed the scratch and lump on my forehead.

"I really need to…"

He interrupted before I could finish my sentence.

"No, you're coming with me!" He gently took hold of my hand and started to lead me back down the steps to the limousine, and that same electric tingle that I felt the first time he shook my hand gripped me again. I could not understand it, but I knew that I didn't want to go with him right now, so I tried to free my hand fro his, but I cringed in pain when he just tightened his grip. The muscles in my arm began to throb from my injury. He noticed right away that I was in pain, and he quickly lifted me into his arms to carry me the rest of the way. Tears began to trickle from my eyes, more from the weakness that I felt being near him, as opposed to the pain in my arm. He put me in the car, slid in next to me and asked the driver to just drive around for a while. I turned my head to face the window, embarrassed now because I didn't want him to see me cry, but the ordeal of the day and the tension and fear I had gone through finally caught up with me and I began to cry uncontrollably. He put his arm around me and pulled me close to him. With his free hand, he turned my face toward him and pressed my head to his shoulder. I couldn't help but notice his hard muscled chest, and the sweet aroma that came from him that had so intoxicated me before. He stroked my hair and gently rocked me in his arms and eventually between his sweet scent, the rocking, and his fingers gently stroking through my hair, my crying slowly subsided. We rode in silence for quite a while, and I wanted to stay like this forever, safe and happy with him so near. Finally reality hit me, and I began to pull away from him and sit up straight in the seat. His arm remained resting on the seat behind me for a few minutes, but finally he did pull it back to his side.

He asked, "Are you hungry? It is past suppertime and I am starving." I looked out the window and was surprised that it was beginning to get dark.

"How long have we been riding? I asked wide-eyed.

"It doesn't matter," he said, "as long as you feel a little better now."

He told the driver to take us to an Italian restaurant that he knew was only a couple of blocks away.

"Honestly Rafe, I'm not hungry at all. I've already eaten." I lied.

He cocked his head to the side and looked at me severely, indicating he knew I was lying. But he didn't press the subject any further.

"Never mind Joseph," he told the driver in Italian.

"Just take us to the Appian Way Regional Park."

"Rafe, I really think I had better go home. I've spoiled the better part of your day, and it's getting late. I'm sure you have other engagements this evening." I didn't want to go to the park. That meant questions, and I wasn't ready to answer and of his questions.

He looked at me with a curious smile, and was very quiet for what seemed like an eternity, and finally, he said:

"Becca, I really need to talk to you this evening. I've been waiting for you all day long and this really can't wait, so if you could spare me just a little of your time. I will make sure you get home soon."

What could I say? The poor man had spent the better part of the afternoon with me, while I sat in his car and cried like a child. I owed him that much. And since he hadn't asked me where I had been, I thought maybe I could escape his wrath at least for tonight.

"I'm sorry Rafe I am being selfish. Of course, I'm happy to talk with you."

I smiled at him, and he smiled back, but there was something bothering him, I could see it in his eyes.

When we arrived at the park he spoke to Joseph again in Italian, telling him we were going to walk for a bit. He got out of the car and taking me by the hand of my arm that was not hurt, helped me out of the car. We walked for a few minutes in silence, past bubbling granite fountains, with cherubs holding up the urns the water came from. The sweet scent from the figs that were growing in abundance on the trees perfumed the evening air. We walked along the cobblestone paths until we came upon a small gazebo that had flowering vines growing up and around its posts and the gazebo itself was lit up with tiny clear LED lights that made the whole scene appear to be a setting amongst the stars. It was absolutely breathtaking. The thick carpet of freshly mown grass gave a magical aura to the enormous pine trees in the foreground.

Rafe stopped, and looking at me said:

"Would you like to sit here for a while? It seems to be relatively private."

"Oh yes! This is absolutely incredible it looks like a fairytale. I have never been to this park before. I'm glad you decided to stop."

It was hard to believe that just a few minutes earlier I had wanted to go home.

He led me to a white rod iron bench that was elaborately decorated with swirls of carved iron that made it look like something from the Renaissance era. He motioned for me to sit down. He started to sit next to me, and then as if something warned him not to, he just stood in front of me looking deep into my eyes. It didn't take me long to become completely absorbed in his gaze, and I wished he would take me in his arms again. I wanted to kiss his beautiful lips so badly, that I had to look away from him because I was afraid my expression would give me away. I couldn't speak, so I fidgeted with the lace on my shawl.

"Becca do you want to tell me where you went today, or do you want me to tell you what I already know?"

I looked up at him in total shock. How could he possibly know? I wasn't prepared for this at all. I didn't know what to say. I had to take the chance that maybe he was just bluffing and maybe he didn't actually know, but was instead trying to get me to admit to something he suspected.

"And just where do you think I went Rafe? I didn't know my personal business was anyone else's."

"It is my business when you go somewhere that I absolutely forbid you to go. Obviously you didn't take our conference seriously!"

His eyes never left mine, and I knew he was waiting impatiently for me to give him an answer. I noticed that a muscle in the side of his jaw had started to twitch. I sighed deeply and reached into my purse, pulling out the skeleton key and handing it to him. There was no sense in making him angrier. I had dealt with enough angry men for one day. His eyes still never left mine as he rolled the key around in his hand for a few seconds.

Finally, I said,

"Say something please! I can't bear the way you are looking at me. I just couldn't help myself. Nicholas…er…Mr. Baragio called before I left work yesterday and…"

"I know he called." He said cutting me short, "I don't want to know all the preliminary details, I only want you to tell me why you deliberately disobeyed a direct order?" He continued, "obviously you can't follow orders from your superiors. You are off of the case Becca, the only thing you will be allowed to do from now own is type your paranormal stories, and if you disobey me again, I will make sure you are fired and return to the United states."

Now I was really angry.

"If you listen to me for one minute Rafe, I'll tell you why I disobeyed your order."

"Why should I listen to you Becca? You clearly didn't listen to me."

The twitch was becoming more prominent and the gold flecks that I noticed the last time we argued were beginning to appear in his eyes again and the cobalt blue was beginning to burn that darker blue color again.

"Do you want me to tell you or not?" I defiantly stared at him, waiting for him to answer.

"It better be good Becca."

I told him everything that happened except for my altercation with Nicholas. I finally finished the explanation with. "…And as you can plainly see I made it back safely, and no one was hurt, and you have the key."

His expression was livid.

"No one was hurt! No one was hurt!" He cupped my chin in his hand, turning my head from side to side. "Your mouth is cut, your nose has been bleeding, you have a huge lump on your forehead, and a cut above your eyebrow, and you're trying to tell me no one was hurt! Becca! Who did this to you? I will destroy them!" Now his eyes were full of rage.

I stared at him momentarily, deciding if I should tell him or not. He dropped his hand from my chin and grabbing me by the shoulders, he began to shake me.

"Tell me Becca!"

I winced in pain, and my shawl fell from my shoulders and it was then that he saw the large red welts that had left the perfect imprint where fingers had been wrapped tightly around my arm. There was an area from my elbow to my wrist that was swollen, and black and blue. He looked horrified as he looked back down the length of my arm.

"It's nothing Rafe, in comparison to someone being killed. It is over, leave it at that."

"Oh it's not over, you can count on that! Becca you are going to tell me who did this to you."

He had the most pained expression on his face as he let go of me, and I didn't know until later that it pained him to know that he hadn't been there to protect me.

I pulled my shawl back around me and walked down the gazebo steps onto the grass, wanting to get out of the light. When I reached the cobblestone walkway, he reached out and took my hand and turned me to face him.

"Becca, we are not leaving this place until you tell me who did this to you. We'll stay here all night if we have to. You are going to tell me who did this."

I finally gave in. I was so tired. I just couldn't go on making excuses. In almost a whisper I said,

"It was Baragio, Nicholas Baragio."

Rafe took his fingers and traced it softly from the lobe of my ear down the side of my cheekbone to my chin, lifting my face to look into his eyes.

"This could have been so much worse Becca. That's why I didn't want you to go in the first place. These are dangerous people we're dealing with. A woman has no business up against men like these."

My mind was on repeat over and over. Thinking. Please, please kiss me Rafe. I think I only heard what he was saying as background noise. His hand was pleasantly cool on my chin, and I could still feel the tingle from the tracing of his finger down the sides of my face. I don't think I had ever wanted to be kissed as badly ad I did now by this beautiful man.

He quickly looked away from my eyes.

"Becca, I promise you this; Baragio will pay, and he will pay dearly for what he has done to you. Let's get you home now. I know that you must be completely exhausted."

We walked in silence now along the impressive cobblestone walk back toward the limo. I could feel a tension between us, almost like there was something left unsaid. I was happy that the first part of this ordeal was behind us.

I wondered how I would ever convince him to let me return the Fatima Letters to Luther Amaddon. I hadn't mentioned his name to Rafe yet, and decided that it could wait until later. I knew we weren't finished with this conversation. After he had gotten over the shock of my bruises he would have many questions for me.

We walked a little further and suddenly, without a word, he took hold of my hand and led me over to one of the crumbling catacomb walls and pushing me up against the stonewall he only said:

"God forgive me!" And pulling me close to him, with one hand under my chin, and the other pressed firmly against my back, he tilted my face up to his and cobalt blue eyes hungrily stared into mine and before I had a chance to whisper one word, his mouth covered mine. He kissed me softly at first, but as I responded to his embrace, he kissed me more passionately. I entwined my fingers in his luscious hair pulling his mouth closer to mine completely lost in the moment. He became more passionate; softly tracing my lips with his tongue until I eagerly opened my mouth to taste the sweetness of his hungry embrace. I became lost in ecstasy as his body molded closer to mine, and his hand slid down my back to my waist, pressing me to him. I thought I would die in this sweet moment. My ears began to ring, as his kiss became more and more intense, and then, he pulled his mouth from mine and hungrily kissed my throat, moving further down my neck leaving a hot pleasurable sensation along the path of his kisses, and then just as suddenly as he began the kiss, he abruptly pulled away. Holding me at an arms length from him, he said:

"Oh, Becca, I am so sorry. Please forgive me."

I couldn't catch my breath. My chest was heaving, and the swooning feeling was beginning to subside very slowly. Through my breathlessness, I heard myself say,

"Please Rafe, don't stop. I have wanted this since I first met you. You don't know how much I have thought about a moment like this."

"STOP! Becca, this isn't right."

"What could be wro…"

"Becca, I shouldn't have kissed you like that, or let myself get carried away like I did. I can't talk to you about it now. I'm sorry. Come on, I'll take you home."

I frowned, confused. I had to know what was going on.

"Rafe, did I do something wrong?"

There was a terrible sadness in his eyes. It hurt me to see it there, especially since I didn't know why.

"No, Becca, I did!" And with those final words, he took my hand in his and led me back to the car. Only then did he let go of my hand as he opened the limo door for me.

He gave the driver directions to my flat as we rode the rest of the way in silence. He wandered in his thoughts and I wandered in mine. As we arrived at my house he walked me to the door and with a sad look playing in his eyes he said;

"Becca, I promise you Baragio will pay for what he did to you."

I looked at him, "When will I see you again?" I needed more of him and I hoped this wasn't going to be the end.

He lowered his head and sighed, "Ill see you in the morning. Come to my office, I'm sure Mr. Ferrachi will want to hear your story also. Bring Mr. Bellini with you if you like. We need to debrief you since you won't be on the case anymore."

I was dumbfounded.

"You aren't serious are you? Are you really taking me off the case?"

"I told you I was." He said, "That has not changed. Be in my office by ten-tomorrow morning.

He lowered his head and kissed me on my forehead, and our eyes locked again oh so tenderly. I was beside myself with fear that I would never feel his strong arms around me again, or his lips softly kissing mine.

"Rafe, please tell me this is not the end!"

His eyes looked the saddest I had ever seen.

He deeply sighed again, turned and walked away.

The rest of the evening seemed like it took a lifetime to get through. My mind was full of sweet memories and questions. This day had been more eventful then anything else in the last six months. Rafe's kiss and the reaction I had, followed by his sudden rejection had me completely perplexed. I could have stayed awake for the majority of the night if I had not been so exhausted. I couldn't think anymore. Rafe, Baragio, Amaddon, The Pope…and oh my god, what if Rafe was married? Maybe that is why he apologized, and told me he should not have kissed me. I couldn't think at all anymore, and in spite of everything, I fell into a deep sleep.

The next thing I knew, it was morning. The sun was shining through the window. It was another beautiful day. Then reality hit me. I didn't want to think of the previous day, but the pain in my arm as I stretched, brought everything flooding back into my mind. I was sore all over but thankfully when I looked in the mirror I didn't have the lump on my forehead anymore. Only a light bruise and the small cut on my eyebrow which could be covered with makeup, remained. My bottom lip just looked a little plumper than usual. I checked over my arm, and it still looked pretty bad, but at least it wasn't swollen more than it had been yesterday.

With the intention of lessening Rafes anger, I opted for a long sleeve shirt.

Thinking of Rafe brought up the thought again, what if he was married? I pray that it isn't true. I decided then and there that it would be the only reason I would not want to be near him again.

When I arrived at the office, the first person to meet me was Heidi, and as always full of news.

"Rebecca, David Rafe was here looking for you several times yesterday. He finally insisted on me giving him your address. I hope that was okay. Oh and by the way, I asked Mr. Bellini if Mr. Rafe was married, and guess what? He's not! So, if you aren't going after him, I am. He is just absolutely drop dead gorgeous.

I found myself both elated and disappointed at the same time. If he was married, I knew why he reacted the way he did, but since he wasn't, I couldn't fathom why he would break our embrace so abruptly.

I couldn't think about it now. I told Heidi that it was all right that she gave him my address and then asked her if Mr. Bellini was in his office. She nodded yes and motioned me in.

At ten-o'clock sharp Mr. Bellini and I were sitting in Mr. Ferrachis' office waiting for our meeting with him and Rafe.

Mr. Ferrachi came in, and told us that Rafe had a previous engagement and he hadn't yet returned, but he began talking to us about my indiscretion yesterday anyway. I had already filled Mr. Bellini in on the important business details

and evidentially Rafe had done the same with Mr. Ferrachi.

"Miss Malone, Mr. Rafe doesn't want you to deliver the Fatima papers considering what you went through yesterday to get the key. In fact he wants you debriefed and off the case. But since his departure this morning, I have already spoken to Mr. Baragio and after speaking to his superiors, I was told if we removed you as our messenger, they would simply dispose of the Pope and find another way to fulfill their wishes. They assured me that we would not be happy about the way that they would go about it. So despite Rafe's wishes, you are still on the case. Mr. Baragio will call with instructions sometime tomorrow."

I looked at him and smiled,

"What about Mr. Rafe? Won't he try to stop me from going? He was pretty adamant about me not returning to see Mr. Baragio."

"Miss Malone, I don't blame him for being angry. That was a pretty dangerous stunt you pulled yesterday. First, directly disobeying orders. Secondly, not even letting anyone know where you were going. However, I have Mr. Baragio's assurance that we will know where this meeting is to take place. So you won't have to worry about sneaking around. You are lucky you aren't losing your job, as I will convince Mr. Rafe that what you did was for the security of the Pope. Truthfully I already think he knows that. He just wants to trust that you will do what you are told so that you won't be in any danger," he winked. "So you just let me worry about him, okay?"

I nodded, not knowing what else to say or do. I couldn't imagine Rafe taking this as calmly a Mr. Ferrachi thought he would.

Mr. Bellini gave me hell all the way back to the office for disobeying orders and putting myself in danger. I suspected he was actually angrier with me for upsetting Rafe than he was worried about me. He began to shake his finger at me, which meant I was about to have a lecture from him.

"Rebecca, do you have any idea how high up the proverbial ladder Mr. Rafe is in the Vatican? No I don't suppose you do. I've been told that his authority is actually higher than the Popes', if that is possible. Do not ever make him angry again. Do you understand? How did he find out where you were anyway?"

"I honestly don't know Mr. Bellini. Believe me, somehow he knew. Don't worry. I won't do anything that stupid again. It was a terrifying experience. Especially when we went to a different address. I just hope that Mr. Ferrachi's decision isn't going to upset Mr. Rafe to much. But if you are saying that his authority is that high, wouldn't he have the last say on whether I continue or not?"

Mr. Bellini thought about that for a few minutes, then he finally looked at me and said: "I don't think that Mr. Rafe would want to do anything to further endanger the Pope. I'm sure that when he thinks about it in that light he will come around. Plus

We have the added assurance of knowing where the meeting is to take place."

When we returned to the office, I had a pile of work waiting for me from the day before, as well as the days mail to still go through. I immediately got to work reading, trashing, writing and more reading. I was totally immersed in my work when my desk phone rang. I answered in my usual greeting and the voice on the other end belonged to none other than David Rafe.

"Hi Rebecca."

It worried me, because he used my given name and not the familiar "Becca." "Hello Mr. Rafe, what can I do for you today?" I hated sounding so formal but then I was at work and didn't want anyone suspicious.

"May I take you to lunch today? Say around 12:30 p.m, or are you busy?" His voice sounded friendly enough. Maybe he would explain himself to me, or maybe he was going to take me off the case. Bust as long as I was going to see him that was what was the most important to me.

"12:30 p.m. would be fine Rafe. That is usually when I take my lunch hour anyway."

"All right I will be there with my car. I will come up and get you. I'll see you then."

After I hung up the phone, I managed to keep my mind occupied until lunchtime by digging back into the stacks of mail on my desk. One of the letters I opened was of particular interest to me. It only said,

(Dear Miss Malone,

Be prepared for a paranormal story like you have never written before, It will affect the entire catholic church from the highest authorities down to the average catholic. In fact it will affect all of Christianity as we all know it. Be prepared to see visions, and happenings that have never been seen on this earth before. We want you to cover the story for as long as there is a story to cover,

Sincerely,

The Other Side

PS Expect to hear from us soon)

I read it over and over, trying to decide whether it was a hoax or something of importance. I decided that with everything that was going on right now that we would have to place importance on any letter like this whether we thought it was a prank or not, at least until we had the Pope back safely at the Vatican. I buzzed Heidi and asked if Mr. Bellini was free to see me for a few minutes.

"Just a minute Rebecca, let me check."

She put me on hold, but within a few seconds was back on the phone.

"He said to make it fast as he has work to do. I hope it isn't bad news, he's in one of his grumpy moods today."

"It's okay Heidi, I won't take long."

I took the letter with me to his office. He opened the door before I even had a chance to knock.

"Come on in Becca. What have you got for me?"

I sat down in the chair he motioned me to and handed him the letter.

He read it and handed it back to me.

"What do you make of it Becca?"

"I don't know, but I think considering the case that we are on that we shouldn't overlook anything. My first inclination is to think it is a hoax. It is pretty bizarre, but I still think we should pass it on to the authorities don't you?"

"Yes, I do, but make sure you make a copy of it for us. Is that all you have for me? I have a really hectic schedule today."

"That's it."

He walked me to the door and when he opened it there stood Rafe chatting with Heidi. She was right about him. He was absolutely gorgeous. Always impeccably dressed, and so handsome he looked like he belonged in a fashion magazine. He looked over at me immediately and smiled. I noticed his beautiful cobalt blue yes seemed peaceful today. There didn't seem to be any torment or anger that I could read.

Mr. Bellini rushed ahead of me and shaking Rafe's hand said:

"Well hello there Mr. Rafe, and what brings you to our office today?"

"I came to take Becca to lunch."

Heidi caught the Becca part right away and as Rafe's back was turned to her she put her thumb and forefinger together in a little circle, giving be the okay sign and winking. I only caught if for a second, but looked back at Rafe quickly because I was afraid she would make me bust out in laughter. She was so shy, it was something I would have never expected to come from her. I felt like I was getting to know her a little more every day and I liked what I saw.

"Becca, are you ready?" It was Rafe getting my attention.

"OH! Yes, I'm sorry." I smiled anyway, just thinking of Heidi's little gesture.

As soon as we got in the elevator he looked at me and said:

"What was so funny when you were watching Mr. Bellini's secretary in there?"

"Oh, nothing important Rafe, she just tickles me sometimes with the little expressions she makes."

We walked down to the limousine and the same driver was waiting, holding the door open.

When we settled in the car, Rafe instructed him to take us to St. Peters.

"I hope you don't mind Becca but since you seemed to enjoy the park so much yesterday I took the liberty of picking us up box lunches. I thought we could eat lunch in the garden at St. Peter's."

"Oh, that would be wonderful, but are we allowed to do that? " I asked, looking at him skeptically.

"Don't worry, I have permission! You will love it. The gardens are always beautiful no matter what time of year it is."

He was right, when we reached the gardens; I had to admit it was beautiful. There were flowers in bloom that you wouldn't normally see this time of year, and the rose garden had every variety and color of rose that you could imagine. We sat under a large pine tree that had been trimmed back just for that purpose. The birds were singing and the sun was shining brightly in the fall sky. It was a perfect day for a picnic. Rafe spread out a white tablecloth on the grass and took a bottle of wine, two glasses and different kinds of cheeses and bread along with Italian olives and grapes out of the basket and we had a luncheon feast. It was such a relaxing hour. When we were finished he leaned back against the tree with his arms behind his head and studying me, he inquired:

"Becca, do you mind me asking how much you weigh?"

"No, not at all. I weigh 110 pounds. Why?"

"Oh no reason, I was just curious, and what are you about five foot six?"

"No, I'm five foot four, and I wear a sized five shoe. Is there anything else you want to know about me?"

"Well, I can see for myself that your hair is so black that when the sun hits it just right it has a nice shine to it, so it must be natural. And I never noticed until today in the sunlight how very green your eyes are. I knew they were green, but today they are almost emerald green."

I blushed and stared at him for a few minutes before I said,

"Okay Rafe. Why all the questions? Is it really curiosity or is there a motive behind it?"

"No motive, really. But come to think of it you are a pretty tiny thing to be taking on strong men. Don't you think?"

"Rafe, I really don't want to hash through yesterday, if you don't mind."

"No. Honestly Becca. I was just curious. I won't bring up yesterday again if you don't either. Except I do want you to remember the promise I made to you about Baragio. I did mean that, and I will carry through with my promise."

His eyes took on a determined look and I knew that he was serious and I knew that he most definitely would not forget it. Though I secretly wished he would.

"Okay. Now it's my turn to ask you questions Rafe."

He looked at his watch.

"Do you think we have time?"

I saw the amusement dancing in his eyes.

Darn it Rafe you planned it this way, I said to myself.

"No I don't suppose we have time," I said looking at my watch. But next time it's my turn. Deal?"

He just looked at me and smiled.

"Deal"

We gathered everything together and walked back to the car. When we were almost back to the office, I remembered the letter.

"Oh Rafe, I almost forgot. I received this letter today and it may be a hoax but you need to take a look at it. I will need a copy when we get back to the office and you can keep the original."

I handed it to him and he read it in silence, and I noticed a slight frown come across his face.

"What, Rafe? What is it? Is it important?"

"I don't know, but I will study it and see if I can figure out anything.

"Well, there was not a return address. I looked on the envelope as soon as I got it. The envelope is still on my desk if you want it."

"Definitely," he said as we parked in front of the newspaper building.

Before I got out of the car I looked up at him.

"Rafe, I want to thank you for a very pleasant lunch. I really enjoyed St. Peters garden and the lovely conversation, even if it was only about me."

"You're quite welcome Becca. Have you ever been inside St. Peters Basilica before?"

"No, I hate to admit it. I never seemed to have the time to get over there."

He looked at me and smiled, as if he already knew I was going to say that.

"Maybe we can take a little longer lunch tomorrow and I can take you to see it."

I couldn't believe he was asking me out for lunch again tomorrow.

"I would love that."

I spent the rest of the afternoon working through my mail until Mike came over and plopped down in the chair across from my desk.

"Pretty busy today aren't you Rebecca?"

"Yes Mike, I hate to be rude, but I need to get through as much of this as I can before I leave today. Missing yesterday didn't help much."

"I noticed that you had another lunch date today."

I just ignored him and kept on typing.

"So that was David Rafe, huh?"

"Yes Mike, that was David Rafe."

My eyes never left my computer screen.

"I noticed that he called you Becca. Pretty friendly don't you think? For just meeting him?"

I finally stopped typing and looking at him said:

"We aren't jealous now, are we Mike? You've heard Mr. Bellini call me Becca several times, I'm sure. It has been your choice to call me by my given name."

He flashed me his most charming smile.

"I happen to like the way Rebecca sounds, it suits you. It sounds classy, and yet romantic at the same time. Actually, it was the way that you looked at him that got my attention."

"Oh, and how was that?"

I just shook my head at him, amused at his slight jealous tone.

"Well, kinda like you couldn't wait to leave with him. You know what I mean?"

"No Mike, I don't know what you mean. I think you're seeing things that are just not there. My association with Mr. Rafe is strictly business," I lied. At least I hoped I was lying.

He just stared at me for a second, and then said:

"Are you free for lunch tomorrow?"

I quickly looked away and started typing again.

"No. I have a previous engagement tomorrow for lunch."

"Oh?"

This really caught his attention.

"You wouldn't happen to have another lunch date with Mr. Rafe would you?"

I hated to be rude to him, so I smiled as I said:

"Mike, do you really think it is any of your business?"

He shrugged his shoulders and put his hands up in a mock 'I'm backing off gesture," and said:

"Okay, I get the picture, I'll ask you another day."

"That would be great! Now Mike, truthfully, I really need to get to work."

He got up from the chair and gave me a knowing smile, and walked back to his desk.

That evening all I thought about was Rafe. He seemed so totally relaxed today and comfortable with me. There was no sadness in his eyes. Our conversation had been light and fun, even if I never got my turn to question him. The one thing that really had me puzzled was that he never once mentioned anything about taking me off the case or if Mr. Ferrachi had said anything to him. Maybe Mr. Ferrachi hadn't spoken to him yet. I still couldn't believe that Rafe hadn't mentioned my debriefing, because it was something I knew that he would have wanted to be in on. Oh well, I wasn't going to dwell on it. I just wanted to remember the light laughter, and the contented feelings we shared with each other. Hopefully tomorrow would be more of the same.

Chapter 3
THE PRISON

The next morning it was pouring down rain, and according to the weather station it was going to most of the day. I wondered if Rafe would still keep our lunch date. I didn't have to wait very long for an answer, because as soon as I walked in the office Heidi let me know that I was supposed to call Mr. Ferrachi right away and when I did he let me know that I had an appointment.

"Rebecca, Mr. Baragio called this morning and they would like you to bring the Fatima letters today at 12:30 PM. I have sent Sister Mary Angela to pick them up from the Pope's apartments and bring them here, so if you could meet me outside the Papal Palace at noon, I will give them to you along with the directions Mr. Baragio sent.

My stomach did a little flip flop as I thought of meeting Nicholas Baragio

"He did give you the directions then as he said he would. But what if they take me somewhere else like they did last time?"

"No need to worry about that Rebecca, we have it all covered."

"Mr. Ferrachi please, don't have me followed, or they will kill me and the Pope."

He said,

"Don't worry, it is covered. That's all I can tell you. We won't do anything to jeopardize you or the Holy Father."

"All right, I will see you at noon then."

"You are a brave girl Rebecca, and the Holy Father and my office will always be indebted to you for this sacrifice you are making."

"Thank you, Mr. Ferrachi."

I hung up the phone and said under my breath,

"I hope I'm not making myself the sacrifice."

Mr. Ferrachi never mentioned Kate to me, so I assumed he must have spoken to him. I didn't want to have to give him the reason I was cancelling our lunch date so I asked Heidi if she would call his office and tell him I was sorry, but I would have to miss lunch today because I had been called away on business.

"I'd be happy to call him Rebecca."

She smiled a silly little grin.

"Maybe he'll ask me to take your place."

"Maybe," I said. "You never know."

I laughed and thumped her on the arm.

The hours until noon seemed to speed by faster than I would have liked for them to. The next thing I knew, I was sitting in a cab waiting for Mr. Ferrachi in front of the Papal Palace. He came running out the door and handed the address to the cab driver and motioned me to roll down my window as he said,

"Good luck and don't worry about anything. Here are the letters and make sure you come back here as soon as you are finished with your business and hopefully you'll have the Pope with you."

I just nodded my head, and rolled up the window, and gave a nervous little sigh.

Wouldn't it be great though if it would be that simple. Somehow I just didn't think Nicholas or Luther would be that amiable to deal with. I was sure that they would

want more than just the Fatima papers before they released the Pope.

I had no idea where we were going. Had it been for a different reason I probably would have enjoyed the drive. We were driving through a lot of ruins. Finally, I couldn't stand it any longer, so I leaned forward and asked the cab driver.

"Ma'am, I have been instructed to take you to the carcere in old Rome."

"Excuse me Sir, but could you tell me what that is?" I was becoming tense, I hated not knowing where I was.

He looked in the rearview mirror at me and said,

"Carcere, simply means prison. The prison is in the Old Roman ruins at the foot of Capitoline Hill, one of the seven hills of Rome. The prisons name is Mamertine Prison and it is an accepted belief that it is the prison where St. Peter and St. Paul were incarcerated. It is one of the most sacred places in Rome. It is beneath the San Guieseppi dei Falegnami Church that was build over the prison centuries later. They say the prison itself was built in the 7th Century BC. You will find it an interesting place to see."

"Grazie," I said to him. One of the few words I knew in Italian.

I sat back and wondered why they had picked a prison as opposed to the house I was in last time. I wondered it the Pope would even be there. Well, at least it was a known address, so surely nothing too bad could happen there since it was the middle of the day. That helped me relax a bit.

Finally, when he pulled over to the curb, he looked out the window and said,

"Ma'am, it appears to be closed. Do you want me to leave you here anyway?"

It figures, I said to myself. "Yes, it's okay to leave me here. I have someone who is coming to meet me." I started to pay him, but he shook his head and told me Mr. Ferrachi had already taken care of it. I would have to remember to thank him.

I stood alone, wondering if I was going to be met by the black limousine again, when suddenly, there standing beside me was Nicholas Baragio. It startled me when I saw him and I got a little jumpy. He just laughed.

"Follow me, Miss Malone."

There was no car, so I assumed we couldn't be going to far. He took me beneath the church, unlocked the door of the prison and we went in. He locked the door behind him as we entered. The room was a strange trapezoidal shape. I looked around the Pope and Luther were nowhere to be seen. Nicholas walked over to the stairs and led me to a lower level. The stairs took us down to a room that resembled a dungeon; except for a small alter in the middle. There was a plaque on the wall that said something in Italian. The only word I recognized was Peter.

I looked around and no one but Nicholas and I were down here either. I turned and looked at him, raising an eyebrow, and he said,

"Don't worry, Luther will be here soon. He wanted to make sure the Pope was dressed differently so no one would recognize him. I see I left my marks on your arm. Maybe next time I tell you something, you will listen to me."

"You disgust me Nicholas. Could I please wait upstairs until Luther gets here?"

"No! You had better stay right where you are unless you want some of the same medicine you got last time. Or maybe you enjoy being hurt. Is that what it is? It has been my experience that some women really get turned on by that."

I didn't move, and shivered in disgust. I certainly did not want to be hit again. He watched me for a few seconds and then he began to circle me, looking me up and down and I started to cringe inside. I wanted to reach out and slap him as hard as I could, but I tried to remain calm. I didn't want an altercation with anyone this time. I had learned my lesson well the last time. His phone rang. He talked someone for a few minutes and then threw his phone in the corner.

"We have plenty of time to get to know each other. Luther is having some problems with the Pope, so he'll be a little longer than expected. Give me your purse."

It wasn't actually a purse. It was a messenger bag and had my phone and the Fatima letters in it. I started to say no, but decided against it. As I reached out to give it to him, he jerked it out of my hand and threw it in the corner along with his phone.

I was wearing my hair up today and I'd worn a green skirt and a green and white sheer blouse with matching high-heeled shoes. I wished I had brought my sweater from the office. The more covered up I was, the happier I would be, as Nicholas was not missing one inch of my body as he looked me up and down. I wanted to throw up.

"Take your hair down! He said.

"Why?" I glared at him questioningly.

"Let's not start out wrong here Miss Malone, don't make me do it myself or you might regret it.

I quickly pulled the pins from my hair and it came down cascading to my waist. He took in a deep breath and kept circling me.

"Now, unbutton your blouse and take it off slowly."

That was it, that is when I couldn't stand it any longer and I lost my temper. I spit in his face.

"You pig. I will not do another thing you ask me to do."

I started for the stairs, but he grabbed me by the hair and hurled me to the floor and was on top of me in a minute. He held both of my hands high above my head so that not only could I not do anything, but neither could he.

"I'm going to make this slow." He said, grinning through yellowed teeth. "We have about an hour before Luther gets here, and I'm going to take my time and make it very painful."

He let go of my hands and sat up. I doubled up my fist and started hitting him, but he just laughed as he caught both of my wrists in his hands, standing up and pulling me to my feet. Then he shoved me away from him.

"Do you want to do what I ask you now, or are you having to much fun wrestling with me?"

I flew at him, catching him off guard, and brought my knee up and kicked him as hard as I could in the groin. He crumpled to the floor moaning in pain. I ran for my messenger bag, turned and kicked him in the face as I ran past him. The spike of my heel pierced his cheek. I ran to the stairs and looked back to see if he was still down. I ran up a few steps and right into Luther.

"Where are we going Becca? Is Nicholas giving you a bad time again?"

I began backing down the stairs, staring in disbelief at the Pope, who was not only in street clothes, but he had been beaten so badly that it took two men to drag him down the stairs.

"Oh my God! What have you done to him? He is hurt so terribly."

I stared at Luther, not believing the Popes demeanor. He didn't act like he even knew he was alive.

"Let's just say we had a little disagreement and I won." Said Luther.

He looked at Nicholas and started laughing and looking back at me said,

"It looks like you and Nicholas had a little disagreement too, and you won. It's a good thing I got here when I did or you might have killed him.

He laughed louder.

Nicholas was slowly rising to his feet, still stooped over in pain and holding the side of his face that was now bleeding profusely.

Luther looked at him shaking his head.

"I told you not to mess with her Nicholas, why couldn't you have just left well enough alone?"

"Luther, she kept trying to leave when she saw you weren't here. I can't believe it! Her high heel has gone all the way through my cheek!"

Luther looked at Nicholas and when he saw all the blood, he turned and looked at me and said,

"You know you are going to have to pay for this, and if he doesn't feel up to making you pay, than I will. I will not tolerate anyone hurting my people."

"Oh, but it is okay if he throws around a defenseless woman? You just sat and watched him knock me around the other day."

"I stopped him before you were hurt to badly. And from the looks of him, I wouldn't exactly call you defenseless. Now give me the Fatima letters."

He reached his hand out for me to give them to him, but before I pulled them out of my messenger bag, I looked at him and asked,

"Will the Pope be going with me?"

"That depends on the Pope." He turned and looked at Pius XIII.

"I have one more request I would like him to fulfill before he leaves our friendly company."

The Pope was hanging on the arms of two men and if they hadn't been holding him up, I am positive he would have collapsed on the floor. His eyes were swollen shut .

I gave Luther a dirty look. I was so disgusted with both of the men that I couldn't look either of them in the eye.

"Do you really think you left him in any shape to do anything for you? He doesn't even seem to be coherent."

Luther stared at me with amusement in his eyes. I thought I caught a glint of hatred there also, but if I did it disappeared before I could really take note. He turned to the Pope once again and kicked him hard on the shinbone. I winced, but the Pope didn't move at all except from the force of the kick that moved his body. I looked at Luther with an 'I told you so' expression.

"Oh don't worry sweet Becca, we have ways of making him come around. All he has to do is make a tape that we can send to the radio stations denouncing the Catholic Church for the fraud it is, and he will be free to go."

I looked at him wide-eyed, I couldn't believe what I was hearing coming from the man's mouth.

"He will never agree to that, and you know he won't. I—can't believe you could ask him to do such a horrible thing. You are a diabolical man."

"Why thank you Rebecca, that is the best compliment I have had all day. I enjoy it when people tell me I am evil."

I didn't know what to say. This situation was getting worse by the minute. He really seemed to enjoy hurting the Pope and I couldn't understand why.

"What could he have done to you that is so horrible that you would treat him like this? He is a good man. Please let me take him with me. You have your letters, and he is not in any condition to do anything let alone to speak into a microphone denouncing the very tenets his life is based on. Can't you see that he won't last much longer? Isn't there anything I can say to change your mind?"

He stared at me for a minute narrowing his eyes and then looking at Nicholas Baragio, he said,

"I'm quite bored of her now. Are you well enough to take care of her, or do you want me to do it for you?"

Nicholas looked at me with eyes filled with hatred and said,

"I feel well enough. I have a big score to settle with her, she could have scarred me for life. Can I do whatever I want to her?"

Luther Laughed.

"Obviously you can't do what you would like to do or you wouldn't still be standing stooped over. You can do what you like to her, short of killing her. I want her alive when she goes back to that pompous ass who thinks he's so great."

I had no idea who he was talking about, but when Nicholas started walking towards me I noticed that the place on his cheek where I had punctured it with my heel was not bleeding anymore. In fact it was completely healed! It was as though I had never done anything to him. What on earth was going on here? This was really beginning to scare me. Something was obviously terribly evil about these people, and I felt trapped. Out of the corner of my eye I saw Luther motion to the guards and they let the Pope slump to the floor.

The next thing I knew one of the guards had grabbed me from behind and was trying to pull my arms behind my back. I started squirming and kicking as hard as I could, trying to break his hold. Nicholas picked up a candleholder that was made of solid brass and he hit me hard across both legs, breaking them both below the knee.

"You bitch! You'll never kick anyone again. Now you know what pain is."

My legs immediately gave out from under me and the pain was so intense that all I could do was scream and scream. The next thing I knew he was coming at me with a knife. I tried to move my body to the side, but the knife went in above my right hip. I began seeing stars in frond of my eyes. I was on the verge of passing out. He was on the floor sitting on top of me and slapping me.

"No, no, Miss Malone, don't pass out on me now! I want you to be awake when I slash that pretty face of yours."

I could feel myself slipping into unconsciousness, when suddenly, he was being pulled off of me and thrown across the room. My eyes immediately opened to see Rafe pulling him up from the floor by his throat. Thank God I thought in relief. Rafe kept slamming him against the wall over and over until Nicholas was unconscious. He rushed over to me, his eyes full of pain.

"Oh Becca, Becca I'm so sorry."

He lifted me enough so that he could cradle my head against his chest. I put my fingers in my mouth and bit down hard to keep from screaming. I was in agony. My body hurt everywhere. Blood was trickling from my mouth again where Nicholas had broken open the cut from when I had bitten my lip before. Rafe tried to pull my hand out of my mouth, but I kept shaking my head and writhing in pain.

"What a touching scene. You always were good at saving people, weren't you?"

It was Luther.

He knew Rafe? I was conscious enough to notice that Rafe looked at me with complete shock in his eyes. And then I remembered that I had never told him about Luther Amaddon.

"Becca. Has he been here all along?"

I just nodded. I didn't want to take my hand out of my mouth long enough to talk.

"I really would have never let you come here if I would have known he was here. Do you know who he is?"

He had such an incredulous expression on his face when he asked me.

"Luther," was all I could imagine to say.

"You didn't actually think I was going to tell her anything else did you?"

Luther laughed.

"I would have never got her to come here."

About that time Nicholas pulled himself to his feet, but stayed where he was. He looked like a whipped puppy. Rafe just glared at him, daring him to make a move.

Luther looked at me; eyes full of hate.

"Do you remember what I told you Becca? What would happen if you gave anyone directions?'

He pulled a long golden dagger from beneath his black suit jacket and walked over to the Pope and stabbed him through the heart. The Pope barely flinched; it confirmed my fear of how near death he already was.

I could hear my screaming. It sounded like someone else, but it came from my mouth. The Pope, such an innocent person lay dead on the floor.

Rafe was in front of Luther in a split second. I was losing consciousness again, but not before I felt the wind begin to blow very hard in the room, and I heard Luther say,

"This isn't over Rebecca, I will make you pay for your betrayal.

Then I saw a beautiful strong muscled angel with beautiful wings and golden brown hair holding a sword in front of him, facing Luther. Luther backed away, but the wind became so forceful that it blew him and his two guards through the wall of the prison. The expressions on their faces read of terror and their bodies seemed to disappear as soon as they were on the other side.

Nicholas Baragio, started for the stairs hoping to leave, but the angel grabbed him from behind and quickly drew his sword across Baragios' throat and cut off his head and threw it to the floor.

I must be delirious were my last thoughts as I slipped into oblivion. I woke up once in extreme pain. Rafe was beside me. He was doing something to me that was hurting very bad. His hand was on the stab wound on my side and he was pressing on it with a lot of force, and was causing me excruciating pain. I thought maybe he was trying to stop the bleeding.

"Please Rafe, don't hurt me anymore, just let me sleep. I can't stand it. Please stop."

"Becca it will be fine I promise it will only hurt for a little bit longer and then you won't feel the pain." He looked up from whatever he was doing and kissed me softly on my hand.

"I feel so much better just knowing that you are here." I whispered. "Please stay with me. I am so afraid. What is going on? I don't underst…"

His hands were on my legs now and I held my breath as long as I could, and then I started to scream. Then I passed out.

When I woke up again in was dark, and I sat up startled, because I didn't know where I was.

"It's okay Becca, you're safe at home now." Said Rafe. He came and sat behind me and tenderly laid me back down, then taking a wet wash cloth he began to softly pat my forehead, and then he moved down to my neck and arms. When he lifted the blankets back to tend to my legs I began to flinch before he even touched them. But surprisingly I had feeling in them again and I could feel the coolness of the cloth against my skin. I tried to move my left leg and was able although the pain was acute.

"Don't move, you aren't all the way healed. It will take a while before all the soreness goes away completely. You will need to rest for a few days. I'll be here to take care of you Becca. I won't leave you. Please don't be afraid anymore. I'll protect you. Just go back to sleep and rest and heal."

That was all I needed to hear. Those words were music to my ears. He wasn't going to leave. I knew when I woke up he would be here, and I didn't need to be afraid of anything because he would protect me. I could hear the telephone ringing in the background, but my eyelids fluttered closed and I was restfully sleeping before he answered it.

The next morning I was full of questions.

"Why aren't I in the hospital? Aren't my legs broken? What about the gash in my side?"

I was filled with worry.

"Aren't you even going to say you are happy to see me still here?" Rafe smiled, his most infectious smile.

"Rafe, of course, that is the best part of all this chaos. You are here with me. Thank you so much. But why aren't I in the hospital?"

"Becca, wait! Let's take one question at a time okay? You aren't in the hospital because your injuries didn't turn out to be that bad. The bones in your legs were just bruised real bad."

"No Rafe! They were broken I couldn't even move them. I had no feeling in them at all. I heard them snap. They were broken!"

"Becca you were so frightened. You were delirious. You just thought that you couldn't move the…"

"No! I know what I felt. I just don't understand any of this Rafe. Please! Tell me the truth!"

"I would never lie to you Becca. Your legs are not broken." He said, bending over the bed and stroking my hair. "You can move them. But I suggest you keep them as still as possible until the bruising subsides a little bit more. In a couple of days they will feel fine."

I shook my head, not believing what he was telling me, but when I tried both of my legs moved and all the feeling was there.

"But…"

"Rebecca! Relax! We'll talk about it more this afternoon. I have to go to the Vatican and when I get back I'll explain everything. Don't worry you won't be alone. Mr. Bellini is sending Heidi over to sit with you. As soon as she gets here I have to leave."

About that time there was a knock on the door and he went to let Heidi in.

Rafe told Heidi to take care of me, and thanked her for coming. He stood in the doorway but didn't come back in the bedroom. I knew it was because he didn't want to answer any more questions in front of Heidi. He knew that the more I remembered, the more questions I would ask.

"I will call and check on you Becca, and I'll be back as soon as I can." Then he turned and walked out the door.

Heidi looked at me and back at Rafe as he closed the door.

"Huh," she said more to herself than to me. "I wish he was checking on me instead of you."

I started laughing. 'Oooh don't make me laugh. It makes my side hurt!"

But I laughed anyway.

She sat on the bed beside me, fluffed my pillows behind my head and folded the blanket back so I could sit up and talk to her.

"Rebecca, I just can't believe you took that bad of a fall. You're lucky you didn't break your legs. Mr. Bellini said you caught the edge of the gate when you fell and cut your side pretty band and they had to have the Vatican doctor come and stitch it up. Are you in a lot of pain? Mr. Rafe told me to give you one of these pills if you got to uncomfortable. So make sure you tell me okay? Oh, and before I forget, Mike Warner asked me to give you this card."

She handed me a sealed envelope.

I set it on the nightstand, because I didn't feel like reading it right now. So that's the story they are telling everyone. I fell down. I still couldn't believe my legs weren't broken. I wiggled my toes.

"Oooh that hurt!"

"What's wrong Rebecca?" asked a wide-eyed Heidi.

"Oh nothing, I just was checking to see if my toes would wiggle and it hurt."

She went down to the end of the bed and pulled back the blankets.

"Well, I guess so! They are swollen and you are black and blue from the tips of your toes to your knees. Gosh, you must have strong bones."

"I suppose I must."

Why did this seem so wrong to me? Was I that delirious? Like Rafe said.

Heidi sat quiet for a few minutes and then changed the subject.

"I guess the Vatican will be really busy today, and buzzing with people."

"Why?" I said.

"Oh my gosh, didn't you know that the Pope was killed in an airplane accident on his way back to the Vatican?"

It all came flooding back to me now. The Pope was dead. An image of Luther shoving a dagger into the Popes chest flashed across my mind. Of course they couldn't tell anyone that he had been killed. I shivered in fear remembering Luther's threat to me. He thought I told Rafe where I would be. How did Rafe get there so fast? I shivered again, and put my hands to my head. I didn't want to think about any of this right now. My side was beginning to throb badly.

"Are you cold Rebecca?"

"No please give me one of those pills, I am beginning to feel worse."

She got me a glass of water and handed me the pill. I laid back on the pillows and closed my eyes, but couldn't sleep. There were just too many things to remember.

"Rebecca, I'm going to go in the other room and listen to the news an let you get a little rest."

"No Heidi, please don't leave me." I began to imagine that I could hear Luther whispering to me, but I quickly said something so she wouldn't know I was afraid.

"N-No, lets just visit for a while. Turn the television on in here. I'd like to hear the news also."

"Okay, how about if I go and get us a cup of coffee first. Doesn't that sound good?"

Actually it did and so I nodded. She came back with two cups of coffee. I looked at her quizzically.

"Heidi Morans! Since when did you start drinking coffee?"

"Since I heard the Pope died. He was such a good Pontiff. Everyone loved him so much. I just can't believe he's gone. Do you realize how busy we are going to be for the next few weeks?"

"No, I don't want to think about it right now. Could you go ahead and turn the news on?"

St. Peters Basilica already had the doors draped in the long black banner which was customary when a Pope passed. There were several news vans all over Vatican Square, just waiting to interview anyone that looked like they might have authority. I wondered how security was going to pull this lie off.

Mr. Ferrachi was speaking to one of the reporters, explaining that the plane crashed in some jungle, and that it was kept quiet until the Pope's body could be returned to the Vatican. He was being prepared for a proper funeral and interment and it would take place tomorrow at St. Peters Basilica at 10:00 am. After that the Cardinals would have their conclave to elect a new Pope. That was all she shared. He then waved them off, telling them he was too busy to answer their questions. When they continued to follow him he ignored them.

I noticed that the Swiss Guard was everywhere. I didn't even know there were that many Swiss Guard employed by the Vatican.

Heidi and I continued watching the coverage, changing the channels, but soon became bored because the Priest, Bishops and Cardinals were all asked the same questions, just by different newscasters.

I started getting very groggy from the pain pill Heidi had given me earlier and I fell asleep. When I woke up it was getting dark and Heidi wasn't sitting on the bed. I became frightened that I was alone and when I turned to look to the other side of the bed, Rafe was sitting in the chair smiling at me.

"Hello sleepy head." He came over and sat down next to me touching his hand to my forehead.

I sighed, feeling better just knowing he was there.

"Where's Heidi?" I asked.

"You've been asleep for a good while. I got back about two o'clock this afternoon and she left a little after that. It's seven o'clock now. You've got to be hungry. I'll go and fix you something to eat." He started to get up, and I grabbed his hand.

"No! You promised you would answer some questions when you got back."

He started to pull away. "Becca, let's get some food in you first and then I'll answer all the questions you want."

I squeezed his hand.

"No Rafe, now!"

He sat and stared at me for a minute.

"All right Becca! What do you want to know?"

"Rafe, how did you know where I was? I could have been in any of those buildings. The church, upstairs, down the street. And how did you get into the room without any of us even knowing you were there?"

"Becca! Please, just one question at a time! The only way that I would let Mr. Ferrachi send you on this little caper was if he let me follow you. Otherwise you would have never gone. Speaking of capers, why didn't you tell me that Luther Amaddon was at the other meeting?"

"Rafe, you answer my questions first, and then I'll answer yours!"

"Okay, lets' see, you were screaming. I could hear you from outside, so I hurried into the prison because that is where the sound was coming from. It didn't take much to realize the screaming was coming from downstairs. Everyone was preoccupied with you. You were in such agony you wouldn't have noticed me entering. When I saw Baragio sitting on you getting ready to slash your face, and the blood coming from your side, I wanted to kill him. I couldn't think of anything else but to kill him. I also thought your legs were broken because of the way they were twisted behind you. All I can tell you about that is that they weren't broken. Now before you ask me anything else you answer my question or I'm not going to answer anymore of yours. Why didn't you tell me that Luther was at your first meeting, and just what do you know about him?"

"Rafe" I smiled. "One question at a time, remember? You just asked me two."

He just looked at me, shook his head and smiled.

"Sorry, you can answer them one at a time. Let's hear it!"

"Well I was going to tell you about Luther. He seemed to be in charge of whatever their terrible operation was. He was so strange, and after you told me I was off of the case I was afraid to tell you or Mr. Ferrachi that anyone else was involved. I thought if there was a chance that you would let me go, then telling you about him would ruin my chances. What I told you about Nicholas was bad enough without adding any other weird players to the story."

"Well you were smart not to tell me Becca, because you would have never gone if I knew he was there. I feel guilty as it is now, after everything that has happened."

He looked at me with the pain in his eyes that I was getting so used to seeing. I'd be so happy if I could see the relaxed look that was on his face the day in the Vatican Gardens. That now seemed like a hundred years ago.

"Please Rafe, don't feel guilty. None of this is your fault. It was those filthy pigs! You had nothing to do with the way that they treated me. It's actually my fault that Luther killed the Pope. He told me that if I told anyone where to find me that he would kill the Pope."

"Becca, you didn't tell anyone where to find you, that's not your fault."

He took my hand in between both of his and held it so tenderly.

"Rest assured that Luther thinks it's my fault. I know. I remember him telling me that I would pay. Oh Rafe, I never thought I would be afraid of anyone in my life, and I am so afraid of him."

"Just exactly what do you know about Mr. Amaddon Becca?"

He looked down at our hands when he asked me, and I had the distinct feeling he didn't want me to see the expression on his face.

"Nothing except that he is a vile, cruel and diabolical man. I pray that I never have to see him again."

"You are right about that, and if I have my way you will never have to meet again, but we have to be very careful. He's very crafty, and he will be out to get revenge in any way he can."

I cringed remembering my guttural emotion when Luther touched my hand. Rafe looked at me questioningly.

"Becca, is there something you aren't telling me? I just noticed that you just had a little involuntary tremble."

"No! Just thinking of everything that has happened in the last few days."

"Well, we are going to stop this talking now and feed you. Then if there is anything else you want to know you can quiz me after you eat. You need all the strength you can get to heal fast."

He stood up and before he could leave I asked him, "Rafe, could you please help me to the restroom so that I can wash my face?"

He helped me walk to the bathroom door, and then he went into the kitchen. I still had so many questions to ask him. Some of them he might not even be able to answer.

I unbuttoned my pajamas so that I could look at the wound on my side. Oh my God? It wasn't there. I kept looking at the spot where I knew I had been stabbed. It was sore when I touched it, but there wasn't a single spot on me, no stitches, not even a scab. I had to know what was happening. Something beyond my reasoning was going on here and I started shaking uncontrollably with fear as I just stared at the place where the stab wound should have been. I pulled up the legs to my pajamas to look at my legs. They hurt too, but aside from a little bruising, they looked fine. Why was I healing so fast. Heidi just told me that my legs were bruised very badly. She checked them this afternoon. As a matter of fact, she was the one who told me that Mr. Ferrachi said the Vatican doctor had stitched up my side. That was just last night, and I was now all healed except for the soreness. Why hadn't

Rafe said anything to me about any of this? He just said he saw me bleeding. He was the one that was putting pressure on my side. Now I was really full of questions.

I began to cry. My life had changed so much just in the past few days and now I felt like I had lost control over everything in my life. I wasn't used to not being able to explain everything that happened to me, but this was beyond reality. I ran cool water over my eyes again so they wouldn't look like I had been crying. Rafe was whistling a beautiful tune when I walked into the bedroom and he had a sandwich and some soup waiting for me.

He noticed right away that I had been crying.

"Becca? What's wrong? Did you hurt yourself by getting up to soon?"

I went over and sat on the edge of the bed, putting my head in my hands. I said,,

"Oh Rafe, that's not it at all! I can't eat right now. I am so very confused. You have to answer something for me. Please, I just can't eat right now.

He knelt down in front of me, and pulling my hands away from my face, he cupped my chin in his hands. "What is it Becca? What's bothering you so badly?"

I pushed his hands away from my chin and bent and pulled up the legs of my pajamas.

"This! Hardly any bruising! The pain is endurable. I really thought they were broke and…"

"Wait just a minute Becca. I told you about your legs…" I quickly cut him off

"…And Heidi told me they were bruised very badly. Do you call this bruised badly?" I pointed to my legs again.

"What about the cut on my side Rafe? Why is it all healed? It was bleeding heavily last night. I even remember you holding pressure on it to stop the bleeding. I need some answers. This is so confusing. Heidi said that Mr. Ferrachi sent the Vatican Doctor here last night and he stitched my side. Are you going to try and tell me that these stitched healed and disappeared in less than twenty four hours and no trace of a scar? And there are a few crazy things that happened that I don't even want to discuss right now. I know you have the answers Rafe, you have to because you even saw the blood coming from my side, you just told me so a little while ago. Tell me Rafe, I can handle it. What is going on?"

He just stared at me through those beautiful cobalt blue eyes. I could tell he was debating on just what he wanted to tell me.

"Don't leave anything out Rafe. I want to hear it all!"

The expression on his face was one of bewilderment he had that terrible look of anguish in his eyes. He lifted me from the bed to stand in front of him, and looking down into my face he said,

"Becca, I can't tell you right this minute. I promise to explain everything but I just can't bring myself to give you an explanation right now."

"Why? Please tell me why? I am so confused over this that…"

Before I had a chance to utter another word, his lips were on mine, and they weren't tender and light this time. His kiss was full of desire and his lips parted mine, and his arms pulled me close to him so tightly that I could feel every muscle of his body molded against mine. My head began to spin and my breath came out in short little gasps. He must have mistook the passion, thinking I lost my breath because his lips left my mouth and he began kissing down my throat to my collarbone where he traced delicate kisses slowly back and forth across it. Then going back to the hollow of my throat he softly lingered there. I was so breathless from the intense pleasure that my legs began to shake and give out beneath me. When he noticed this, I think he finally realized that his passionate embrace hat affected me to the core of my being. He swooped me up into his rock hard arms and placed me on the bed pressing his long lean body against mine, and immediately he jumped up from the bed, looked at me with eyes full of passion, gasping from his desire. I sat up confused and feeling rejected. This was the second time he had done this to me. What was wrong?

He looked away from me for a moment, and then fixed his gaze on mine once more, slowly shaking his head back and forth, wincing in pain. He said,

"Oh! My sweet, sweet Becca, I have so much to tell you and I am so sorry I have done this to you again." With that said, he turned and walked into the other room.

When I finally composed myself enough to follow him into the living room, he was on the telephone talking to someone. When he saw me he quickly said, "I'll see you in a few minutes then." And he hung up the phone.

I looked at him shocked.

"Rafe what am I doing wrong? Aren't you as attracted to me as I am to you? I'm so

sorry that I can't control myself with you."

"Becca, please! I'm so attracted to you it's sinful. It's not you.. It's me that can't control myself around you. You don't know how hard this is for me. It will all be clear to you as soon as I explain everything, but I just can't tonight. Heidi will be here to stay with you for the night I have to leave."

What did he mean he was leaving?

"Rafe!"

The tears began to roll down my face. Now it was sheer frustration intermingled with the confusion.

"Please, I'm begging you…"

The doorbell began to ring. I had no choice but to compose myself. I wiped the sleeve of my pajamas across my eyes and tried to look as nonchalant as possible.

Rafe walked to the door to answer it. He never looked back at me once. Then in an even calm voice he said.

"Heidi, I'm so sorry to call you out on such short notice and so late at night, but I have some business that I have to take care of immediately!"

She batted her eyes at him,

"It's okay Mr. Rafe, I would come and stay with Rebecca anytime. Don't feel bad about it."

Rafe walked over to me, but he would not look into my eyes as he gently kissed me on the forehead.

"I hope I can get back tomorrow Becca, but if I can't, I'm sure Heidi wouldn't mind staying with you one more night."

Before I had a chance to say anything. Heidi said,

"Of course Mr. Rafe. I really don't mind."

I looked at both of them as serious as I could and said,

"It's okay I will be going to work tomorrow. No one needs to worry about staying with me. I feel just fine."

They both said at the same time,

"No! You are not!"

And then Rafe went on to say,

"Rebecca, tomorrow is Friday, there is no reason for you to go back to work on the last day of the work week, and everything is hectic right now with the Pope's funeral tomorrow."

I just glared at him.

" I'm stubborn when I want to be Rafe. I thank both of you for taking such good care of me. But I guarantee you, I feel well enough to work. I need to have my mind on something else beside myself and I'm going to work. I will ride in with Heidi. That's my final comment on the matter."

Rafe looked at me now with anger in his eyes.

"We'll talk about this tomorrow Becca!"

He closed the door behind him on his way out.

Heidi looked at me a little puzzled,

"What was that all about? If I didn't know better I would have thought the two of you had been quarrelling."

"Nothing, I just feel that I want to get out of here and go to work. It's not like I have some strenuous job or anything."

"Oh!"

She giggled.

"I thought maybe Rafe had a hot date tonight or something until I saw him kiss you on the forehead. That about blew my socks off. Let's have some wine."

"Okay Heidi, let's."

She had a way about her that always lifted my spirits.

Chapter 4
THE BRIDGE

Heidi and I arrived at work about six thirty the next morning because we wanted to beat all the crowds that soon would fill Vatican Square for the Pope's funeral. We both immediately began to work, Heidi so she could attend the funeral and I had the intention of catching up on all of the mounds of mail that had accumulated on my desk in my absence. I was anxious to see if there were anymore strange letters like the one that I had previously received but after I quickly scanned through most of the letters and didn't recognize anything close I began reading through some of the more interesting pieces picking out the letters that I thought would be worthy of correspondence.

At eight a.m. the rest of the staff started filtering in. Mike came over and sat down beside me and I thanked him for the card, which still sat on the table next to my bed, unopened.

"Rebecca, you look like hell! Why did you even bother coming to work today? You look like you could use a good weeks rest. Mr. Bellini is going to be so upset when he sees you have come back to work so soon. I've been covering all your calls for you, but I didn't dare touch any of that spooky mail that you get."

He laughed, and I suddenly realized how much I had missed his lop-sided grin, and the fun-loving mood he always seemed to be in.

"Oh Michael, I've missed you!" I said giving him a big hug, which completely took him by surprise.

"I needed a little laughter today. I think I needed to get out and be around people."

"And I thought it was just me you would want to be around. I should have known better." He said.

"Mike, stop it. Sometimes you can be so irritating." I laughed and resisted the temptation to ruffle his hair.

"One minute you say you need me, and the next I'm irritating? Sounds like you're not to sure about your feelings about me. Hmm, maybe I do have a chance."

"Stop it!" I grinned. "I'm completely sure of my feelings for you. You are the one who keeps forgetting. Now get to work, before I start to get grumpy with you."

"Oh goodness, now we wouldn't want to see that, would we Rebecca? Seriously, though, welcome back. But I still think you should have taken a little more time to recuperate."

"That's exactly what she's going to do." It was Mr. Bellini, looking at me sternly. "I haven't been here ten minutes and I have already received a call from Mr. Ferrachis' office telling me that Mr. David Rafe would be here to take you home as soon as his meeting is over. Mr. Ferrachi was none too happy that I let you come back to work so soon. Which is really funny, considering that I didn't know the first thing about it. Thanks for making me look bad, Becca." He sounded gruff but reached over and gave me a warm hug.

"We're all going to the Popes' funeral, are you coming along?"

"Is everyone in the office going? I really don't want to stay here alone."

A familiar voice came from behind us.

"You won't have to Becca, because I am taking you home right now." It was Rafe, and by the expression on his face I could tell that he wasn't too happy with me. He picked up my sweater, and draping it over my shoulders, as he handed me my handbag said.

"Goodbye everyone, Becca will be back to work when she isn't so weak and tired."

He gently put his arm through mine and walked me to the elevator. I only had enough time to wave goodbye to Heidi.

I noticed that Mike had a frown on his face and was staring peculiarly at me, and I wondered what that was all about. Surely he wasn't jealous.

When we were settled in the black Mercedes that Rafe was driving himself today, he looked over at me and shook his head.

"You look so tired today Becca, your lips even have a purple tinge to them. Do you feel weak? You were right last night when you said you could be stubborn when you wanted to be! But you're only slowing the healing process by your stubbornness!"

Without answering him, I looked at him closely. "Are you going to tell me today Rafe? I need you to answer my questions. All my questions! Beginning with why I suddenly become so repulsive to you."

We hadn't driven a half-mile and he quickly pulled the Mercedes over into the first vacant parking spot and leaving the engine to idle, he turned to look at me.

"Is that what you think? That you repulse me? He shook his head, staring at me incredulously. "That is the furthest thing from the truth. Though I can see why you think it. I'm surprised that you even want to have anything to do with me."

There was no doubt in my mind that I was falling deeply in love with Rafe. I had never been in love before, and I barely knew this man, but I knew this was the real thing. My whole being was absorbed in thoughts of him. I wanted to spend all my time with him. I also knew that he felt something for me. I just didn't know if his feelings were as deep as mine because of the way he always seemed to reject me just when he seemed close to making love to me. I had to get some answers from him today or I felt like I was going to lose my mind.

"Rafe, don't you know I-I'm falling in love with you?"

"Oh Becca, please don't say that. You may feel very differently about me when I explain everything to you. Do you feel up to a little drive? It's not the place I had in mind to talk to you, but it will have to do. But only if you don't feel to weak. If you do we can go back to your flat."

"I won't feel any better at home. I just need to know Rafe! I just can't take this bouncing back and forth any longer. It just confused me too much. Just drive, I'll be fine."

He put the Mercedes in gear, quickly speeding out of the parking spot to get into the flow of traffic, which already overflowed the lanes in the direction of Vatican Square. Thank goodness we were going in the opposite direction or we would be sitting in traffic for hours.

He drove to another part of Rome that I had never been to before. He parked in a nice neighborhood that was close to the Tiber River. Like everything else I had seen so far, this site was also beautiful. I was especially fascinated by the centuries' old buildings that lined the streets. We walked a few hundred feet to a bridge that crossed the Tiber. I stopped and took in the beauty of this magnificent bridge. There were ten beautiful angel sculptures that spanned the bridge. Rafe was watching me with an unreadable expression on his face. I turned and looked into the unfathomable depths of his cobalt blue eyes. I then looked again at the beautiful statues and than back at him.

"Oh Rafe. These angels are so beautiful. I don't mean to embarrass you, but with their beautiful features and muscled bodies, if you hadn't been with me when I saw these sculptures, I would have immediately thought of you and your hard muscled body and those same delicate features."

His eyes looked amused for a minute, and then a terrible sadness filled their depths. He took my hand in his and we started to walk across the bridge, void of people, due to the Pope's funeral. We stopped at the first angel who was holding a whip in his hands.

"Becca, this bridge has a long history behind it. One day I may explain it all to you. It is called Castel Saint' Angelo Bridge, which translated into English means the Bridge of the Angels. The sculptures were placed here in the 17th Century and were based on the designs of Bernini. It symbolized the transformation of Rome from the center of the Roman Pagan Empire to the Center of the Catholic Empire. That's how very old the bridge itself is. The span of the whole bridge is faced with Teavertine Marble. It is quite exquisite, don't you think?"

"I am speechless, Rafe. I've never seen anything like it. But then I'm finding that everything in Rome is making me speechless." We continued on to the next angel sculpture.

"Becca, I don't know if you have noticed, but each of these angels is holding an instrument symbolizing the instruments used in the Passion of Our Lord." I noticed he bowed his head when he mentioned Our Lord. It surprised me, but then we had never really spoken much about religion before.

He motioned me over to a marble bench that was in between the next two statues, and we sat down.

He took both of my hands into his, and sighed very deeply.

"My intentions were to take you to St. Peters Basilica, to explain everything to you at lunch the other day. But obviously after our lunch was cancelled, and with the untimely death of Pope Pius XIII, and now his funeral, we couldn't go there. So this seemed like the next appropriate place in Rome to bring you. Promise me that you will not interrupt me until I have finished with my explanation. I can only hope that you will comprehend all that I have to say, and, will think it through before you change your opinion of me. However, I will understand whatever course of action you decide to take concerning us. Please, don't interrupt me, or I'll never be able to finish my confession. It is hard enough as it is."

I stared into his blank stare for a moment. Now, I was scared, and wasn't sure if I wanted to hear this or not.

"Oh Rafe, now I am afraid of what you are going to say. I'm so afraid of losing you. But I need to know what the problem with me is."

"It isn't you Becca, just listen! Please!" I made a motion as if to zip my lips and he squeezed my hand, but never took his eyes from my face as he continued to talk.

"First of all I want you to know that the first day that you walked into my office, I was completely attracted to you. I have never had that happen to me before, and that is what makes this so very difficult for me."

I wasn't sure whether his eyes were welling up with tears from what he was about to tell me, or watering from the soft breeze that now had begun to circle around us, wrapping us in its' warmth.

"The reason I apologized when I kissed you, and the reason I have broken our embrace is because my love and loyalty, in fact my whole reason for existence, belongs to someone else. So you see, these feelings I have for you, even though they feel so right, are actually wrong."

I looked at him shaking my head no. I wanted to call him a liar, to tell him I didn't believe he was in love with someone else. Oh my God, this was my worst nightmare. I would have never thought of this in one hundred years. I kept quiet, not because I didn't want to say something, but because I couldn't. The tears began to stream silently down my cheeks. Rafe took a long slender finger and wiped the tears away, while he reached in his pocket for a hankie.

"No Becca, it isn't what you think. I might as well just come out with it, because I can see that I am only making matters worse. I have been involved in many investigations in many different countries during my lifetime and I solemnly swear to you, there has never been another human being in this world I have cared for, like I do for you. My loyalty belongs to someone else, not because of my own actions, but because of what I was created to do. This is going to be difficult for you, but I can always prove what I say to you is the truth. So please remember that as I speak." Now that he had my full attention I didn't want to miss a single word he had to say, but the tears continued to flow, as I knew this couldn't be good no matter what it was.

"My real name is Raphael, not David Rafe, I am one of the Archangels who stands before the throne of God. I have been to this earth many times in the past, and this time I am here to avenge his law. I take on human form whenever I am on earth in the service of God, but this is the very first time that I have experienced the human feelings of love for a woman. I do love you Becca, which you can be sure of. I have had to return to heaven three times already to talk to the Master about my feelings for you. Being the loving God that He is, He wants me to work this out on my own. My love for him is eternal, and the only other love I knew up until I met you, was the love that we have for all creation".

I could tell that he knew that I was in complete unbelievable shock. This couldn't be real. It was too bizarre and I was having a terrible time absorbing anything that he was saying to me. My mind just kept repeating over and over, "I know this is a strange nightmare. It has to be." I kept listening to his musical voice, watching the pained expression on his face as he explained his role in heaven to me.

"Becca, it would not be right for me to become involved permanently in any other kind of a relationship aside from my love for all creation.

There are seven of us who have duties in heaven that are serious, and our undivided attention needs to be upon He who created us.

If you and I retain our relationship from today forward we will have to redefine it, and be very careful of our actions. I am so sorry Becca that I have involved you in any of this sadistic mess. So you see, none of it is your fault. I can only tell you that my feelings for you are those of a man who is very deeply in love with a woman, and I would desperately like to claim you as my own. But it's not possible." He lifted my chin and looked into my eyes. "Becca, don't you see this pains me so badly. I want to be with you forever, but the most I can promise you is my time here, and to heal the wounds that I have caused you. I am going to give you time to think about this, and if you decide you never want to see me again, I will love you still, forever. But I will understand."

I couldn't take my eyes off of him. My beautiful Rafe, No Raphael, he could never be mine. I didn't want to live, and I knew I couldn't live without him. Before I ever answered him, I knew I could never stay away from him as long as he was on this earth. All I could manage to say was,

"But, I love you so much, please Rafe, don't leave me."

I stood to look up at the angel sculpture behind us. I looked once again as Rafe, he had the most wounded expression in his eyes, and it was then that I realized this absolutely tormented him to the core of his being. None of this was his fault either. At this moment we were just two souls who had happened to fall in love with each other. Of course his loyalty would be first to his creator. I understood that perfectly. But I also knew that it didn't matter to me who, or what he was I would love him forever. He must have seen the glint of resignation in my eyes, because he stood up and took me in his arms holding me against him, though not as tightly as usual. He kissed me gently on my forehead and said, "Oh my poor, poor Becca. I vow to make this up to you if it takes eternity."

I looked up into his beautiful angel eyes and as I lightly stroked the side of his face, I whispered, "Don't look so sad my beautiful angel. My love will always be yours as long as God gives me breath in this body. I will belong to you."

We stood and held each other for what seemed like an eternity, neither one of us wanting to let go. It almost felt like a goodbye, but at the same time I felt completely relieved of all the anxiety that had been built up from the first time Rafe kissed me. It was a bittersweet anguish. Finally when we did break our embrace we walked along the whole span of the bridge arm in arm, looking at each of the beautiful sculptured angels and the amazing architecture of the bridge itself. The breeze felt cool on our faces, and every now and then it would dance and swirl around us, engulfing us in our little world of ecstasy.

We rode in silence back to my flat, and when we were almost there it hit me, the angel at the prison who cut off Nicholas' head. As if he read my mind Rafe looked at me and said. "It was me."

I looked over at him wide eyed, "But how did you change so fast? Never mind! I don't think I could handle your answer right now."

His hands gripped the steering wheel, and he smiled at me. "You would be surprised at the things that I can do."

If nothing supernatural ever happened to me again, I knew I could be sure of one thing. This was going to be one interesting experience.

He dropped me off at my flat, and as he held the door open for me to get out of the Mercedes he gave me a light kiss on the cheek and said:

"I'll be back in a little while." And then he sped off into the night.

Once, inside, I fed Mr. Boots and settled on the couch. I turned on the television set to watch the news of the Popes' funeral. It made me so sad to see them carrying his coffin. All I could think of was how terribly he had been beaten, and how frail he looked the day he was murdered. Just as I began to change the channel I noticed that the light was blinking on the answering machine, so I forgot the TV and went to retrieve my messages. As I turned on the machine, the first was a familiar voice I recognized as Nicholas Baragio! But how could this be? I saw Rafe…er…Raphael cut off his head with my own two eyes. I had to play the message again, because the sound of his voice shocked me so much that I didn't hear the message he left. All he said was,

"Wasn't that a beautiful funeral Rebecca? You can be sure that the next one will be yours, but not until I have finished playing with you.

Luther promised me that much, but he wants to be the one to finish you off. I look forward to seeing you again! Soon!"

I didn't listen to the other two messages, I was afraid to. I quickly ran and locked my doors and windows. I was terrified! This had to be someone playing a bad joke on me. But I knew that it wasn't a joke. I shut all the blinds on the windows and went into the kitchen and made myself a stiff drink to calm my nerves a little bit.

It seemed like an eternity before Rafe came back, but finally he was there, knocking on the locked door. I was almost afraid to open it, and he probably thought I was crazy when I said, "Who is it?" because I never asked that question when someone knocked. When I let him in he looked at me strangely.

"Becca, what on earth is wrong? You aren't afraid of me now are you?"

I shook my head no, and the words poured out of my mouth. "Listen to my messages!"

He played back the message on my answering machine, and I noticed that he had a menacing expression on his face. "I should have burned him and asked for him to be banned to hell as soon as I cut off his head! I was too preoccupied with your injuries. I am going to have to take care of him once and for all."

The other two messages were from Heidi and Mike. Heidi called to say she wouldn't be over this evening because the Popes' funeral had upset her too badly. Mike had called to invite me out to lunch with him when I came back to work. When Rafe listened to Mikes' message he raised a quizzical eyebrow, and looked at me curiously. I just ignored him.

"Rafe, I saw you cut off Nicholas' head, how can he still be alive? I saw you throw it on the floor he was dead!"

"No, Becca, the only way you can kill a demon for good is to ban him to hell and I didn't do that. He is back and probably out to get more revenge than he ever was before. You can't ever be left alone now. You are no match for the demons in Luther's' army.

He walked with me over to the couch and sat me on his lap. "There are so many things that I have to explain to you so that you can begin to understand the workings of our realm as well as to ensure you are prepared for them. You are such an innocent and frail human and the only weapon and protection you have is me. It is my fault that you are in this much danger, it was my weakness for you that kept me from being more astute."

"No Rafe, if I would have listened to you in the first place and never put myself into this dangerous situation, you would not have to protect me at all. You did, after all, try to warn me."

"Maybe, maybe not Becca. Sometimes these shrewd demons have a particular person picked out for a reason, and I feel like your reason is me. They are smart, they knew I would have feelings for you, and you are just a pawn in their whole scheme of diabolical entertainment. Don't be afraid. We are stronger than they are."

I smiled weakly at him. "I'm not afraid Rafe, as long as you are here to protect me."

My heart began to pound, because I knew he couldn't be with me every minute. But I also knew that he would always make sure that I was protected, as long as it was in his power. I knew also that he had a much stronger Commander that Nicholas had.

"Why don't we change the subject for the evening Rafe. Tell me about your life."

"Before we do that Becca, you have to know one very important factor, and I am not telling you this to frighten you, however I'm sure it will. I am telling you so that you will always be on your guard, and always call me when you are in grave danger. Luther Abaddon is Satan"

He stared at me with an expression that was serious and I knew he was waiting for my reaction.

"Oh Rafe, this all seems so impossible. Please don't tell me anymore tonight or I am going to be a basket case. How can any of this be happening? No! Don't tell me now. I can't handle it right now. Please, just tell me more about yourself."

I learned that he can do all the things that we humans can do, but a lot of our necessities aren't essential for him to survive, like eating and sleeping or breathing. Angels never get sick or tired. Their spiritual life takes care of them and sustains them. Of course he is stronger and faster than a human. He has the same emotions as a human, sadness anger, joy, and love, and now passionate love.

He told me about different times that he had been sent to earth as far back as the Old Testament era. One book of the Bible was even written about the time he came and healed a blind man and his wife. It is the Book of Tobit, or Tobias. It is one of the books that was omitted in the King James; version as its authenticity was questioned. I was continually interrupting him, because I was so full of questions.

"Just how old are you Rafe?"

"I have no idea, God created me before he created man, so I have been around for a very long time."

I stared at him trying to digest that bit of information when another thought came to mind. "Would you prefer I call you Rafe or Raphael? Where did you ever come up with the name David Rafe?"

"My duties on earth require that I go by my human name of Rafe. So please continue to call me Rafe, I love to hear your voice say my name. Especially when you are asleep!"

"What! How embarrassing. Do I really talk about you when I'm sleeping?"

"You did when you were napping the other day, you even said you loved me. But of course I imagine that it was only due to the fact that you had taken a pain killer." He turned and grinned at me.

"Oh no Rafe, I honestly do love you." I looked at him, thinking to myself, 'why did circumstances have to be like this?' I knew we could make each other happy. I didn't tell him what I was thinking because I was sure it would only hurt him if I brought the subject up again. I was up against something bigger and more powerful than anything on earth. God was not someone to take lightly. I sighed and wondered why He let this happen. I didn't know whether it was a test for Rafe or for me.

Rafe was quietly watching me. He was probably trying to fathom what was going on in my mind.

This whole situation made me feel like I had a noose around my neck being pulled tighter, and tighter, squeezing until when he finally had to leave me, all the life would be choked out of me. I didn't care what kind of horrid things I would have to go through as long as I could be with him. Finally, I looked up at him.

"Okay, continue, how did you get the name David Rafe?"

He smiled at me again. I could see the relief in his actions that I didn't bring up the subject of our former discussion.

"My Father gave me the name David after King David of course, and Rafe is short for Raphael."

"I guess I am actually calling you by your nickname then when I call you Rafe, aren't I? That makes me feel much better. I don't feel like I'm cheating you out of your angelic name."

We sat and talked for hours, I enjoyed hearing about a life that was completely outside of my imagination; the holiness of heaven and how it is such a peaceful, tranquil place, the beauty that is beyond anything that we find on this earth. It is a place of eternal happiness. I imagine it as a place where fairy dust is falling from eternity, sparkling every object it touches. I found out that the meadows are speckled with all the different forms of animal life, and whether they are predator or prey, they live side by side in perfect harmony. Flower gardens are everywhere putting off the most beautiful intoxicating scents, all from every imaginable species and color. It is never to hot, never to cold. The whether is perfect. People do not just live in houses, but they live in stunning mansions, decorated outside and inside in perfect taste. I was sure that just the little bit that I grasped, that there is nothing in comparison to it on this earth. That is why it is so very hard to understand as a human. I had nothing to compare it with, because as Rafe said, "There is no comparison."

I finally fell asleep while listening to this beautiful creature tell me about the perfect life that he led. I only woke once that night, and that was when he lifted me into his perfectly muscled arms and carried me to my bed and covered me with the Dresden quilt that was folded across the back of the overstuffed chair that decorated the corner of the room.

When I woke up the next morning, I stretched my body. It felt good to be alive. Then I remembered everything Rafe had told me, and I lay for a long time trying to digest it all in my mind. It all seemed so impossible. He said he was here to avenge God's law. What on earth did that mean? What was happening that was so important that God would send one of his Archangels here? It had to be something historical. "I can't think about this. It is just to above my understanding." I said these words out loud evidently, because as soon as I finished Rafe said:

"Well Good morning!"

I turned, startled, looking to see where his voice was coming from. He was sitting comfortably in the chair looking at me.

"Did you sit in that chair all night?" I said to him, holding my hand over my still pounding heart.

"Becca, I didn't mean to startle you! I was so busy watching you stretch your beautiful body that I didn't even think of you not realizing that I was here. I watched you all night. You didn't seem to have any nightmares, and at least I know that you still love me."

"It would have been nice if He..." I pointed up to the ceiling. "...would have created you to sleep, maybe then you wouldn't know all my secrets." I rolled my eyes, embarrassed, because I knew that as long as he was with me, he would know everything I did as I slept.

He just laughed as he came over and gave me a friendly peck on the cheek. I guess this is what he meant when he said we would have to redefine our relationship. I didn't care, as long as I could look at his beauty and be with him. I was too much in love with him to ever care the same way about another man.

He sat silently for a few minutes and then he took hold of my hands and pulled me up from the bed, and we walked hand in hand into the living room.

"Becca, I know this is all very hard for you to comprehend, but as each day goes by you will understand a little more. I don't want to give you all the specific details at once. It would be too much for any human to grasp, and I don't want to frighten you anymore than you already are. You are going to have to trust that I will inform you as needed. Now lets start the morning on a lighter note. Do you want any breakfast?"

I shook my head no. "Just coffee. I'll go and make it. Is there anything I can get you?"

"I'll have some coffee."

"But I thought..."

"Becca, I said eating, and drinking weren't necessary for us, I didn't say we couldn't do it, and I happen to like coffee very much. It is one of the pleasures you have on earth that we don't have in heaven. But then in heaven, we wouldn't even think of any of the foods you have here on earth. We are perfectly content in every way."

I set our coffee and some cookies I found in the cabinet on the coffee table and went and sat beside him on the couch.

"You do know Rafe, that my mind is having a really hard time accepting all of this. I guess God didn't program us to know what actually takes place in heaven, at least not to the extent that I am learning from you. These are ideas that I have never given that much thought. I was taught to worry about getting to heaven, not what it would be like when I arrived."

"I know, and It's sad that preachers don't teach more about heaven instead of damning everyone to hell for all their little imperfections. Heaven is nothing like any of those preachers teach, Becca. There is much more to life that we have there, and so much of it is already in the Bible if they would just open their eyes."

I watched him as he took a bite out of one of the cookies. It was obvious by his expression that he wasn't too pleased with the way it tasted. He set it back down on his plate like it was Limburger cheese or something. He took a drink of his coffee and caught me looking at him out of the corner of his eyes.

He put his coffee cup down and turned and looked at me. "Becca, there is something that I have to talk to you about, and it is serious so listen to me carefully. It isn't something you can just decide you don't want to think about."

"It's a bad habit, Rafe. It's always been easier for me to push things that I think are unpleasant to the back of my mind, rather than try to work them out."

He smiled knowingly in my direction. "So I've noticed," as he continued. "You can't be alone, ever. Luther sees you as one of his enemies now, and I guarantee he is out to destroy you. For your own good, don't ever think of him as Luther again, only as Satan. I know how frightening this is to you, but you have to make it a reality.

Because that is exactly what it is. You need to be on your toes at all times and be aware of everything that is going on around you. Do you understand me?"

I wanted so badly to go back to a few days ago, before I ever met any of these characters. But I knew if I could, I wouldn't have met Rafe, and he was my life now. So I sighed and nodded my head. I was no match for Satan, but I knew I had to do this for whatever small amount of time I had left to spend with Rafe, and he was my life now.

"Good! Do you really think you are strong enough to go back to work for at least half of a day? I have business at the Vatican, at least until noon every day, and I don't want to leave you alone here, and even if Heidi could come and stay with you, I doubt very much her help would be any protection from Satan. I'm sure you agree with me."

"Rafe, I was ready to work yesterday, and no one thought I should be there. You even made me leave early remember? I will be fine. I can work for the whole day. You don't need to be that worried about me. Honestly!"

"You are nowhere ready to work for a whole day. I hate sending you for even half a day. You were right about your legs being broken and the gash in your side."

I looked at him in total surprise.

"I healed you Becca! I know how long it will take you to be physically and completely healed. I only sped up the process of healing. Your body is the only thing that can complete the process, and only with cooperation from you, by resting and taking it easy. Your body is in a fragile state right now, so don't question me when I say I want to bring you home at noon every day. If I have an emergency to handle, well, we will cross that bridge when we come to it."

"Oh Rafe! It would be so much easier on you if I wasn't a burden to you."

"Don't you ever say that! You are the most important thing on this earth, and I want you well and healthy. You only stand to benefit by listening to me."

"Rafe, please know that I will do anything you ask me. I don't ever want to go against your wishes again. Look where it landed me the first time I went against you."

"No Becca, those were orders you disobeyed. Not wishes! Don't ever cross me that way again. I don't think that you want to see me angry."

He didn't smile when he said this to me, and I knew that there was truth behind his words.

"My biggest concern is for you to regain your strength. I know with all my heart you don't have the strength to get away from Nicholas yet. You don't even have the strength to run on your legs. So let's take this one day at a time. Now go and get dressed. I have plans for our day!"

Thrilled at the notion of spending the whole day with him, I quickly retreated to my room with no argument, excited as a child who was going to a candy store.

"Where are we going? What do I need to wear?"

"It's a surprise. Wear something comfortable, maybe a pair of slacks and a sweater. And no high heels!"

I put on the new Versace slacks and matching powder blue and cream colored sweater that I had purchased last week, glad to not have to wear a dress for a change. We had a strict dress code at the Newspaper Office, because it was inside Vatican City. We had to wear dresses below the knee, or long skirts and at least elbow length sleeves on our blouses and sweaters. I wore my hair casual today, falling down around my shoulders, almost to my waist, with just a little bit of curl to it.

When I appeared in the living room he looked at me appreciatively, saying:

"Well at least no one can say I don't know what I am doing when I fall in love with a mortal. You look beautiful. Do you have a scarf? I would like to start the day by taking you to St. Peters. Is that okay?"

"Of course Rafe, I am just happy being with you, no matter where we go." I said as I walked back into the bedroom to grab a cream colored pashmina from my bureau drawer and wrapped it loosely around my neck.

When we arrived at St. Peters there were surprisingly few people lingering in the great room of the Basilica. It appeared more elaborately decorated that it ever had in any of the television programs or pictures that I had seen. But then, colors and objects are so much more brilliant when we can see them with our own eyes. I was especially overwhelmed with Michelangelo's frescos than anything else except for maybe the huge pillars that surrounded the altar that is said to be placed in protection over St. Peter's tomb.

Rafe seemed so at ease and at home with the décor of this beautiful place. He knelt beside me in the pew with his hands folded the way that you see the great saints, or angels at prayer in religious pictures. His eyes were fixed on the huge tabernacle, where it is said that Jesus is in the Blessed Sacrament. His lips were moving, but I could not hear a sound. I felt suddenly ashamed for spending my time looking up at the ceiling and all around at the beauty of the décor while he was in prayer, so I knelt there beside him, folded my hands, and closed my eyes in prayer also. I thanked God for sending Rafe to earth asking Him that I not offend him in any way. I knew he had a special reason for Rafe and I meeting and whatever his plan was for us I wanted Him to give me the courage and fortitude to accept it.

Rafe finally reached over, and touching my hands said: "I have another chapel that I want to show you that is more private than this where we can sit and talk."

The chapel he took me to was the Popes' private chapel. There were black streamers across the entrance, but Rafe proceeded inside anyway. The chapel was decorated with an altar and a tabernacle as well as a crucifix attached to the wall. That was it. Pope Pius XIII had been a simple man, poor in spirit and shy. I could see him in here praying. It fit his humble personality.

"What are you thinking about Becca?"

We were sitting in one of the small pews and as I looked around there wasn't another person in the chapel. We were alone and could talk.

"I was just thinking how sad it was that Satan killed Pope Pius XIII. I will never forget how tired and worn he looked last week when I saw him, but he wasn't to tired to give me his blessing. Then when Lu…Satan killed him. It was so horrible. He was so near death before that and so despondent. The Pope knew it was Satan, didn't he Rafe?"

Those deep blue eyes were penetrating mine again, seeming to read within the depths of my mind.

"Yes, he knew. Oh Becca so much of your world is about to change. No matter what you see or hear, please, don't listen to anyone or think you should follow something you see. Listen only to me. That is the only way I can promise you safety."

"Is it the end of times Rafe?" I didn't want to hear the answer to the question, but I knew I had to ask. He was looking at me so sadly and with such a serious expression.

"Becca, you cannot divulge one word of the conversation we are about to have with anyone, because Our Father could change everything I am telling you in the blink of an eye. I can't tell you everything, like I said; I only want to prepare you. This isn't just the end times Becca. It is the end."

"You mean it is the end of the world?"

"No, those are men's words, it is the end of things the way that you know them now. I am sure that you have heard it said, he will create new heavens and a new earth?"

I nodded, I had heard the priest talk about it before, but I never paid much attention.

After all, people had been talking about the world ending for as long as I could remember.

"There will be new ways Becca, and new rules. What you have on earth now will be destroyed and a lot of things as you know them will be destroyed as well. That is why I am here. It is going to be the ultimate battle between good and evil with the angels of heaven and the demons of hell at war. It will be the battle to end all battles, and I really detest the idea that you will be here to endure it. I can only tell you God has a plan for everyone on earth and their destinations must be fulfilled. I cannot change that. That is between you and God, and what he has in store for each and every one of you."

I put my hands to my temples. "Don't say anything else for a minute Rafe. Let me think, let this sink into my mind."

We sat in perfect silence. All I could think about was all the innocent people, all the people who didn't even believe in God. I became frightened for them. Damn! I became frightened for myself.

"What about all of the innocent people, and all those who were never taught to believe about God? What about them Rafe? It isn't fair. I know that the world has become a rotten stink hole But there must be people in every walk of life who are good left. What about all of them? This is it then? The time is now and there is nothing we can do about it?"

He put his arms around me and I was grateful, because I knew that I was on the verge of becoming hysterical.

"Becca, Becca, how many generations has the human race gone through? So many have turned their backs on God. Now they say that this generation is being taught to believe that it is only ignorant, uneducated people who believe all the fairytale stories that are Gods actual word." Now he pressed his knuckles to his forehead. "I wish it were different Becca, but man has done this to himself. If it makes you feel any better those who have led a life of good will be rewarded with good, while those who have led a life of perdition will be damned to perdition, and those who know no better, or are in between will have a short time to change their ways for the good of their souls. But our Father has given this world long enough. He is Love, and it has pained us in Heaven to know how much He has loved human kind to be repaid the way He has been, by the very ones he has created. In the end, it is Satan who will pay. It is his undoing's that circumstances have not been different since the beginning. He deceived a woman and she in turn deceived her mate. Now he will have to pay, and I am here to make sure he does, and when God sends the rest of his army, the battle will begin." He was almost livid when he finished speaking and I had no doubt how much he really loved God and hated Satan, and I thought to myself, he couldn't think much of the human race right now either.

"Oh Rafe, I am so sorry you are right of course. It is something we have known all of our lives, and I resign myself to the fact that this is the payment for our actions. I will do whatever you want me to do. Just please don't leave me until you absolutely have to."

He put his arms around me and squeezed me very tight. When he released me he said,

"Becca, let's just enjoy the rest of the day." And with those words we knelt in prayer a little longer, and then we left the chapel.

When we got back into the Mercedes I looked at him and said:

"Rafe. I only have one more thing to say to you. Thank you for the confidence you have placed in me, and I promise to help you in anyway that I can."

He squeezed my hand and smiled that beautiful smile I had grown so fond of.

"That means more to me than you will ever know Becca."

We spent the day seeing a few of the sites that I hadn't yet been to in Rome. The last place that we visited for the day was atop one of the seven hills in the city. There were huge cliffs that looked down to the river far below. We walked in the forest and it was so peaceful and quiet. The birds seemed to be singing sad melodies , giving me the impression that they already knew what was about to take place on our planet.

When we reached the summit of the hill it frightened me to look over the cliff to the river below. Rafe just laughed and held my hand, pulling me back from the ledge. We sat on a huge boulder overlooking the scenery below and it was so breathtakingly beautiful. Just the history of Rome is enough to induce a person to sit and imagine the ancient city at the height of it's glory spread out beneath. Rafe climbed down from the boulder and walked a few feet from its side. I watched him, wondering what he was thinking at this very moment, but decided not to disturb his thoughts. Suddenly it became very windy, leaves began falling from the trees and the dust off the cliff began to blow in my face, stinging my eyes as it hit me. I lifted my arm to shield my face with one hand while holding tightly to the boulder with the other hand. For a moment, I became frightened that the wind would blow me off the huge rock.

"Rafe, where are you? I can't see anything with all of this dust blowing in my face."

Then just as suddenly as the wind had come up, it became still and quiet. Where Rafe had been standing stood the most magnificent angel. His body was completely muscled and his features were extremely beautiful and handsome all at the same time. He was tall and his skin had a shimmery glow to it. The sight was absolutely breathtaking. I was momentarily speechless. He spread his huge wings, flapping them lightly as he walked toward me. I knew in an instant it was Rafe. He did this to convince me. To make sure I really did believe his story. He was so stunning, and he was the first to speak.

"Becca! Don't be afraid, it is only me. Are you afraid?"

"No." I stammered, "I, you, ah, you didn't have to prove anything to me Rafe. Oh my God, you are so beautiful. I don't know what to say."

"But you aren't afraid?" His eyes were still the beautiful cobalt blue that you could lose yourself in, and that put me a little bit at ease.

"I'm not afraid of you Rafe. I'm just flabbergasted by your beauty. I have never seen anything so beautiful in my entire life."

"Becca, I want to show you something that is beautiful and that you probably would have never had a chance to see in your lifetime if you hadn't met me. But I need you to calm down. I don't want you to have a stroke."

"Rafe the most beautiful thing that I may ever see in my life is standing right in front of me. I am looking at you now."

He just laughed and glided towards me, swinging me up into his arms, as he walked to the edge of the cliff with me howling, "No, No" all the way. When he flew off of the edge I buried my head into his granite hard chest squeezing my eyes shut and not moving a muscle in my body. I could hear the flapping of his wings and feel the soft breeze flitting past us.

Finally he said, "Becca. Open your eyes. . I won't drop you. Don't you trust me?"

With my eyes still squeezed shut, I lifted my head from his chest and I heard a weak little whisper come from my lips. "I do. I trust you will all my heart. I trust you with my life."

He started laughing again. "Are you trying to convince me or yourself?"

The whisper was just an octave higher. "Both, I guess!"

"Becca, please open your eyes. Now!" I opened my eyes and looked up at him. I could still feel the strange tingling sensation in my body that I felt whenever I looked into his eyes or was near him. "Look around Becca, I promise you are safe."

I looked around, and of course he was right as always, it was beautiful. Soaring through the air, and being held by an angel. I really began to enjoy this angelic joyride that he was taking me on. He pointed out all the different sites as we flew past them. It was hard to visualize how very large the city actually was from the ground. The Vatican state looked so tiny from up here. We flew until it was nearly dusk and then we landed back on top of the cliff next to the boulder where just a little earlier I had been sitting peacefully. He set me down gently and held me close for a moment. I could tell that he wanted to kiss me just as badly as I wanted him to. There was a warm desire for him, deep inside of me. But we just stared at each other for what seemed like an eternity, neither one of us wanting to spoil the moment. When he finally did release me he merely kissed me on the top of my forehead and we both sighed, deeply, in unison.

Chapter 5
THE PARK

The following day we both left for work together. As Rafes' duties require him to be on the job earlier than me, I arrived at the newspaper office a few minutes after Heidi.

"Hi Rebecca! Is it all right for you to come to work now? I thought you were resting for a while."

"I'm just working half of a day for now. By the way Heidi, when are you going to start calling me Becca? Every time someone calls me Rebecca, I think they are either angry with me or they don't know me well."

"Oh that would be just great! I haven't been angry with you, and I suppose we have come to know each other rather well. I would be delighted to call you Becca, my dear friend."

"Good" I laughed "…and Heidi, thank you for being such a great friend. Has anything new, besides the obvious, been going on around here that I should know about?"

"Well the only important news right now that I know of is that the Cardinal's have all entered the conclave to begin the selection of a new Pope. Today should be the first day we will see if they have made a selection. Black smoke means they have and white smoke means they have not. It should be pretty interesting to see whom they pick. I think whoever he is; he will have a tough time living up to Pius XIIIs reputation, don't you?"

"Yes, I doubt there is a man devout enough to fill his shoes. I hope that there is though."

I walked back to my desk to sort through some of my mail. I wrote a short article on the Pope emphasizing how much he would be missed.

When I started going through some of the mounds of mail, there was one letter addressed to me personally. There was no return address. I hated it when that occurred because I could never respond to them, and I wasn't willing to print anything that I didn't have a return address, which allowed me to verify the information sent to me. I opened the envelope with my letter opener carefully. In bold print on a single sheet of paper, it only said, SOON BECCA, SOON! I immediately thought of Nicholas Barragio. I bet it was from him. Obviously he wasn't going to leave me alone until he made sure I was dead. I put the letter back in the envelope and shoved it in my purse to show to Rafe later. I had to be strong. I couldn't let these little reminders from Nicholas get to me or I would go crazy. Regardless, I shivered at the thought anyway.

The next letter I came upon spoke of the food shortage in both Ethiopia and China, One third of the population in both of the countries had already died of starvation and parts of Asia and Africa were quickly facing the same ramifications. The woman who wrote this letter was an American from China. She was married to a Chinese diplomat, and she claimed that an Angel had appeared to her, warning that the world was about to come to an end. She was told that her husband was a good man. The Angel wanted her to try and convince him to pray for enlightenment so that his soul would be saved. She spoke of all the prophecies that most Christians knew about that were going to take place anytime now. If she only knew how right on target she was. I set the letter aside to call her later to see what else she had to say. Perhaps if she was reliable I could print her story. It might give our readers some food for thought.

Without realizing it, I started thinking of all the horrible things that could potentially happen and now that I knew it wasn't just a possibility, but a reality, it was beginning to truly frighten me. Would we live through it? Was Rafe connected to me because I was going to die a horrible death planned by the devil? Was Rafe sent just to comfort me while I was still here? I didn't know. I hated not knowing. Maybe it would be easier that way. I hoped that I wouldn't suffer, but I did know that if Nicholas Barragio had anything to do with it I would suffer worse than a lot of people. I can remember those yellow teeth, and how he seemed to undress me with his eyes. I cringed at the thought of it.

"Rebecca!"

The voice startled me, and I let out a little yell of surprise.

"Mike, you just scared me half to death." I still could feel my heart pounding frantically under by blouse.

"I'm sorry Rebecca, but you looked like someone scared you before I even said your name. Are you all right? I've been really worried about you lately."

"Oh Mike, thanks. But I am fine, really. I'm healing very nicely and before you know it I'll be back to work full time. Right now I have permission for partial days, but that's okay, as long as I get out of the house. I'm not a person to sit still for very long."

He shrugged his shoulders and said, "Don't you think it's time for a break? It's ten thirty already. You want to go and get some coffee?"

I shook my head no. "Mmm, I better not…Since I'm not here all day I probably just need to keep working until its time for me to go."

"Becca, Mr. Bellini asked me to take you down to the cafeteria. He said that you had been working nonstop since you got here. So come on, let's go get some coffee and donuts."

I looked towards Mr. Bellini's office and as if to verify what Mike was saying. Mr. B was on the other side of the glass door pointing at the elevator, motioning for me to go. I had to laugh. He watched out for me just like an old papa bear. I nodded my head yes, as I got up from my chair to leave with Mike.

We had no sooner gotten on the elevator and pushed the button for the ground floor when the elevator shook so violently that I almost fell down, and probably would have if Mike hadn't been there to help me keep my balance. The shaking seemed like it lasted forever, and I could feel the elevator banging against the walls. The lights flickered and then went out. Then, Thank God, everything stopped shaking. The only trouble was that the elevator was stopped and evidently was between floors because we couldn't open the door. It was so dark that I couldn't even see my hand in front of me. Mike pushed the elevator emergency button. It didn't work either. We both started hollering

"Help" and pounding on the sides of the elevator in hopes of someone hearing us. But no one seemed to hear a sound.

"It must have been an earthquake!" Mike said. "I can't imagine anything else that would have happened so suddenly." He lit his cigarette lighter to see my face.

"Oh there you are, you can't see anything in here can you?"

He took hold of my hand and pulled me closer to his side. I think he was probably just as frightened as I was. We kept trying to push buttons and holler, but no one came to our rescue. Finally I started getting really hot. It was becoming stuffy in this tiny little cubicle.

"Mike, I have to sit down on the floor, I am so hot that I feel faint." I sat down and wiped the edge of my sweater across my forehead. The next think I knew, Mike plopped down beside me.

"You better take it easy Rebecca, don't let yourself get too upset, you're just trying to recuperate. We just need to sit here patiently and wait until someone discovers we aren't around. It shouldn't take them to long to figure out where we are" He patted my hand and moved a little closer to me.

"Well let's just hope there wasn't a lot of damage because if there was and they have other people to tend to, it's going to be a long time before they get to us."

Just about then the elevator began to shutter again. This time a little more violently that before. It was a good thing I was sitting on the floor, or I know I would have fallen for sure this time.

"Rebecca, I hate to admit it, but I'm getting a little anxious myself now, I've never gone through anything like this before, and I don't like being in closed in places like this."

"Neither do I Mike, but we have to remain calm." There was another thunderous shake and the recessed ceiling light fell out of its fixture and hit me on the side of my head, shattering as it did. I reached up to feel my head and I could feel the blood oozing from one of several cuts. This is just what I needed. Another scar decorating my head.

"Rebecca, what was that? Did it hit you?"

"It was the ceiling light Mike, it just cut my head a little bit. I'm okay." I said

I could hear him fumbling around, but I could not see anything. Then he was trying to feel my face and my head. I could tell that he had a piece of cloth in his hands.

"Here Rebecca, take my handkerchief and wipe your cuts. Are you sure they aren't deep?"

"They will be fine Mike", I said reaching for the handkerchief.

"They are just little scratches." I lied

Most of them were but one of them was oozing blood pretty fast and I had to put pressure on the handkerchief because the blood was starting to run down the side of my face. I was beginning to get a little headache and my head began throbbing. I knew it wasn't anything to worry about, but it was an aggravation that I didn't need at the moment. It was bad enough just being trapped in here.

We sat in silence and when I heard Mike's slow steady breathing I knew he must have fallen asleep. Men, they could sleep anywhere, no matter what was going on. There really wasn't anything either of us could do, except wait. Finally I nodded off myself. When I woke up Mike had moved closer and was slumped over so his head was lying against my shoulder. I could hear banging somewhere.

"Mike! Quick! Wake up. I think they are trying to rescue us"

He jumped to his feet and began hollering,

"We're in here, were in here."

Suddenly the elevator began to move, but it was going up instead of down, and then right before the doors opened the lights came back on. We both had to squint our eyes and shield them with our hands. We had been in the dark for so long that our eyes were extremely sensitive to the light. When Mike was finally able to adjust his eyes to the light, he looked at me in horror.

"Oh My God Rebecca, you have blood all over your face and down the front of your dress. I thought you said you weren't cut badly."

"Oh Mike, it's okay! Facial wounds always look worse than they actually are. The skin is so thin on your scalp and forehead that it bleeds a lot. That's all. I'm fine."

The doors to the elevator were finally pried open, and Rafe and Mr. Bellini in addition to half the staff were standing on the other side.

Rafe frowned when he saw that I had blood all over me, and looking at Mike he said,

"Couldn't you have shielded her a little better that that Mike?"

Mike just looked down. I noticed he had a sullen expression on his face.

"Rafe, please! We couldn't see anything in there. It was pitch black."

Without giving me a chance to say anything else, he lifted me in his arms and started for the stairs as I protested.

"I am perfectly capable of walking. Put me down!"

He just ignored me and took me to the car. He put me down in front of the door and opened it for me, waiting until I got inside before he went around to the drivers side.

"Becca, I can't believe you are this accident prone. Are you alright?"

"Rafe, I am fine, they are just a few little cuts from the light fixture that broke when it hit me on the head. Was that an earthquake?"

"Yes!"

He looked at me with a very serious yet sad look and said,

"Becca, It has begun!"

My heart skipped a little beat and I realized that no matter how brave I tried to be, I really was terrified of what was to come.

"Becca, did you know that you and Mike were locked in that elevator for four and a half hours? I know you have to be tired. You've had too much excitement for one day. It is going to be a full time job just keeping you from getting hurt."

He turned and looked at me, smiling as he slid his hand down the side of my face to my shoulder, and the familiar tingle began to overtake me again. I almost told him he had better stop touching me at all if he wanted us to redefine our relationship, but I couldn't as I enjoyed it to much.

"Rafe, I received a letter from a woman today that said one third of the populations of Ethiopia and China had died of starvation. Is that part of it too?"

"Yes, and there will be many more disasters worse than that until one third of mankind is wiped out, and as it says in the Bible, these are just the birth pangs. I hope all Christians are watching the signs like this woman appears to be."

I completely forgot about the other letter in my purse, with everything that had taken place today, and I just laid my head back against the headrest in exhaustion. I thought to myself, what a very tiring week it had been. We rode in silence for a few minutes and finally Rafe looked over at me again and said,

"Becca, you really need to rest when I get you home. Are you up to eating out first?"

"You know I think I could eat an elephant right now, that's how famished I am. Mike and I were going to get coffee and donuts when the earthquake hit, but obviously we didn't make it. Was there very much damage from the earthquake?"

"No, not really. The worst things were that most of the elevators got stuck and some glass cracked. I felt sorry for the people that work in Vatican City though because you could tell that they were very frightened by it. You have to promise me to try and keep your wits about you, because we are going to go through some pretty tough times and I won't be able to spend every minute with you. I'll try and make sure someone who can protect you will be around at all times though. Do you think you can keep calm? That is what will save you"

"I'll try my best Rafe, that's all I can promise you. I kept my head pretty good through the earthquake. Whoever would have thought that the light fixture was going to fall in the pitch black and hit me in the head?"

"Just your luck." He chuckled.

He pulled into the parking lot of one of the hotels that had an excellent restaurant inside. There was one on the roof of the fiftieth floor and one on the ground floor. He wanted to take me to the top so that I could enjoy it revolving and take in the sites of Rome while we ate. But we were informed when we got inside the building that the restaurant on the top floor was closed just as a precaution because of the earthquake. We did have a nice dinner at the ground floor restaurant, as I thought about it while we were eating, after the shake up I just endured, I probably wouldn't have enjoyed sitting in a restaurant that was rotating. My stomach gave a little lurch just thinking about it.

When we got back to the flat I went to sit on the couch for a while, but Rafe suggested I go in and lie on the bed and try to take a little nap. It was still pretty early in the evening, so I said I agreed.

I had been asleep forty-five minutes when I started having my old familiar nightmare again. This time I was running through the streets of Rome, trying to hide in the same church that had always been in my dream. I was running again but this time the hand that had reached out to grab me time and time before finally caught me, and I must have started screaming, as the next thing I was aware of, Rafe was sitting on the bed cradling me in his arms and gently waking me up.

"It's okay Becca, it's okay. You are just having a bad dream. Wake up sweetheart. Come on quit screaming now. I'm here." He was wiping the tears from my eyes with his handkerchief and just kept rocking me back and forth. I put my arms around his neck and buried my head on his chest. Than he lifted me from the bed and took me out into the living room and laid me on the couch.

"What on earth frightened you Becca? You were really screaming. I hope I am not frightening you too much with everything I've been telling you."

"No Rafe, it's not you. It's the same nightmare I seem to have over and over. I have had it for a long time, and I'd rather not talk about it right now, if you don't mind. I am so happy that you were here though, or I would have certainly woken up in a cold sweat. You aren't leaving tonight are you?"

"I told you I wouldn't leave you unless I absolutely had to. Just lay here and rest, okay? I'm here!"

I couldn't go to sleep for a long time but when I finally did, I slept the rest of the evening peacefully through the night and didn't wake up until the sun that was shining through the sheer curtains of the living room windows. Rafe was across the room sitting comfortably on the loveseat that matched the living room furniture. Boots was curled up at his feet.

"Well hello! You actually had a good nights rest Becca. That makes me much happier and I'm hoping you will feel better today. You slept for about fourteen hours. Your body really needed to catch up with all the rest you've missed and the huge stress you've been through."

I had a brush in my purse that was on the table next to him and I asked him if he minded getting it out for me. When he reached into my purse the threatening letter I got yesterday fell out. I still didn't think anything about it, but when he looked at it, his face went pale.

"What's wrong Rafe?"

He held the letter towards me, and he looked like he was going to be angry.

"When were you going to tell me about this, Becca?"

"What?" I had completely forgotten about it.

"SOON, BECCA, SOON?"

"Oh my god, er gosh, I forgot all about that. I was honestly going to tell you about it. That's why it was in my purse. I didn't want any of the office staff to see it. I wasn't trying to deceive you Rafe, I swear. I really just forgot."

"How could you forget something like this? You can't take these things lightly Becca. You know who this is probably from don't you? It is either from Satan or Nicholas." He turned the paper over and then back to the front. "Is this all there is? Where is the return envelope?"

"That's all there was Rafe, nothing else, not even a return address on the envelope. The envelope is still on my desk at work."

"From now on, if you get any mail like this and I'm in my office, please call me immediately. You don't have to read it. All you need to say is 'I got another one.' Please make sure you tell me right away. I can understand that under the circumstances with the earthquake and everything else that you may have forgotten. But don't do it again! I can't protect you if I don't know what is going on."

"Okay, of course I'll call you if I read anything that comes through the mail, phone or messenger. I promise."

"Becca, I just worry about you. You can be independent at times, and this is not the time to show me how independent you are. Satan is a lot stronger and wiser than you, as is Nicholas Baragio. They could break you in two in a matter of seconds. Not minutes, seconds! I hope I have made myself clear on this now! Case closed. Now go and get ready for work. I already called and told Heidi you would be a little late today, so you don't have to do everything in the rush you usually put yourself through."

I turned the news on the television when I went in the bathroom to get ready. I stopped in front of it when I heard the anchorman telling that several of the big farms of the United States and Baja California had been wiped of their crops by a strange breed of locusts that scientists were baffled by, a species they had never seen anything like them before.

The news station panned their cameras across vast regions of farmland that was completely barren. It looked so strange to see just sand and dirt where crops and grass once carpeted the ground. There weren't even any weeds and the leaves on the trees were eliminated completely.

The anchorman commented that if things continued at the rate they were going, not only would there be no crops, but the livestock would have nothing to eat. It appeared to be a gruesome situation. The broadcast immediately went from the locust to a story about a strange flu virus that was already at epidemic proportions in some of the Mideast and the neighboring countries. This virus caused large welts on the body, with an incurable pneumonia that followed. Many of the people in Israel were already succumbing to its affects. The CDC was trying desperately to identify the virus so that they could come up with a vaccine for it. Before it infiltrated the world.

I thought it was strange that no one seemed to be in panic about theses two news stories. Life was just going on as usual. But of course, I might have reacted the same way if Rafe hadn't warned me.

I quickly took my shower and dressed in my mint green suit. I put on the high heel shoes that matched the satin piping that edged the border of the sleeves, collar, and button plackets of the jacket. I found a deep green patterned scarf and lightly draped it across my shoulders. I pulled the sides of my hair back with a fancy comb and let the rest fall loosely down my back. When I went back into the living room Rafe eyed me appreciatively. I tried to act like I didn't notice.

"Rafe, did you happen to be watching the news a few minutes ago?"

"Becca, you look absolutely beautiful today, that color brings out the green of your eyes." He said, ignoring my comment. He walked across the room towards me, and then stopped about a foot away from me, eyes filled with yearning, but he kept control of himself and only sighed. I could feel my body begin to slightly tremble at the anticipation of his embrace, but I knew he could not be disloyal. Nor could I. I had to be satisfied with just the nearness of him and the time we could spend together. This was going to be very difficult. I would have to be very careful how I dressed from now on.

I would have to pick out more simple clothing that didn't flatter my figure like the suit did. I couldn't bare not fulfilling the physical attraction we had for each other, and it wasn't fair to flaunt myself in front of him, when we both knew it was impossible to placate our desires.

"Becca, please tell me you aren't going to wear those shoes."

I looked down at my shoes that perfectly matched my suit and then back at him.

"Why? What's wrong with them?"

"You can't wear those stilts with your legs not completely healed yet. You won't be able to walk before the day is over," He said.

"Oh Rafe, I so am used to wearing heels all the time. I hadn't thought about that. How about if I take a pair of flat shoes along with me to put on when I get to work, so that I at least look decent going to and coming from work?"

He looked at me with somewhat of a condescending twinkle in his eyes, "I guess I can go along with you that much Becca, if you promise to change them as soon as you get to work."

He was so much stronger than I was, he seemed able to shake this feeling of lust, but for me it lingered. I wanted so much to reach out and just touch his hand, but I knew I would not be able to stop with that. I wanted to press myself up against his muscular body and kiss him passionately. Oh this was torture! But it was sweet torture. Better than not having him here with me.

"What are you thinking now Becca?"

He knew, I could tell by the amusement dancing in his eyes. I know my face had to turn all shades of crimson, but I merely looked at him calmly and said,

"I was just thinking about the news."

"Oh!"

He said laughing quietly now.

"That's exactly what I was thinking of too."

I couldn't help myself; I looked at him and said,

"Oh? And you found the news amusing?"

Now his face turned red. He smiled at me and said,

"I think we had better change the subject, before one or both of us get into trouble?"

I just laughed.

The rest of the day went by quickly enough. I had a lot of work to do. Surprisingly, there were more Christians getting suspicious about the state of the world than I would have suspected. I wrote an article commending the people who were watching the world and told them that the only thing they could do now was to pray and keep steadfast in faith.

At 11:30 Rafe called to say he would be a little late, but should be, by to pick me up about 12:30. He thought it would be nice if we went on a little picnic assuming I wasn't too tired. I assured him that I would be fine. My day seemed to be going along smoothly.

True to his word he arrived at 12:30. He took me to a little park that was bordered by the Tiber River. I looked out the window at the water, and it immediately made me sad because I thought back to the day on the Bridge of Angels when Rafe told me we would have to redefine our relationship. I don't think it had really impressed on my mind as much as it did at this very moment. My eyes filled with tears, but I continued to look out the window until I was sure that the breeze blowing in the slightly rolled down window had dried all the heartbreak, which I felt in each tear. Still I would not ever give up this time I had with him, so I didn't want him to see the sadness, and finally when he softly said my name I turned and looked at him with the brightest smile I could muster.

The little park was absolutely beautiful. It looked like we had been dropped into a virgin place of nature, untouched by human hands. The trees overlooked the bank of the river, their branches pointed town toward the waters edge as if they were secretly trying to hold hands with the river. It made for a beautiful shady area for us to sit and watch the swans floating effortlessly on the water. Their arched necks and black eyes and beaks giving them the majestic look that God had planted on them at creation. There were beautiful tiny blue butterflies, flitting amongst the little white flowers that peaked their perfectly round petaled heads out from amongst the blades of grass. The river seemed to be singing a soft melody to all of nature, and the slight breeze was answering with its loving soft refrain.

"Rafe, how did you find this absolutely perfect spot for us to picnic? I just can't believe the beauty before my eyes."

"I have come here many times by myself, when I just wanted to get away from all the hustle and bustle of human life. It reminds me so much of heaven. You are the first person that I have ever brought here. It feels so right to share it with you Becca."

I looked over at Rafe. He was sitting with his hands behind his head resting against a tree trunk, and he seemed as relaxed as he did that day in the Vatican Gardens. I wanted to enjoy this day forever. Just sitting quietly with this wonderful creature that had stolen my heart. I realized that God had created this most beautiful Archangel with all the majesty of a Greek God to serve Him and be part of His heavenly court. Of course he would be perfect, and I wondered how this special Angel could have fallen in love with me, just an ordinary human. All the angels of heaven had to be so much more beautiful than any creature on earth. I was so thankful that he found me an attractive being at all. If things would have been different, I could see myself spending the rest of my natural life with him. Still, I would be forever thankful for having the opportunity no matter how short of a time I would have, to love this beautiful soul. I stared at him as if to imprint, no to brand him, into my memory to keep with me for all eternity.

We ate in silence, perfectly content to be quiet and listen to all the sounds of nature around us.

Finally Rafe looked at me.

"Becca, I have a gift for you, to always remember me. I hope you wear it always."

He reached into his pocket and pulled out a blue velvet box. I opened it and there inside was a beautiful golden angel pendant. The angel was kneeling and blue sapphires were sprinkled across the bottom of the pendant as if to represent water, and it looked like the angel was scooping up the sapphires as though from a bubbling brook. On the back of the pendant was engraved:

"For Becca, My Personal Angel, Love Raphael"

"When you look at this Becca, always think of me fondly, and the perfect day we spent together among nature, in a place that I thought was enough like heaven, that I wanted to share it with you."

Tears began to immediately sting my eyes. I tried not to cry, but the tears rolled sadly down my cheeks.

"Rafe never in a million years will I forget you. You are all I ever wanted, and all I will ever need. Please put this around my neck and I promise I will never take it off. Never!"

He put the necklace around my neck and his fingers lingered there for a few minutes until I could not stand it any longer and I turned and faced him, wrapping my arms around him and crying.

He stroked my hair, holding me against his chest, and then he gently took hold of my shoulders and pushing me away he looked into my eyes and said:

"My beautiful angel, I did not intend for my gift to make you sad. I don't ever want you to think of me sadly, just hold this angel, and always remember, you have an angel in heaven who fell madly in love with you."

I smiled weakly at him.

"I'll always remember, Rafe. I don't ever want to do anything that would make you sad either. I know your life in heaven is perfect. I just want to make your time on this earth as perfectly happy as I can."

With those words said we hugged each other, not in a romantic way, but more in an eternal bond. It was as if at that time we were like the two swans on the river.

Bonded as mates forever. Whatever may come.

We spent the entire afternoon at the park that no one but us seemed to know about. We talked, and laughed and really got to know each other's innermost thoughts and deepest desires. Of course my desires were more on a human plane than his. We listened to each other, completely oblivious of the time, and oblivious to what was going on in the world around us. We didn't talk or worry about how much time we had to spend with each other. We thoroughly enjoyed our time together. I knew that this would probably be the most perfect day that I ever would spend with anyone. We walked around the park enjoying it's beauty. When he jumped over a creek and I tried to follow him if it had not been for his angel powers to guide me across I would have landed right in the middle. We both rolled in the grass; laughing about what a site I would have been in my beautiful suit all wet and muddy. I took a handful of mud and rubbed it all over his face as he was teasing me, and then I jumped up to run before he could catch me. But he had me caught before I even got all the way to my feet and just rubbed his face all over mine, transferring the gooey mess to mine and then as if to make it perfect, he took two tiny white flowers and stuck them right on the tip of my nose in the little pile of mud he had put there.

The time slipped by and when we finally decided to leave, the sun was quickly fading. He brought forth his real angel persona, because he was afraid I would stumble in the dark. He lifted me into his arms and we flew to the place where the car was parked. It would never cease to astonish me when he made the change. He was magnificent as a man, but so much more regal as an angel.

By the time we got into the car we realized that we had spent so many hours at the park that we were famished again. But since we had covered each other with mud, we decided to just make sandwiches and soup at my flat.

The next few days were filled with happenings inside the Vatican. A new Pope had been elected, and most people were very happy with the choice the conclave had made by electing a Mid Eastern Cardinal, who was well versed in most of the major languages and a very popular man among many of the worlds delegates. He had very modern views and planned to make some major changes in the Catholic church.

Rafe was very disappointed with the choice the other cardinals had made, but he said it was all in the workings of Satan, and it would come to this eventually.

He had a very difficult time justifying how humans could be so ignorant of what was happening around them when they had been amply warned for centuries.

On the other hand, he was very sad for those people who knew what was happening, but could do nothing to rectify our human mistakes now. It was to late. We would have to suffer all of the plagues and pestilences that were only just beginning to be waged upon the earth.

Two days after the Pope was elected, some very strong earthquakes devastated a major portion of the United States. Major damages were done in cities from San Francisco, down to México. Parts of the states of Oregon, Washington, Nevada, and Arizona were hit as well. Millions of people were without homes, and the water supply from the Sierra Nevada Mountains to the Los Angeles valley was completely destroyed.

Even though there had been so many signs in just a few short weeks, people still seemed oblivious of their obvious warning.

We had so many stories to cover at the office that we were kept extremely busy, and our days flew by so fast that we were through an entire month in no time.

This morning I was so busy with paranormal stories that I didn't take my morning break because I wanted to finish the story I was working on before Rafe came to pick me up. But by about 11:15 am, I was so hungry that my stomach began to growl loudly. I was afraid everyone in the office would hear me, so I decided to take the elevator down to the first floor to get a snack out of one of the vending machines that lined the lobby

I had my back turned to the front entrance and was just about to stoop down and retrieve my crackers and cheese; when a familiar voice said from behind me:

"Alone at last!"

I turned to see Nicholas Baragio standing very close to me. My heart began to pound wildly, and I actually thought I was going to have a heart attack right there in the lobby.

I started to scream, and he clamped his hand over my mouth and said:

"Don't draw any attention to us Rebecca! You are coming with me!"

He twisted my arm behind my back, and with his hand still clamped over my mouth started to pull me backwards to the door.

Suddenly, another voice spoke out:

"Excuse me, can I help you sir?"

Nicholas quickly released me as Mike came from the elevator. We were right in his view.

I sighed a huge sigh of relief, and quickly went to stand behind him. Mike looked first at Nicholas and than at me.

"Are you all right Rebecca?"

Then looking back at Nicholas with an annoyed expression on his face, he said:

"Just what is going on here?"

Nicholas merely smiled at him and said,

"I am sorry. This was a case of mistaken identity. You see, I thought she was my sister who ran away a couple of years ago, and when I saw her I was anxious to take her home to my worried parents, but I can see now that I was completely mistaken."

With that said, he gave a little bow, and said:

"Forgive me Miss."

And walked out the door.

Mike ran to the door with me right behind him to see which way he had gone, but when we reached the doors, Nicholas simply vanished.

Mike turned to say something to me, and nearly fell over me because I was standing so close to him.

"Rebecca, tell me what is going on!"

My eyes were full of tears and I was shaking uncontrollably. I just shook my head and shrugged my shoulders, but he took me by the hand outside to the bench in front of the building.

"Ever since you met this David Rafe guy, you have been acting like you are scared to death. Does this by any chance, have anything to do with him?"

I looked at him in disbelief and stuttered,

"N—No, how can you think that! How can you even think that? Rafe would never do anything to harm me."

"Rebecca, look at me! I know you don't want to hear this but I am in Love with you. I watch every move that you make. I know how you act normally, and you have not been acting normally. Whoever this man was, you obviously are terrified. I am under the impression that the two of you knew each other. For some reason I also feel that this Rafe guy is involved in some way. You can always talk to me Rebecca, now , tell me, what is going on?"

"Mike, stop! Please! You would be afraid too, if someone came up behind you and clamped his had over your mouth. He told you it was a mistaken identity. Let's just leave it at that."

Mike shook his head.

"You are still shaking pretty badly. Look at your hands, and your mouth is quivering."

He put his arm around my shoulder.

"Let's just sit here for a few minutes until you calm down."

About that time Rafe came walking up to us. One look at me, and he looked at Mike and said:

"Mike! What has happened to her now?"

It sounded more like an accusation than a question.

Mike looked furiously at him for a moment. Without saying a word, he turned, and looked at me and said.

"You tell him!"

He turned to leave and then as if rethinking the situation, he turned and looked at me once more and said:

"I'll be keeping my eye on you, Rebecca."

He looked again at Rafe with an expression of disgust. Then he stalked away from us to the elevator.

Chapter 6
THREE DAYS OF DARKNESS

Rafe sat down on the bench next to me.

"What is wrong Becca? What was that all about?"

He nodded his head toward the spot where Mike had been standing.

"Rafe, please don't be angry with him, if it hadn't been for Mike I don't know where I would be right now."

I continued to tell him the whole episode that had taken place at the vending machines. He looked at me in wide eyed horror. I hoped he would have a new found respect for mike, but all he said was,

"I thought I told you never to be alone! Oh Becca, how soon you forget. Tell me everything that was said. Don't leave out a single word."

I continued telling him everything that happened including everything that Mike had said, but I conveniently left out the part where Mike said he loved me.

"Rafe, I don't know why, but Mike suddenly doesn't seem like he trusts you very much. He thought I was afraid of you and that all of this had something to do with you."

"Becca, are you blind? Didn't you know that Mike is in love with you? I don't know how much more obvious he could be about it. He seldom takes his eyes off of you. He doesn't like me because he's afraid I might ruin his chances with you. You didn't tell him that you knew Nicholas did you?"

"No, of course not Rafe. I hope that he bought Nicholas' explanation. I just don't want him getting bad ideas about you."

"Becca, I'm more than capable of handling Mike. I do owe him my thanks for choosing to follow you and get off the elevator at precisely the right time though, don't I?"

"Rafe, I really don't think that he was following me."

"Becca, I'm a male. I know he was following you."

I decided not to argue the point any further. I didn't need both of these males, as he put it, angry at each other, especially since I loved one as my soul mate, and the other as my friend.

"I should be upset with you Becca. You need to pay more attention to everything you do, and everywhere you go. If you don't you will end up in Satan's clutches again. I told you he is out to get you. He is way out of your league; you are dealing with demons, not humans. I told you that you don't stand a chance against them!"

He lifted my chin to make me stare in his eyes, his voice was soft, pleading, but the fiery yellow specks were there dancing in the depths of his eyes. I knew it wouldn't take much to anger him.

"Are you going to listen to what I'm saying to you this time?"

I started to pull my chin out of his grip. I was beginning to feel like a little child being scolded. But he pulled my face around to look at him, with a little more force this time.

"I'm not playing games with you Becca, I am serious. Do I need to drag you around with me everywhere I go and include you in everything I do? Because I will. Believe me, I will. You are much too precious to me for you to take these matters lightly."

There, I did it. I made him angry. It wasn't my intention, but I could tell he was angry now. Why did I always seem to do things at the wrong time?

"Rafe, I promise you, I will never do anything like that again. Now, can I please have my chin back? I am entirely to blame. I don't want Nicholas to ever get his hands on me again, much less, Satan. I'll make sure I'm never alone. I promise. I'm sorry if I angered you."

He just shook his head back and forth, releasing my chin and looking at me, saying more to himself than to me,

"To independent, just too independent."

He stood up and taking me by the hand led me toward the elevator.

"You need to check out for the day, don't you?"

"Yes."

I looked into his eyes again and they had softened somewhat, but I would have felt much better if he would at least smile at me.

Later that day, while listening to the news at home, I learned that many of the college students in the United States and England no longer believe in God or any higher being. At least eighty percent believed that we came to be by some form of evolution, and that only people who were ignorant and uneducated believe in the Bible and the stories it held. I hated that Rafe had to hear such things coming from civilization. It had to make God's entire heavenly court feel like their efforts had no

Purpose. Especially since everything they knew from all eternity was the love of God for all mankind. Now to be told by the very people God had created that he didn't exist had to be the biggest blow that could be dealt to them. I looked over at Rafe to see how he was reacting to this horrid news, but I saw no reaction. He turned and looked at me and patted my hand.

"It's okay Becca. Don't worry about me. We have known this was going to happen for centuries. We have watched it slowly progress. That is why the end must come. That is why we are here today. Only those who believe the truth will take notice of the disasters that are going on around them. That is why I told you I am here to avenge God. Not only me, but also Michael, and Gabriel, Uriel, Chanmel, Japhiel and Raguel, all seven of the Archangels of God will fight against the evil that has taken over the earth, so that it will be cleansed of the crime of unbelief and evil. Then will come the beginning of the new heavens and the new earth that the Son of God began with his death and resurrection.

Listen to me carefully Becca; the one hundred and forty four thousand elders have all been signed. Now the wrath of God as sent by the angels has been loosed upon the earth. Only the just will survive, but not until they have had much too suffer. You have to be strong. I can't impress on you how strong you have to be, and that is why sometimes I get so exasperated with you. I feel that you are not placing enough importance on this. Maybe it's not your fault, because you have never experienced anything like this before. But you must pay strict attention to me in order to survive."

I began to feel a twinge of nausea in the pit of my stomach because I knew that Rafe in all seriousness was looking out for my well being to keep me safe from all the terrible events that were taking place on the earth, like the giant volcano that had erupted in Hawaii just a few days earlier that had filled so many people that the seas were filled with the red of their blood, but scientists tried to explain it away as just being a red tide that had been caused by the volcanic eruption. Only those people who were well versed in Biblical Prophecy or had their own special Angel to explain these happenings to them like I did, would understand the truth. Many strange things were taking place around the globe that science tried to explain away by thwarting Christian explanations. The saddest part of the whole ordeal for all of us Catholics was that our new Pope was agreeing with the scientists, instead of warning his sheep.

"You are beginning to see the devastating effects of this whole prophetical warning, aren't you Becca?"

I nodded my head yes and gave a deep sigh that didn't relieve my fear one iota.

"Oh Rafe, I am so very scared. On the one hand, I want to go on as long as you are here, and on the other hand, I would rather it all ended fast for me, if I can't spend my life with you. Maybe that's why I get so foolish at times."

His eyes became wide with concern as he took a hold of me, looking sincerely into my eyes and saying,

"Becca, don't ever, ever think like that. Your life is so important to me. If you love me like you say you do, you will want to live, because I would never be able to forgive myself for making myself known to you, let alone falling in love with you, if I thought you wanted your life to end. Please! Don't ever talk like that again. You just can't think that way."

I could see the hurt that I caused and it made me feel guilty. Sometimes I wished I would just bite my tongue before I spoke. I wanted to take him in my arms and hold him there forever.

"Rafe, forgive me please. How many times I speak before I think when it comes to you. I have to always remember that I'm not dealing with an ordinary human when I talk to you. I am so grateful for your love and your trust in showing me who you really are. Living without you would be much better than ever thinking that you were sorry you ever loved me and trusted me. I am so, so, sorry I ever thought anything so selfish. I'll never think that way again. I promise."

I got down on my knees in front of him and laying my head in his lap I said in a whisper,

" I'll do whatever you say. I'll take great care of myself, and I promise to be as brave as I can, just never be sorry you fell in love with me, or showed me who you are. I want you to look down from heaven and be proud that you know me. I can't and won't ever cause you any sadness if I can at all help it."

"Becca, you are my sweet, sweet, personal angel from God. No matter what I say, I could never be sorry I fell in love with you. I just wish that I could spend…Oh never mind. Just know that I will love you always."

If an angel could cry, and maybe they do, I would swear that he was about to cry, and all I could do was put my arms around him and hug him.

The rest of the evening we were both very quiet, each of us lost in our own thoughts. It almost seemed cruel to me that we would ever have to be separated from each other. But then we could not blame anyone for our falling in love with each other but ourselves. No! I really didn't believe that. I believe in fate. I felt that we were destined to fall in love with each other. I couldn't believe it was a plan of Satan; I had to believe that it was a plan of Gods. If Satan had planned it, Rafe and I surely would have made love by now. We both were trying so hard to be faithful to the life that God created Rafe for, Maybe God wanted him to be happy here on earth, and maybe he wanted me to feel what true love felt like as well as being protected before life as I knew it came to an end.

I finally fell asleep on the sofa with my head in Rafe's lap I don't know how he could sit still for so long, but I stayed there the whole night through feeling safe as a little babe in its mother's arms.

I don't know what time it was when he woke me. I only knew that the lights were out and it was pitch black so I figured it had to be somewhere around three o'clock in the morning.

"Wake up Becca, you have to wake up now."

"Why?" I asked groggily. "It's still dark, it's not time to get ready for work."

""Becca, come on, wake all the way up. I have things I have to do.

I blinked my eyes, yawned and stretched, and then smiled at him.

"Oh, and just what do you have to do in the middle of the night Rafe?"

"It's not the middle of the night. It's ten in the morning. We're in the three days of darkness."

"The what?" I exclaimed.

"Oh my God Rafe! Is that when God blackens the sun and moon for the three days and three nights and evil comes upon us?"

"Yes, but don't be frightened. I have some candles and they will give you plenty of light until it is over, and they won't burn out because they are blessed."

He went to the table and lit a candle that brightened up the whole room.

"But you have to promise me that you won't open the door to anyone, no matter who they say they are. If they say it's your Mother, or Heidi, or Mike, or anyone you know, or someone begging for you to let them in. Don't do it. Even if it sounds like me begging for you to let me in, don't listen. Because it won't be me or anyone else you know. It will be the evil spirits trying to get you to let them in so that they can attack you. You are going to hear crying and screaming in the streets, and pounding on your door. But whatever you do. DON'T OPEN THE DOOR! AND DON'T LOOK OUT THE WINDOWS! Do you understand?"

I was horrified; I nodded yes and then blurted out,

"But where are you going to be?"

"I haves to go out and help people. I have to make them believe me, and any who haven't been overtaken by Satan I have to get into their houses and make them lock themselves in like I'm asking you to do. Don't worry, when I get back I can get in on my own.

Remember, if someone says they are me asking to be let in, don't listen. I don't have to ask. I can get in on my own. Tell me you understand and you're listening."

"Rafe! Please! Please! Don't leave me here by myself. I beg you please, I'm so scared!"

"Becca get a hold of yourself! I have to do this! It's my job! I know I said I wouldn't leave you alone, but I have no choice right now. Just please don't open the door! Are you listening?"

" I'm listening! I'm listening! Of course you have to go. I'm sorry. Don't worry about me. I'll be fine. I promise, I won't open the door or look out the windows! Go! Now! Before people start being overtaken by the evil spirits."

He hugged me very close and planted a quick kiss on my forehead, and before I knew what had happened he just disappeared into thin air.

I ran to double check that the doors were locked and the curtains closed on all the windows, but thank goodness Rafe had already made sure all of that was done before he woke me. I went into my bedroom and picked up Mr. Boots from my bed and went back into the living room and cuddled up in the corner of the couch with him. Then I covered us with a blanket.

I heard a thud outside. It sounded like someone or something was thrown against my front door. I didn't hear anything else so I just huddled down a little further into the corner of the couch petting Mr. Boots, probably a little faster than I normally would.

Before long the screaming began. It was horrible. Some people were moaning. Others were crying, and then there were the blood curdling screams. I shuddered at the thought of what the demons were doing to them. It got louder and more intense, with more people joining in. Finally the screaming upset me so badly that I had to cover my ears with the pillows. Even the hair on Mr. Boots back was standing on end. Just when I thought the screaming had subsided a bit, there was a loud knock on my door.

"Miss Malone! Rebecca are you in there? Please let me in. It's Mr. Ferrachi, I have to see David Rafe. Terrible things are happening in the city and we need his help! Please this is urgent Vatican business!"

I started toward the door, and then I remembered what Rafe said!

"Mr. Ferrachi, Ra…Mr. Rafe has already left to help people, please get back to the Vatican. I'm sure he will find you."

"Rebecca quickly, I need you to open the door, these people are after me, and then I heard a giant thud, like someone threw him against the door. Or he threw himself against it. I started backing down the hall back into the living room. Oh! I hoped I was doing the right thing. I had to listen to Rafe. He wouldn't tell me the wrong thing to do. The pounding started once again, but when Mr. Ferrachi saw that I wasn't going to let him in, the pounding finally stopped.

Now I could hear pounding on my windows, and someone was throwing stones against them trying to get them to break. I stood and stared at the closed curtains, waiting for a rock or stone to come crashing through the window, but surprisingly, the windows never broke. It was the screaming that was really affecting me. Not only adults, but also I could hear the cries of children too. I told myself not to cry, that I had to try and stay calm. But the calmness didn't come easy with all the commotion.

I was so tempted to open the drapes so I could better see what was going on, but I was told not to look out the windows either. It made it especially hard hearing all the horrid screams and not being able to see the people that needed help. I started to pull back the cord to open the drapes. NO! My mind instinctively reminded me. Those aren't people who are tormenting me. It is the demons. Thank God I didn't open the drapes.

My mouth was so dry! I had to go into the kitchen to get some water. But when I turned on the faucet nothing came out. I ran to both bathrooms to check the water there. No Water! I hurried back into the kitchen and was thankful for the case of water that Rafe had brought in just yesterday. He knew, he knew this was going to happen I wondered if he knew it would be today. Surely not. I don't think anyone but God would have known the exact time and hour all of these things were supposed to take place. I took two big gulps of water and put the lid back on the bottle and carried it into the living room with me and set it on the table next to me.

Suddenly there was another knock on my door or I should say it sounded like a desperate pounding. I didn't want to acknowledge it. I wasn't supposed to pay any attention to anyone knocking, so why should I verbally answer the knock?

"Becca, this is Heidi! Heidi Moran. Please let me in. I'm afraid to be by myself at home, and it is getting so terrible out here."

She began crying, then the next thing I heard was her scream.

"Becca! Please! There are dead people all over the streets. I can't stay out here by myself. I'm just so afraid. Open the door." The knocking became more desperate, and the pounding got louder and louder and so did her screaming and crying.

I started toward the door,

"Just a minute Heidi! I'm coming."

There was no answer from the other side, but I could hear her breathing when I got to the door. A voice from within me said, Becca, don't open the door.

"Becca, please open it now, they're about to get me!"

When I got to the door, I just turned my back, and slid against the door to the floor. I sat there covering my ears and crying, "I can't, oh God, I can't." I was sobbing now because I could hear Heidi begging and pleading for me to let her in, and her voice started to sound like it was getting further and further away. I could imagine some horrible monster dragging my friends off one by one and killing them. I sat on the floor leaning against the door for the longest time just crying and feeling very guilty. All was beginning to get quiet again when unexpectedly another crashing bang jolted me back to the present moment.

"Becca, let me in, hurry. NOW! It's Raphael. Please let me in before the demons get me. You are my only hope. I've tried to save as many people as I could today. But it is useless now. Satan and his demons have overcome everyone, and I am too weak to let myself in like I told you I would. You've got to listen to me. Becca, sweetheart, please hurry and open the door."

I knew I had to open the door. Rafe had given me to much information for it to be a demon. They wouldn't think I knew his real name. They also wouldn't know that he told me not to open the door even if it was him knocking. I stood up, wiped my eyes with the back of my hand, sniffled, and reached for the doorknob. But before I could turn the lock someone reached out from behind me and grabbed my arm and pulled me away from the door. I turned wide-eyed to see Rafe holding my arm. He grabbed my other arm and pulled me close to him, wrapping his arms tightly around me. He nuzzled his face in my hair and I could hear his muffled voice say with relief.

"Oh Becca, I almost lost you. Thank God that he sent me back when he did. You would have opened the door thinking you were letting me in and the demons would have surely have abducted or worse yet, killed you. I know you must have had a horrible time tonight not letting anyone in. I am just thankful I got back when I did."

"Oh Rafe, I am so sorry. I really thought it was you. I mean the demon said it was Raphael. I couldn't imagine that they would think I knew what your real name was. Thank you! God thank you, for saving me."

"Becca, God sent me back in the knick of time. Don't feel bad. God told humanity that the devil could deceive the elect if it were at all possible. The demons are angels also. They are as wise as Gods' angels. He created them remember. They just became bad angels who want all humanity to ignore God so that they can be banned to hell."

"Rafe, is it over?"

I looked at him, hoping to see some relief in his expression, but all I saw there was dread.

"No Becca! It will last for three whole days and three whole nights. Then it will be over, at least this part of the suffering. But now I can stay with you until I'm called out again. Don't tremble, you are safe now."

He walked me back into the living room and after he got me settled on the couch he went into the kitchen and came back with a glass of wine.

"Here, drink this. It will calm your nerves a little."

I took the glass of wine from him and I had to hold onto the wine glass with both hands because they were shaking uncontrollably. Rafe noticed immediately and sat down beside me and after he told me to take a drink, he took the glass from me and set it on the coffee table and put his arm around me pulling me close and stroking my hair, and rocking me back and forth until I began to calm myself. The shaking slowly subsided. He kissed me lightly on the forehead.

"You're safe Becca. Drink your wine now, it will relax you and make you feel much calmer."

I took the glass of wine and gulped the whole thing down in one swallow. He looked at me unbelievingly and then started to laugh.

"You wanted to calm down immediately didn't you?"

"Yes, can I have another please?"

"Becca, I wanted you to calm down, not to get drunk. I think you'll see in a few minutes that you feel much better. I don't think you really need another drink, do you?"

I looked into his soft cobalt blue eyes, and I shook my head no.

"I guess not."

I was hoping that the wine would make me sleepy, and I wouldn't have to think of this day anymore. But after a few minutes I realized I was becoming pretty calm, but I wasn't sleepy at all.

"What time is it Rafe?"

He looked at his watch,

"It's three thirty in the afternoon. Why?"

I didn't answer I was preoccupied. No wonder I wasn't sleepy, only about twelve hours of this day had gone by in this horrid darkness and we still had about fifty hours to go. Finally, I said;

"Oh no reason, I just wondered."

I really hoped he didn't have to leave again because I didn't know if I would be able to withstand the demons, especially after I almost let them in because they tricked me. I wondered just how much they knew about me. They could probably talk me into anything if they really wanted to. Where was my faith in God? I needed to get a hold on myself. I knew it was too late now for any of us to decide to change our ways. Now all we could live on was faith, hope and love. There was nothing left for us to do. God was finally tired of us showing him lack of respect and destroying the earth he gave us to tend.

Rafe was watching me. His eyes never left me. Finally, in a quiet voice he said:

"Becca, what is on your mind?"

"Nothing Rafe. I'm fine now, honestly."

"Becca, I really want to know what you are thinking. Don't do this to yourself or to me. I'm not blind; I can see something is troubling you. Come on tell me. I don't want to have to beg you to tell me!"

I looked at him. He knew me so very well. I never could fool him when I was trying so hard to hide my fear from him.

"I was just wondering just how strong I could be against the demons when I almost gave myself to them willingly by almost opening that door."

I shuddered just thinking about what might have happened. Luth… Satan had promised to kill me.

"You have to be very careful. Now that you understand how hard they try to deceive. You will be more on guard. Just remember don't open the door to anyone. It won't be a real person. No matter what they say or do. I know it is not easy, but you have to keep that going over and over in your mind. It's not really them it is evil. I know you can do it Becca. That was a horrible trial, and I don't know what would have happened if I hadn't showed up when I did. But now you know the truth. You heard the voice that sounded like me, when I was standing right here beside you. So I hope that you can be certain now that it wasn't me, and it won't be anyone else except the demons trying to deceive you."

"This is all so horrible Rafe. I will just feel safe if you can stay with me as long as possible. What would I do if I didn't have you to protect me? I shudder to even think about it."

The candle was still glowing where he lit it this morning. It hadn't burned down one single inch. The flickering from the flame seemed to only accentuate the sharp planes of his face giving him that statuesque appearance again. I couldn't help but marvel how beautiful he was. I decided to concentrate on him to take my mind off of everything else that was going on. It wouldn't be hard. Studying him was one of my favorite pastimes. I wanted to memorize further everything about him, every tiny little detail that I might have missed, before he had to leave me forever. My heart skipped a beat realizing that I wouldn't have him for long. I absentmindedly reached up and touched his face, tracing the fine line of his jaws. Passing my fingers gently over his lips, that when not smiling seemed to have a pouty expression to them, just made him all the more endearing. He looked down at me now with a quizzical expression in his eyes, but he never said a word. It was almost as though he knew what I was doing and didn't want to disturb me. I moved my fingers up to the fine laugh lines that bordered the sides of his eyes. Than I ran my fingers through his silky brownish blonde hair, that had just a touch of curl to it. I loved the feel of his hair. It felt like fine baby hair, but it was thick and luscious. I slid my hand down the side of his face down his long neck that I so wanted to plant tiny kisses on, to the first button that was unbuttoned on his shirt and ran my fingers across his stone hard muscle chest feeling the massive hair that grew there. I felt him gasp under my touch, and he reached up and caught my hand, pulling it away, and pressing the palm of my hand to his lips. The warm familiar tingling was back in a flash. How could he make me feel like this when all he was doing was kissing my hand? I looked into his eyes and I could see that he was agonizing over my inquisitiveness, but seemed unable to decide that I was going to take advantage of the situation. I couldn't help myself. I wanted as much of him as I could get before he was gone. I kissed the inside of his wrist and then I pulled myself up so that my upper body meted against his and I started planting slow kisses on the hollow of his neck. He gasped again, and before he had a chance to react, I entwined my finger in his gorgeous hair and pulled him close so that my eager mouth met his. He started to return the kiss with a fervor like I had never experienced before, and then he pulled my arms from around his neck and gently pushing me away from him and gasping, said,

"No Becca, please don't do this. I can't bear it."

His words only enticed me into an emotional frenzy and I pushed my body as close to him as I could, boldly kissing his neck once again.

He started to fight me to some extent, but I only kept pursuing him more by the minute, kissing him and pulling my arms from his grasp and wrapping them tightly around him so that my body was molded to his and when I found his lips once more, I kissed him passionately and shamelessly. I could feel myself sinking into a feverish desire. I wanted him and I wanted him now. But in the blinking of an eye he broke the embrace, having to use more force on me than before. My lustful eyes looked into his surprised gaze as he held my hands against my sides, I suddenly came back to my senses. I began to feel embarrassed and ashamed of my brazen actions. How could I tempt him like that? I felt like a tramp! He was still breathing heavily when I pulled myself away and started to retreat to the kitchen. I was so mortified that I could die, but as I struggled to get away, he pulled me back down on his lap and once again he began to stroke my hair slowly as if he were trying to comfort me.

"Oh Becca, don't run away my little vixen. If I were but a mortal man I would have taken advantage of you in a second. I knew you could be passionate, but I didn't know that you had it in you to try and molest me! You know why I had to stop you."

He lifted my chin and looked into my eyes.

"Don't be ashamed Becca. I will cherish that embrace forever. I'm just sorry that I couldn't take advantage of your weakness."

"No Rafe, I'm sorry that I tried to take advantage of your weakness. I wasn't weak at all. Yes, I'm ashamed. I'm ashamed that I made it hard for you and ashamed that I may have angered God. He has every right to wipe me off the face of this earth right now! I behaved like one of the harlots in the bible."

"Becca stop! God forgave the harlots of the bible times, and you are not a harlot. You are simply being human, with human feelings. You love me, and you fear losing me, just as I do you. What you did was purely natural."

I wanted to ask him to leave so that I would never tempt him again, but I was too weak. I couldn't. I vowed to myself to never put him in this position again. I could tell it was torture for him to break our embrace. I had to find something to do in this horrible darkness that would keep me occupied so that I would not put either of us in this kind of a predicament again. But at the moment nothing came to mind. He was the first to break the silence.

"Becca, it is getting very late. I think you need to try and get some rest. Did you want to go into the bedroom to sleep?"

My eyes gave away the fear that suddenly grabbed me.

"No Rafe, I think I just want to sleep out here on the couch again. I can't stand all the crying and screaming."

It was quiet now but who knew when the horrific sounds would start up again.

"Rafe, do you remember when I got the letter at the office, and it said I would be seeing all kinds of strange things taking place? Things that had never happened before? This must be one of the things the author was writing about!"

"Becca, I am sure that letter was from Satan or one of his demons. I don't know hwy they involved you in this, unless it is because they know more about our relationship than I had realized. But like I told you before, you have to be very cautious right now."

The next two days went by without more incidents. The demons must have moved from Rome to another part of the country because it stayed relatively quiet and calm. The horrible darkness continued to haunt us though, and the only thing that gave us any light was that one lonely candle that Rafe had lit three days ago. We had plenty of canned food and water in the house so we didn't go hungry or get thirsty, but being without electricity had its drawbacks. We couldn't have any hot meals and all we could drink was the bottled water. We couldn't use the phone or get any news from the television. It seemed odd when I realized that it was the same all over the entire earth. The thought made me feel uneasy as I contemplated what might be in store for us next. Finally, after exactly seventy-two hours, everything went back to normal, or so it seemed. The electricity was back on, the water was running and all of our modern conveniences as we knew were in working order again. The first thing I wanted to do was to look outside. But Rafe convinced me to wait until he went outdoors and made sure it was safe and not too horrifying that it might put me into a state of shock. While he went outside, I did the second thing that I wanted to do. I took a shower. By the time Rafe came back into the house I was dressed and ready to head out.

"Becca, it isn't a very pretty sight out there. Bodies are lying all over the streets, and there are poor souls who didn't make it out of their cars. Automobiles are crashed into trees. Some were stopped in the middle of the road, some have been hit from behind by other cars. Most likely from the terrible darkness."

He went over to the television set and turned it on. He had to search through many unreceptive, snowy channels until he finally found a news station that was working. Ironically it was a news station at the Vatican.

We listened, horrified as the newscaster proceeded to tell the world that a meteor had blackened out the sun and the moon could not give off light as there was no reflection from the sun. he said that most of the citizens had died because they had panicked in the darkness and had terrible accidents. All this information came from the World Science Center. I couldn't believe my ears. This was all being blamed on Mother Nature. The majority of the population would probably believe this because so many of them had been taught not to acknowledge a creator anymore. They presented film that had been shot all over Rome showing the dead in the streets and on their lawns, in cars, in homes. It was the scene that Rafe didn't want me to see. He turned and looked at me as if he were anticipating my reaction. I looked at him and sighed heavily, shaking my head in awe.

"I know this is terrible for you Becca, but I really shouldn't try to protect you from seeing it because things are going to get a lot worse and you will eventually have to see some of the horrible plagues that mankind has brought on himself. I'm sorry, but that's all I can tell you. Do you think you can handle it?"

"What choice do I have Rafe? I never thought I would live to see the days our parents and grandparents said would happen one day, and yet here I am a part of it."

"Yes you are right in the middle of it and you have to be very strong and brave to survive it. You can't let the horror of this situation cause you to act foolishly. You are going to see horrible things, things that you never thought of in your life. Just keep your senses about you and you'll make it through this war to end all wars."

He was completely solemn and I knew he was worried, first of all, because I was so stubborn and secondly, because I was so human.

"Rafe, I will promise to do the best that I can."

"That's not enough Becca. You have to do better than the best that you can. When you think you are handling things the best you can, please try a little harder."

"Aren't you going to be with me most of the time Rafe?"

I knew he had business to attend to, but hopefully he would spend the rest of his time with me. It would be unbearable to go through this by myself.

"I can't promise you that now Becca. As soon as the war between good and evil begins Michael and all the other Archangels will join me and we will gather our armies together to fight the final battle against Satan and all his evil spirits. It will all depend on how long the battle takes before I can come back. For now, I am here. You are safe. My job now is to heal the broken souls. I will be attending to those poor souls who may want or need it."

Our attention was drawn back to the newscaster who just informed the world that it was estimated that Rome had lost one third of it's citizens during the meteor eclipse. No one thought to correlate it with the warning of the Three Days of Darkness. Then the world was informed that Mr. Josef Ferrachi, the Commander of the Vatican Swiss Guard had lost his life when his car drove over an embankment and landed a hundred feet below on the freeway and was struck by another vehicle. I looked in astonished disbelief at Rafe.

"Then he really was at my door, asking me to let him in wasn't he Rafe?"

"I don't know Becca, probably not. We are told that it is all evil spirits that are trying to trick people into believing it is friends or relatives."

"Oh Rafe, I will just die if anything has happened to Heidi. She was here too."

"Becca! Calm down. I happen to know that Heidi is fine. I dropped candles off at an elderly couples house and Heidi was there. It just so happened that they were her parents. Heidi wasn't here."

I sat on the floor and curled my legs underneath me, leaning on the coffee table with my chin in my hands watching the goldfish swimming in the bowl. I loved to watch the fish when I was upset or nervous. Watching their fluid movement through the water usually proved to relax me. It certainly wasn't much help right now though.

"Becca?"

Rafe interrupted my focused attention on the fish.

"This is going to put extra work on me now that Mr. Ferrachi is gone. I will have to find a replacement for him, and that may take a few days. I want you to go to work with me. If the newspaper office is open you can go to work, otherwise I will take you to work with me."

I looked over at him.

"That would be great! I feel so bad about Mr. Ferrachi. I really never got to know him very well, but I know he was a very professional and an astute man"

He looked at me deep in his own thoughts.

"Yes, that is two good men we have lost from the Vatican. The Pope, and now Josef."

"I didn't even know his first name was Josef, Rafe. That's how little I knew him. We had a strictly business relationship, but he was always kind to me.

I went back to my fish watching. I stared attentively at the fishbowl, but I was really thinking about this beautiful earth that God had given us that we had so abused. I don't think most people even think about it one way or another. They have just lived here and lived the way that they wanted. Not many of us can say that we lived our whole life in union with the laws of the Bible. I had to admit to

myself that I was terribly frightened; not only because of the tings that were taking place, but for my eternal soul as well. If I was allowed to go to heaven would I even know or recognize Rafe, or would I be so happy to be in the presence of God that our relationship would never come to mind again? I hoped not. I didn't want to forget him, ever.

What if I was left to remain on earth? That would be so lonely because I don't think I could love anyone ever again the way that I loved Rafe. I didn't want to think about that possibility. I turned and looked at Rafe again. He was watching me intently.

"Becca, are you okay?" He asked.

"Yes, I'm just lost in my own thoughts, so sorry that as humans we let our civilization ever get to this point. It really makes me angry and sad that we are about to lose everything because of our mortal stupidity. This earth is so beautiful and not only have we literally destroyed it ourselves, but we have doomed ourselves and our children in the process."

"No Becca, that isn't exactly true. Yes, mankind has doomed itself, but only with the influence of Satan and all his wily ways. But there are those people who have passed the test. Some who are already high up the ladder on the way to heaven, and who will be led to the new heavens, and those who have not yet quite achieved their best potential who will be left to start the new earth. They will have a fresh start. The others will be doomed to the fiery pit. But only after they reject God completely."

I looked at him for a minute and then back to my little globe of a fishbowl trying to imagine what that would be like. Since I didn't know anything different than the life the we had now, it was very hard for me to visualize.

We spent most of the day talking about all the things that had brought man to this point. Rafe talked to me about how different things would be once Satan was damned to hell. I got the impression that there wouldn't be that many people who would be left on earth to start it anew, but God had these special people chosen from the beginning of time and they would all be descendants of the twelve tribes of Israel.

"I guess that leaves out any of us Westerners doesn't it?" I asked

"No Becca. What on earth would ever make you think that? There are relatives all over the whole earth that come from the twelve tribes of Israel. They didn't all just remain in the same area for all of these thousands of years."

He looked at me like he couldn't believe that I would ever think such a thing.

"I guess I never thought of it that way. I think of the twelve tribes as all beings of Jewish descent." I said.

He looked at me once again, smiling this time.

"Don't you think everyone on the face of the earth came from the same line at one time or another?"

"No one ever explained it to me that way Rafe. We just never really talked that much about the end times when I was younger, only that we should be ready for them."

"Hmm, how could you be ready if you didn't know anything about them?"

"We couldn't be Rafe. I don't think it would have mattered what anyone told us, we would have never been ready. We are all too concerned with our own problems to worry about what is going to take place in our future. Except perhaps for a select few."

"Becca, you are getting more perceptive every day."

"Yes, thanks to you and your guidance through this ordeal. Where would I be if I hadn't met you? I wonder."

He leaned over and kissed me on the cheek. I was happy this was the way it was meant to be.

Chapter 7
NIGHTMARE

The next day Rafe was very quiet for several hours. I left him to his own thoughts because I could tell he was intent on whatever was going on in the depths of his mind. Later that day he told me we needed to get out and see what was occurring at the Vatican. The first place we stopped was the newspaper office. I was told Mr. Bellini was there along with a few of the staff that decided to come in of their own volition, as they couldn't call.

Heidi was one of the employees that had made it in and when she saw me she ran from behind her desk and gave me a big hug in greeting.

"Oh Becca, I was so worried about you and Mr. Rafe. I'm so happy to see you and I know Mr. Bellini will be too. We are so busy here; do you think you can work? We have been trying to pass along the word to anyone we see that we're open. So if you see anyone who works here make sure you pass on the news."

"I'll do that, Heidi. Where is Mr. Bellini?"

"He went to see if he could get the vending machines on the second floor to work. The ones on the first floor haven't been filled, so there isn't much of a selection there. He'll be back in a few minutes."

"Where is Mr. Rafe?"

"He had to see about a replacement for Mr. Ferrachi, so he is over at Security."

She looked at me and then her eyes filled with tears.

"Isn't it terrible about Mr. Ferrachi? I can't believe he's gone. I didn't know him personally like you, but I talked to him quite frequently on the phone. I really never got to know him that well either Heidi. But I did like what I knew about him and I am sure he is going to be terribly missed, especially by the Guard. They seemed to have a lot of respect for him. Not to change the subject, but has anyone heard from Mike?"

"Yes, he is with Mr. Bellini getting snacks for everyone."

"Did everyone get through the darkness alright?" I couldn't help but ask. So many people had been killed.

"I think so Becca. But then, like you, some of our employees haven't come in yet. I'm sure all their telephone lines are down. I know that the telephone companies are working feverishly day and night to get them repaired."

"What do you think about all of this Heidi?"

"Well, I'm one of the few who don't believe that it had anything to do with a meteor, or a natural disaster. How about you?"

"I'm in full agreement with you!"

The elevator doors opened and Mr. Bellini and Mike came in with hands full of candy bars, chips and cookies. When they saw me they dropped their loot in the middle of Heidi's desk and both gave me a big bear hug as a greeting.

"It's time to celebrate!" Said Mr. Bellini. "Come on everyone, get up here and get a snack. Take a break; we're only missing three employees now. I hope they all show up soon and God willing, everyone is safe after the horrible ordeal we just endured."

We talked and visited for about ten minutes and after we all had our fill of the junk food we resumed work.

I had a lot of mail on my desk, as usual. Mostly it came from people that were convinced our three days of darkness came as a punishment from God for the way we were living our lives. One letter that arrived didn't have a return address and I recognized the small print immediately. I was almost afraid to read its contents. Regardless of what Rafe said, I had to know what was in the envelope. I ripped it open and there scrawled in small print across the middle of the page, just like before was written:

IT WON'T BE MUCH LONGER BECCA, AND YOU WILL BELONG TO ME.

This letter unlike the other was signed though. The signature was scrawled below the writing.

LUTHER
Fear immediately gripped me and my heart began to pound wildly. Just the thought of who Luther truly was terrified me to the core.

I looked up from my desk and Mike was standing there staring at me with a frown on his face.

"Rebecca. What's wrong? You look like you just saw a ghost."

I nonchalantly folded the letter and put it back in the envelope before he had a chance to see it. I hoped that he didn't realize that that it's contents were what was bothering me.

"Well, Hi Mike. So far I'm glad to see you. Don't do or say anything to spoil it."

I smiled at him. He always made me smile. But then I remembered that the last time I saw him, he told me that he loved me. I had to be careful that I didn't give him any reason to think that I might reciprocate.

"Don't change the subject Rebecca. I've noticed how jumpy you've been for the last several weeks. You act like you are scared to death of something. What's going on?"

"There you go Mike, you are going to make me angry. I guess we should all be a little jumpy right now after the three days we just went through."

"Rebecca, don't tell me you believe all this religious junk. It was a meteor blocking the sun. We're lucky it didn't stay there or we would eventually be in a lot of trouble."

"Come on Mike, are you going to tell me that it didn't bother you in the least? I mean it was completely out of the normal realm of things we are used to."

"I was concerned yes, but after we found out what caused it, I don't think we necessarily need to dwell on it any longer. But you were jumpy before that ever happened. I'm just worried about you, Rebecca. You know I would do anything in this world to help you or keep you safe. I just want you to know I'm here for you. Okay?"

I could tell that I hurt his feelings by not letting him into my inner thoughts. He turned and went back to his desk without saying another word. I wanted to go after him. I had never intended to hurt him. I knew though, that it was better for me to leave well enough alone, so I returned to my work. It would be nice if I could get Heidi and Mike interested in each other. They would make such a cute couple, but she never showed any interest in him, and of course he thought he was madly in love with me. Once he realized that I had no intentions of becoming interested in him, maybe he would turn his affections elsewhere. That was another reason I couldn't feel bad when I hurt his feelings. I liked him so much, as a friend. It was hard to keep from apologizing when I upset him.

I put the letter in my sweater pocket, with the intent of placing it in my purse later. We all were absorbed in the mounds of work that the three days of darkness brought us and the day sped by.

The evening was strangely quiet. Rafe seemed to be preoccupied and I assumed that it was because of the decision he had to make about replacing Mr. Ferrachi. I didn't want to bother him so I remained quiet, reading a book and periodically looking over at him. He never looked up at me though. Finally I began to feel a little uneasy. This just wasn't like Rafe at all, he was usually so attentive, I told myself that if I had on my mind what he had on his I would be preoccupied as well.

At 10:00 pm, I decided that I should call it a night and since he seemed to want to be alone I decided to sleep in the bedroom instead of bothering him all night. I just had made up my mind that there was nothing to be afraid of, OH MY God! I just remembered the letter in my sweater pocket. I didn't know what to do. If I didn't tell him about it he was going to be very upset with me, and yet if I did tell him it would just give him something else to worry about, maybe tomorrow morning.

"Rafe" I said, standing up from the chair.

"I think I'll go to bed. I am really beginning to get very tired."

I realized that it was the first full day I'd put in at the office since my attack by Nicholas and it was such a busy day that I actually was exhausted.

"Wait Rebecca, I need to talk to you first."

Uh, oh, that didn't sound good. I slowly sat back down in the chair.

"Come over here and sit by me." He patted the place on the couch next to him. I got up and went and sat down beside him. I don't know why, but I had a dreadful feeling that this wasn't going to be good.

He patted my hand, and I looked into his eyes to see if I could see any signs of emotion there. But for a change there was nothing I could read in his eyes.

"Becca, this morning after I dropped you off for work, I met with all the Archangels and we are about to wage our war on Satan and the unholy of the world. Michael, who is in charge of all of us, wants me to stay with the other Archangels and with my army of angels. Each one of us is in charge of a battalion of our own. You know that I can't say no. It is my duty, and it is what I was created for, to serve God in heaven. My only jobs on the earth are the ones that God sends me on. But Michael is in charge of this war and I have to do what he asks me."

My heart began to pound as I listened to him.

"Please don't tell me this is the end Rafe!"

I looked at him closely, looking for some sign of comfort, but none was there.

"Becca, don't make this any more difficult than it already is. Please! I have asked Michael to meet you, and though he is not happy that I fell in love with a mortal human he has agreed to meet you tomorrow morning. I am hoping that when he meets you he will be a little more lenient with me. But even if he is, I won't be able to stay here anymore. I have to trust that you will take care of yourself now, and pay attention to what is going on around you. You have to do it for your sake, as well as for mine. All people will see Gods armies before too much longer, and there will still be some who decide to follow evil. You'll know when we are coming, because everyone will hear the trumpet blow, and I will announce that we have come to avenge the lord and for those who believe to go into hiding. I want you to go to the park where we had the picnic and I gave you the angel pendant. Do you think you could find it again?"

I just nodded. The moment had finally come, and I could feel my world crashing around me. I was preparing for the literal world to end. But I wasn't even prepared for our little world to end. But I knew, I could tell by the resolve in his expression, that there was nothing that I would be able to say or do that would make him stay with me. He had been honest with me from the beginning about where his loyalties lie. I was to shocked to shed a tear.

"Becca!" he said, to get my attention again.

"It is important that you go there. There won't be many places left in Rome that are safe. I need you to tell me you can find the park. I will come there for you when the war is ended and I will take you to a safe place."

At least I knew that I would see him again and a little corner of my heart grasped at hope.

"I will find it, Rafe. I'm sure I remember where it is. I could never forget that place."

My eyes suddenly filled with tears at the thought of his leaving. He quickly took me in his arms and held me very tight like it was the last time he would ever hold me. He kissed me on the forehead and stood up, looking at me. I saw the hurt and sorrow in his eyes.

"Be safe for me my angel and remember everything that I have tried to teach you.

I love you Becca. Always, always, remember that. I have to leave now. I have left the blessed candle here for your protection. Don't open the doors to anyone whose voice you don't recognize. I will be here early in the morning with Michael before you go to work."

"But Rafe, wait a minute."

He put his finger over my lips, and he turned and left.

As soon as the door closed behind him I began to sob. I went to make sure the doors and windows were locked. My eyes were so overflowing with tears that it was hard to focus on anything. Finally I just sat down on the floor with my hands covering my eyes and cried my heart out.

What was I going to do now? I was all by myself in a world that was about to be destroyed. I never thought of being without Rafe, and yet I should have. I might have been more prepared for his leaving. It was my normal pattern of procrastination. But obviously Rafe wasn't prepared for it to end this soon either. I began to wonder if I would really ever see him again after tomorrow morning. So many things could happen. He could be made to forget me. I could be killed. After all, I was just a frail human and not a very smart one most of the time. I couldn't think about it. I would panic. I got ready for bed, and brought Boots out to sleep with me on the couch. I curled up under the blanket and finally cried myself to sleep.

The next morning, because I didn't know what time Rafe and Michael were coming, I got ready early. I wore a white dress that was smocked in the front with tiny blue flowers embroidered above the smocking. It had a wide belt and the skirt of the dress was very full. I put on a pair of powder blue high heels and draped a white angora sweater over the chair to take with me when I left for work. I looked in the mirror and though my hair had its normal sheen, my eyes had huge circles beneath them just like they did before Rafe came into my life.

While I was thinking about life without Rafe, the doorbell rang, and after I checked to see who it was, I let Rafe and Michael in. Michael was as muscular as Rafe but he appeared to be a little older. I felt intimidated by him. I couldn't believe that Michael the Archangel was standing in the middle of my living room. The three of us politely chatted for a few minutes and then Michael told Rafe that he would like to talk to me alone and Rafe could wait for him in the car.

I looked at Rafe. I didn't want him to leave. Like last night there was no expression in his eyes. He came over though and kissed me on the forehead in front of Michael and said:

"I hope to see you later today, Becca." Then he left.

I stood staring at Michael, not knowing what to say or do.

I didn't have to worry though; it was easy for Michael to talk to anyone.

"Becca. May I call you Becca?"

I nodded yes, and waited for him to continue.

"It's unfortunate that you fell in love with Raphael and I feel sorry to put you through the agony you must be going through right now. But Raphael belongs in heaven with all of us who are of his kind. It is also unfortunate for him that God sent him on so many errands while on earth. I am sure that is part of the reason that he has fallen in love with a mortal. He has been amongst humans so often. Passion is something that we don't normally feel. We love all creation but the love between a man and a woman is something that has until now been beyond our means of grasping. It would be better for Raphael if you forget him and asked him not to see you again. However I will not interfere with your life that way. I can order him to stay with his army and away from you while we are at war, but I can only make suggestions to you. I hope I am not coming across to you as being unkind, because I certainly don't mean it that way. I am only looking out for what is best in the long run for Raphael and what is best in the long run for you, because this relationship can never be, unless Raphael denounces God, and I am sure you wouldn't want him to do that."

I looked at him shocked; I couldn't believe that he just said that. I said,

"Rafe, I mean Raphael, would never do that. He couldn't, nor wouldn't denounce God. He didn't want this relationship to begin in the first place. It just happened. But I can assure you that he has always let me know that his loyalty was with God. I know I cannot expect anything to evolve from our relationship. I would only ask you, if it were in his best interest as far as you are concerned, that we be allowed to have some time together for a proper goodbye. This has all happened so suddenly. I can assure you that he has always had an unadulterated love for me. He has been true to God from the start, and I know he will always remain that way."

Michael looked at me with a small smile on his face and said,

"Becca, you are wise beyond your years, and if Raphael had to fall in love with anyone, I am glad it was you. I cannot promise that I will send him back to you to say goodbye, because we are about to embark on the war to end all wars. But I can promise that he knows how much you cared. It was nice to meet you Becca."

With those final words, he left. I watched from the window as he got into the car with Rafe and they drove away.

I didn't have time to dwell on this right now, as I had to hail a cab and get to work.

Heidi noticed the circles under my eyes as soon as I walked through the office doors.

"Wow, Becca. Did you have a hard time sleeping last night or did you just work too many hours yesterday and you are exhausted?"

"I guess it is a little bit of both Heidi. Don't we all have those days once in a while?"

I tried to keep a cheerful note in my voice because I didn't want anyone here at work to know what was happening between Rafe and I. They didn't even know about a relationship of any kind, so there certainly wasn't a reason for them to know that we wouldn't be seeing each other anymore.

I purposely kept busy as much as possible, but I couldn't concentrate. All I wanted to do was crawl into a hole and die. Michael would tell Rafe he couldn't see me anymore. That was pretty obvious by what he said to me. Would Rafe disobey him? I knew better than to even think that he would. I dabbed at my eyes with a hankie, because no matter how hard I tried, my eyes had a will of their own and kept filling with tears. I felt like someone was watching me and I looked up to see Mike standing in front of my desk. Oh no, I thought, this was all I needed.

"Hi Rebecca."

He sure seemed overly cheerful today. I didn't feel in the least like being cheerful, I just wanted to be left alone. I didn't even want to be here today. I wanted to go home and get away from everything. But I knew that I couldn't. I promised Rafe I would be around people as much as possible to try and keep out of the clutches of Satan. I had to remember that, especially since I got the letter from Satan yesterday that I never got a chance to share with Rafe. I had to remember all of it, even though right now I really didn't care what happened to me.

"Hi Mike, don't you have tons of work to do, because I sure do?"

I thought maybe he would take the hint to leave. But of course, he just ignored me.

"I do." He said. "But it's time for lunch and if you aren't spending your lunch hour with David Rafe I thought maybe we could have lunch together. I brought sandwiches from home and some chocolate cake, it's not homemade but it tastes pretty good for a microwave-baked cake."

Just the mention of Rafes name made my heart ache.

"Oh Mike, thanks, I don't think I could eat anything right now. I'm really not hungry."

"Well, are you?"

"Am I what?"

"Having lunch with David Rafe?"

"No! I'm just not hungry Mike."

"Come on Rebecca, it won't kill you to have lunch with me. If you don't want to eat, the least you could do is come outside with me and keep me company for a while, or is that asking to much?"

I really wanted to tell him to just go away and leave me alone. But I had hurt his feelings so much in the last few days, and since he was in such a cheerful mood. I decided to go with him.

"Okay Mike, but no questions about anything today. Only if you promise me that."

"You got it! I promise! We'll just sit outside and enjoy the sun."

He snatched my sweater from the back of my chair and put it around my shoulders before I had a chance to change my mind.

We went outdoors to the employees' picnic area and sat down at one of the tables. We had only been there a very few minutes when Heidi joined us.

"Hi you two. Do you mind if I join you? Since the phones still aren't working I can take my lunch break anytime I want to today."

I quickly answered before Mike had a chance to protest.

"Sure Heidi, this is great. This will be a first. We would love to spend our lunch hour with you. Wouldn't we Mike?"

I knew I had put him on the spot, bout I knew this was a sure fire way of keeping him from asking me any more personal questions.

"Sure, Heidi. Sit down," said Mike in his cheerful tone.

I couldn't tell whether he was just saying it to be nice or if he really meant it.

The three of us talked for a while and Mike shared his chocolate cake with Heidi. I couldn't eat a thing. My stomach was just a jumble of nerves. Finally, I looked over at Heidi and said,

"Heidi, not to be nosy, but do you have a boyfriend?"

Mike and I both looked at her, waiting for an answer.

"Yes, I'm engaged to Mr. Bellini's' son Carlo. Didn't you know that?"

Wes both looked at her shocked.

Mike shook his head no, still agape.

"No" I said, "but I guess that isn't something you would spread around the office is it?"

"Well no, I guess not, but I'll tell you what" she laughed, "I'd drop Carlo in a minute if David Rafe would look at me the way he looks at you Becca."

Mike looked at both of us shaking his head back and forth.

"That's all I hear, David Rafe, David Rafe. What is so fantastic about that guy?"

Heidi looked at him in disbelief.

"Are you crazy? He's drop dead gorgeous and then some. No offense Mike, but there just aren't to many men that could hold a candle to that man. Don't you agree Becca?"

Before I had a chance to answer, she just looked at me and said,

"Of course you do!"

Mike stood up.

"Okay ladies, lunch is over. Let's get back to work."

"Did I upset you Mike?" Heidi said laughing.

"No, I'm getting tired of hearing about that guy." He shook his head again and looking at me said,

"Why so quiet Becca? I figured you'd jump right in on that one.

"Oh Mike. I just thought you'd been badgered enough for one day."

We all laughed and walked up the three flights of stairs back to the office.

I made myself dig into my work for most of the afternoon because I knew that I would go absolutely crazy if I didn't distract myself with something else besides feeling sorry for myself. Every now and then my stomach would feel like it was churning, and a tear would run from the corner of my eye.

At 4:30 pm all the telephones began to work again, and of course we all started to cheer, until we were swamped with incoming calls.

Mr. Bellini told us that one of our three missing employees' had already called and said he would be returning to work tomorrow.

The last hour of work was pretty hard on me as I began to worry about going home. I would be all-alone for the first time. I prayed that Nicholas or Satan didn't get a hold of me. I had to be strong. I had no choice but to go by myself. Rafe could no longer protect me. I had to keep my wits about myself like he had directed. I lingered around for a little while, afraid to leave, but I made up my mind that I wouldn't be the last one out of the office. When I saw that the last three or four people were on their way out of the building, I picked up my purse and followed them. We were waiting outside the elevator for the doors to open so we could leave, when much to my surprise, as they opened, there stood Rafe. He stepped off of the elevator so that the others could get on, and told them we would take the next one down.

"Oh Becca, I'm so happy that you hadn't left yet. I was so worried that I would miss you."

"Rafe, I can't tell you how happy I am to see you. I really thought I was never going to see you again."

"I told you I hoped I'd see you later today Becca. I didn't know whether I would be able to for sure or not. But when I told Michael as we left your flat this morning that I made a promise that you would never be left alone and that I wasn't letting you go home from work without any protection. What could he say? An angel can't break his promise. I can't stay the night, but I have sent three angels from my battalion to watch over you at night, and you have the blessed candle to keep you safe in the house. I'll plan on getting you home every day, but if something comes up that I can't I will send someone to take you."

He didn't have the Mercedes today. He hailed a cab and gave them my address. When we got into the car her reached over and took my hand and held it in his for the entire ride home. I wanted to lean my head on his shoulder so badly, but I didn't dare. I didn't want to give his leader any reason to get angry with me or to be upset with Rafe. I didn't know where my boundaries were supposed to be right now.

Almost as if he could read my mind, Rafe put his arm around me and said,

"Lay your head on my shoulder Becca, you look totally exhausted. I know how awful this is for you. If it is any consolation, it is the same for me. I thought about you many times today."

When we finally got to my flat and he had paid the cab driver he walked me to the door. I didn't know what to do again. Was he going to come in like he usually did? He opened the door for me, but when I turned to look at him questioningly, he just handed me the keys.

"No, Becca, I'm sorry, I have to go now. I will see you tomorrow."

He held onto my hand for a moment longer, turned it over and touched my palm to his cheek and then kissed it, before he just vanished into thin air.

It was a very long and lonely night. I didn't eat. In fact the thought of food still nauseated me. I wasn't too afraid though, because I knew that the angels he sent were watching over me. Even though I couldn't see them I could feel their presence.

I also had the blessed candle, and its flickering glow gave me a sense of security. When sleep finally did come, the terrible nightmare was back to haunt me. Only this time Nicholas was chasing me. When I started screaming and thrashing in my sleep, it woke me up and I bolted straight up into a sitting position in bed. Oh my God, I thought. What am I going to do to get rid of these horrible dreams? I didn't think I was going to be able to take too many more sleepless nights like this. I got out of bed and went and took a shower and changed into dry nightclothes. I missed Rafe

So much. By the time I got back into bed and fell asleep the alarm clock started buzzing.

Chapter 8
DECEPTION

We were all working furiously in the office trying to prepare the newspaper for the printer so that it would be distributed before the day was over. I had so many stories about the three days of darkness that I couldn't put even a third of them in the paper.

Mr. Bellini refused to let me use the term three days of darkness. I could only use the phrase days when the meteor eclipsed the sun.

"I thought we worked for a religious institution inside the Vatican and were supposed to report anything of religious significance, Mr. Bellini."

"You are right Becca, but our new Pope refuses to let us mention anything other than the meteor, because he doesn't want to start any panic amongst Christians."

"But the three days of darkness was prophesized hundreds of years ago. Christians need to know the truth."

"It doesn't matter Becca, our new Pope thinks a lot of the prophesies that we were given are just stories made up by people for attention."

"Whatever you say I'll print Mr. B, but I don't like it. It just seems inappropriate for the Vatican newspaper to go along with scientists."

We were discussing this when we heard a loud noise like a sonic boom and the building began to sway forcefully. Many employees ran from their desks, while others just sat there dumbfounded not knowing what to do. The people who were running were shouting,

"Earthquake, earthquake, get out of the building fast."

People were crammed around the elevator, but some of us ran as fast as we could down the stairs. During all this commotion, the building began to sway and we heard the sounds of a terrible rumble and cracking sounds as the stairs began to fall down behind us. I had to jump to get down the last two steps because they had already broken off. I fell to the ground and scraped both of my knees.

When we were completely away from the building, we just stood and watched as the building began to tumble and fall, some of it crashing thunderously to the ground. When the dust cleared, the top half of the newspaper building that housed the print office was completely gone, and the rest of the building stood crookedly, with large cracks running up the sides and all of the windows had blown out from the force of the shaking.

None of us had any idea how bad the damage was to the rest of the building and all of the exits were now hidden with the debris. One of the employees from St. Peters came running past us and stopped long enough to tell us that he heard that the Basilica had been completely destroyed. He didn't know whether it was true or not. Thank goodness he had been on an errand for one of the Cardinals or he might have been in the building and been killed.

Many people began to leave in search of their friends and families. The parking lot was broken up so badly that it was impossible to get to any of the automobiles, so most of the employees who had cars had to leave on foot.

I wanted to get home as soon as possible, but of course it was impossible to hail a cab with the whole city in such distress. Since I was about three miles from home I knew it would take me awhile to get there.

Streets were blocked with fallen debris and cars couldn't get anywhere. There was nothing for anyone in the city to do but walk to wherever they were going. I began to walk in the direction of my flat, but since there was so much destruction and so many buildings gone, I soon lost my way.

I stopped to help others who were trying to rescue some of the people who were trapped under the fallen buildings.

There was crying and moaning and it reminded me of the sounds of the three days we had just been through, except that the scene was so much more gruesome because of the devastation from the horrible earthquake that had left buildings crumbled on the ground, telephone poles lying across cars and the roads heaved up from their original flat surface, now looked like a bomb had exploded.

All the destruction and chaos made me soon forget about getting home. I probably didn't have a home anyway from the looks of things around me. This was definitely a major disaster.

A man with a weather station radio said this was a worldwide earthquake. I thought to myself that this should make people take notice. When had they ever heard of a worldwide earthquake ever happening?

Those of us who had been walking around aimlessly began to work pulling the wounded out of the twisted mess of bricks and steel until our fingers were bleeding from trying to move the heavy materials, but we kept digging with our bloodied hands late into the night. Whenever we heard someone crying and begging for help under another heap of bricks, we would run to where the sound was coming from to try and dig them out. Many were wounded fatally and some of them were maimed of legs, arms or both.

I finally became so mentally and physically fatigued that I curled up on top of a big chunk of cement that had fallen from one of the buildings and fell into an exhausted sleep.

The next morning I woke, as I was being lifted by strong arms and carried away from the horrid scene. Since I was half asleep, I snuggled deep into his chest feeling safe, but when I realized it wasn't the deeply muscled chest that I was used to; I opened my eyes wide to look directly into the eyes of Luther Amaddon, better known as Satan. I began to struggle and scream trying to get away from him.

"Put me down! Put me down! Where are you taking me?"

My heart was pounding so wildly and I was so frightened that I hoped I would have a heart attack and die.

"Rebecca, shh, I'm not going to hurt you. I'm just going to take you someplace safe where you can eat and take a shower and rest in a bed. Don't be afraid of me. I mean you no harm. Don't you see, I want you for my own? I have no intention of hurting you unless you force me to."

He sounded so serious, but I knew better than to trust him.

"You need to leave me alone. Leave me here. Rafe will be looking for me." I said.

He laughed. "Don't you mean Raphael the Archangel? You'd better forget about him. He belongs in heaven. One good thing about our rebellion is that we can do whatever we want on the earth and fall in love with anyone we want to. Your angel can't do that. He deceived you by letting you fall in love with him. It was pretty arrogant of him actually. He knew what the consequences would be, and he let it happen anyway. It was cruel. I would never do that, because I don't have to. I can fall in love with anyone, anytime and anyplace and have absolutely nothing to feel guilty about."

"But, Luther,"

I was afraid to call him Satan to his face. I wanted to see Rafe, and I wanted to stay alive long enough for him to try and find me.

"You don't love me, you hate me. You told me you would make me pay the next time you saw me."

"Well Rebecca, I have reconsidered and I don't want to kill you after all. Sometimes my emotions get a little mixed up. I want you to stay with me, as mine."

He held on to me tightly and jumped into the air and began to fly just like Rafe, only I could feel the heat from his body and it felt very hot against my body. I began to get sick to my stomach from fear and from being overheated.

"Just a few more minutes Rebecca and we will be there."

He flew across the Tiber River to a beautiful castle that I recognized immediately as The Castel Sant'Angelo, or the Castle of the Angels. It was connected to the bridge of the Angels where Rafe told me who he really was. I noticed as we flew by that a beautiful statue depicting Michael the Archangel was decorating the top of the castle. Surprisingly, it looked very much like the real angel.

Luther took me to what appeared to be the basement of the castle. At the very least it was one of the lower floors. He had separate quarters housed there. The rooms were decorated beautifully reminiscent of St. Peters' Basilica, but without the religious icons that decorated the Basilica.

Luther was acting like the perfect gentleman. He put me down very gently and summoned a young girl to show me to my room. The room had a king size canopy bed decorated with a white gauze material that came down and cascaded along the floor. The bedspread was white brocade with a tiny tinge of pink bordering the edge of the fabric. Several different pink and white pillows in several shapes and sizes were scattered across the head of the bed, making it very inviting for someone who was as tired as I. I stood and stared at the bed. My bones and muscles still ached from sleeping on the hard chunk of concrete that had been my bed the night before. The carpet was very pale pink plush shag that complimented the bed perfectly.

The young girl took me to another room that had a walk-in shower and there was a huge swimming pool in the corner of the room with a golden cherub water fountain that was dumping water into the pool from a golden urn. Every light in the room was giving off a soft glow.

Looking from the bathroom into the bedroom I saw a huge white marble fireplace that I hadn't noticed before. It was positioned directly on the wall opposite the bed. Its mantle was decorated with exceptionally beautiful statues of different sized angels.

Everything in the two rooms was definitely put there for a female occupant. The décor was extremely feminine.

The young girl whose name I learned later was Ursula looked at me with a strange smile and twinkle in her eyes.

"The Master said for you to make yourself comfortable and take a shower or bath. Here is a dressing gown for you to put on."

The dressing gown was as white as the bedspread, but it was made of the softest velvet with long lace insets at the cuffs of the sleeves and the whole gown was trimmed in rose pink satin piping. Like everything else about the rooms; it was beautiful.

"I will help you bathe and dress and then I am to leave you to rest or sleep, and I will be back to wake you for dinner."

She still had a strange smile on her face when she said these words to me.

I looked at her without uttering a word. I had no idea what to say to this young girl who as far as I was concerned had to be as evil as

Luther My head was throbbing, and my stomach began to growl from the hunger that was beginning to gnaw at me from not having eaten anything since the day before.

I let her help me into the shower and when I finished bathing she handed me a large white towel and took me over to the pool.

"It's heated." She said, "Would you like to take a little swim to help relax your muscles?"

I looked at her again and warily said,

"Yes I'll wade."

She lowered the towel as I slid into the water. She was right. It felt so good against my sore muscles. I waded to the end of the pool and relaxed by the cherub, letting the water from his urn splash across my shoulders. I watched the young girl as she clapped her hands an older gentleman entered the room. She said something to him and he left, only to return a few minutes later with what looked like a large platter of fruit and cheese.

After he left, I waded to the steps of the pool to get out because I was beginning to tire. She had the towel open for me before I even approached the first step.

She hurriedly dried me off, much to my chagrin. I couldn't remember ever having anyone else beside myself dry me off after a bath. She seemed completely unconcerned as she helped me into the dressing gown that fit perfectly and was wonderfully soft against my skin.

After I had my fill of fruit and cheese, she left me to rest. I stood staring at the big bed, and I finally decided I wasn't going to be tricked by Luther. I wasn't going to sleep in his inviting bed. The carpet felt so soft and lush against the bottom of my feet that I decided to lie down on the floor and rest. I must have fallen asleep there on the floor, because the next thing that I remembered was that the room was now dark and I was being lifted onto the bed. In my drowsiness I thought it was Rafe and I whispered his name.

"No, darling, it is Luther."

But I was to tired to realize that this was a real conversation and not a dream, and I rolled over on my side and fell into a deeper sleep, dreaming about Rafe.

The next morning I awoke when the young girl gently shook me and placed a tray with eggs and bacon and a carafe of coffee on my bed.

She looked at me with that strange smile again and said:

"The master wants you to join him in the foyer as soon as you are dressed."

She went to the closet and pulled out another beautiful garment. This time it was a dress. When she started to unbutton the buttons on my dressing gown I pushed her hands away and said,

"Thank you, I am perfectly capable of dressing myself!"

She had a pouty expression on her face as I grabbed the dress out of her hands and began to dress myself.

"The master isn't going to like this." She said.

I looked at her and sarcastically said,

"There's no one to tell your master, but you."

I continued to dress myself without looking at her again. When I was finished and had brushed my hair, with the beautiful mother of pearl handled brush on the dresser, I simply turned and looked at her.

"Well, take me to Luther."

Her eyes widened with horror.

"He is Master to you and…"

I didn't let her finish.

"No, he is Master to you. He will never be my Master!"

She started to say something else, but decided against it and lowered her head as she said:

"Follow me."

This floor of the castle was enormous. We walked for quite a while going up and down different corridors. I knew if I had to walk back by myself I would never find my way, as everything looked the same to me. The castle was cold and damp and the tall vaulted ceilings made our footsteps echo as we walked across the floor.

Finally we stopped in front of two massive doors that were flanked on each side by Vatican guards. I frowned, as I looked at them. What was going on here? How strange. Why would the Vatican guards be standing outside of Luthers foyer? What would Rafe think? The guards snapped to attention and gave the familiar salute that I was so used to seeing in the Papal Palace. When I was allowed to enter, Luther stood up from a massive black leather couch.

"Good morning Becca, and how did you sleep? I hope you liked your room. I had them decorated with you in mind."

I frowned.

"How did you know I would be coming here?"

"Did you forget who I am Rebecca? I know quite a few things. I bet your lover never told you about me, did he? If he had maybe you would have been a bit more cautious than you were. I could have brought you here several times."

I cringed thinking of all the warning I had received from Rafe, just another way that I had disappointed him.

"Luther, how is it you have Vatican Guards?"

I asked, narrowing my eyes as I waited for his answer.

"That is my business, it is of no concern to you." He said.

He looked over at the young girl, who now stood quietly in the corner.

"You can leave now Ursula. I will call you when you are needed."

Ursula bowed, turned and left the room without saying a single word.

I looked at Luther, studying the sharp planes of his face. So unlike Rafes beautiful face, his was menacing. The only thing that saved him from being horribly satanic looking were his beautiful soft brown eyes that could mesmerize you with their gentle stare. I remembered seeing hate in their depths before when he promised that he was going to kill me. The lines of his mouth were harsh even when his eyes looked at you so softly. I studied his hands and forearms, they were muscular and strong, and all I could picture was how many people he had killed with those bare hands, and I shivered at the thought.

"Luther, if you aren't going to kill me, would you mind telling me why you brought me here?"

"Because I want you to fall in love with me, Becca. I will take care of you. As you can see, I can give you anything that you could ever want."

"That will never happen!" I spat. "I have no intention of ever loving you. I would rather be dead. Maybe you had better stick to your first promise. You are despicable."

"That could be arranged too Becca, but I would much rather give you the chance to fall in love with me first. There are many women who would love to be in your shoes right now. I am only horrid to people who have been taught that I am horrid. You see, I can teach you that there is no such thing as sin that you can do anything that you want to do without feeling guilty. The man up above has stuck people with so many stigmas that they don't know what its like to live in a world where they can do anything they like and it is not a regarded as a sin. I guarantee you that you would be a much happier person if you wouldn't believe all that 'thou shall not' crap. Give me a chance to show you just how happy you would be in my world, where anything and everything you desire can become a reality."

I was staring in disbelief at him. Did he actually expect me to fall for this?

"I know you are the God of this world SATAN!"

There I said it. Rafe told me not to forget it. If I continued to call him Luther, it would be so easy to forget that he wasn't human. I had to keep reminding myself that he was Satan and was after not only my life, but also my eternal soul.

He started laughing.

"You're wrong Becca, I'm not after you life. I'm after your love, and will pursue you as any young man purses a woman he wants to love him. But you are right about two things, I am Satan, and yes, I am the God of this world. God gave me that privilege when he banned me here, and with that privilege I can give you anything your heart desires."

"You can't give me heaven though, can you Satan?"

He looked at me and laughed again.

"I can give you heaven on earth Becca, that's what is important. The choice is yours"

"Never!"

"Then you will be my prisoner. But I promise to pursue you for your love, or until you end up dead. The choice should be very easy to make. It would be for me, happiness versus death? Don't be foolish."

"Satan do you really think there is anyone who would actually care if I was your prisoner? I am nothing, and as long as I keep my faith and ignore you, I will keep me eternal soul."

I looked at him completely satisfied, feeling like I had just said the perfect combination of words.

He laughed so loud that it echoed throughout the room.

"You have a whole horde of angels who will be looking for you soon. So don't tell me no one cares if you're a prisoner. I feel sorry for both you and your Raphael, how stupid of him to fall in love with you when he knows he can't have you. It's against his Gods rules. Do you actually think he will break those rules for you? I doubt it, I would! I would! But for now, while he is on this planet, he will worry about you."

I knew he was right, on both points. There had to be a way that I could make Rafe forget me. He didn't need the worry of me when he had this horrible war to fight, and so many souls beside mine to worry about. But, oh my God, I loved him. I didn't want him to forget about me. Just like I didn't want to ever for get about him.

"I can see you are not going to give me an answer today Becca, so.."

He clapped his hands twice and Ursula came back into the room.

"take Miss Malone back to her room and lock the door when you leave. She has a lot of things she needs to think about today. She will be our prisoner for a while."

When the door closed behind me and I heard the key turn in the lock, I immediately went back to check it. Yes, it was locked. What was I going to do? There were no windows and the double doors seemed to be the only exit from the room. I went and sat down on the floor next to the bed.

None of this made any sense. What purpose would Satan have in trying to get me to fall in love with him? The only thing that I could think of was my connection with Raphael the angel, not Rafe the man. If that was the reason I was sad for Rafe because I knew that he would try to save me. Even if he could, it would take him away from the war waged against the earth.

I began to cry because try as I might, I had ended up in Satan's clutches just like Rafe said I would. I couldn't stand the thought of him having to worry about me. I felt so very guilty. I had to do something to keep Rafe safe and away from me. If only I knew what. I sat on the floor for a long time until it finally started getting dark. Maybe Rafe would think I died in the earthquake. It would make him very sad, but at least he wouldn't have to worry about me anymore, and he could give his full attention to the war.

I was trying to think of a way to make him forget me when Ursula brought me dinner. It was an elaborate meal and I was waited on hand and foot. I was so confused about Satan. Why did he continue to be so nice to me? I had made it very clear this afternoon that I didn't want anything to do with him. I was going to have to make him so angry that he would kill me. I could suffer for Rafe, but I couldn't endure the thought of him suffering for me. He had too much at stake.

I had to have a plan. I knew I probably would never see Rafe again, so I felt like my absence from his life would be a good thing for him in the long run. It would also please Michael the Archangel and I'm sure it would please God that I would sacrifice myself to keep Rafe safe with his own kind in heaven. It would be hard for him at first and he probably would never forget me, but time eases all wounds. He was the one that was immortal, not me, and the only thing he would gain from our relationship was the heartache of hurting God. I only hoped that God would forgive me.

I had spent so much time thinking about it, that when Ursula came back to get the tray, I hadn't eaten a single bite. She gave me a worried look and took the tray with her and locked the door behind her once more. When she returned a little later she went to the closet and picked me out another dressing gown but this time she didn't try to undress me, she just laid it out on the bed and let herself out.

I was sitting on the floor with my legs crossed in front of me, and the dressing gown billowed around me when the door opened and Satan came in.

"What are you doing on the floor? Why do you insist on not sleeping in the bed?" he asked. His eyes showed no anger, only concern. But I didn't let that intimidate me.

"I wouldn't sleep in your bed if it was the last bed on earth. I told you, I hate you! You are a despicable creature."

I waited for him to turn on me, but his eyes only softened.

"I know what you are trying to do Rebecca, and it is going to take a lot more than that to anger me. What I actually came for is to find out if there is something wrong with the food. You barely touched anything on your tray. I can't have you wasting away to nothing now can I? If there is anything you want or need, please tell Ursula and she will get it for you. She is your servant now."

"I don't need a servant. I can take care of myself," I screamed at him.

"I know you can. I'm just trying to make things pleasant for you while you are here."

"Do you ever plan on setting me free Satan?"

"No! And why did you quit calling me Luther?"

"Satan is a more fitting name for you, it makes me remember what a horrible demon you truly are, that way no matter how nice you are to me, it is always on my mind that you represent evil."

He just laughed again as he left the room.

I finally fell asleep on the floor again for the second night, and no one came in this time to move me to the bed. I didn't dream all night. I was too exhausted to think of anything so I slept the whole night through.

The next morning I was summoned to the foyer again. I wished I could make a connection with the reason for the Swiss Guard. Had they defected their Vatican jobs?

When I was finally admitted into Satan's office I was still troubled over that question.

"Is there something the matter Becca? You seem to be worried about why the Vatican Guard is here. I can answer that question for you. The new Pope and I are in allegiance with each other. Since he wouldn't want anything to happen to me, he has loaned me a few of his Guard for my protection."

I hated that he could read my mind. I wondered if Rafe could do that. If he could he had never let on to anyone that he read minds as far as I was aware. I looked at Satan for a few seconds and then spat out,

"As if you need any protection!"

"Well, you never know now do you Becca? I may even need protection from you. Have you thought anymore about what we discussed yesterday?"

"Yes I have. I have made up my mind that I would rather be dead. So why don't you just get on with it? It's something that would please the both of us."

He got up from behind his desk so fast that he knocked the chair over as he stood. He came rushing around the desk and grabbed me by both of my arms.

"I should kill you! But I want you to love me so you see, I can't no, I won't kill you. Would you rather be my prisoner forever and treated as such? I don't think you

would, but before you answer, come with me so that I can show you just how beautiful this castle is. You would be its mistress."

He was right the castle was magnificent and had every modern convenience that was imaginable. There were butlers, maids and personal servants. He showed me a large oak cabinet that was full of a variety of jewels, with diamonds, rubies, sapphires and every fathomable gem.

"All this jewelry is yours to wear anytime you'd like. Here is the key."

He handed me the key and I gave it back to him.

"I won't need the key. I won't wear any of your jewelry." I said.

He just turned and handed the key to Ursula and said,

"Put this in the top drawer of her bureau, she will soon change her mind. She still

thinks she's in love with that goody two shoes angel."

I scowled at him. He did know exactly how I felt about Rafe. If he could read my mind how was I going to do any plotting against him?

"You'll plot anyway Rebecca, it doesn't matter whether I can read your mind or not. Why does it surprise you so much that I can? In case you didn't realize it that wimpy angel of yours can read minds as well. Didn't he ever tell you that? Oh, I can tell by your reaction that you didn't know."

This delighted him.

"How embarrassing that must be. I bet you could think some pretty steamy things. I bet he has had a lot of fun with that."

He laughed a little longer this time.

I was stunned. How could Rafe not ever tell me that he could read my mind? I thought about the first day in the Regional Park on the Appian Way when I thought I was hiding the fact of my meeting with Nicholas and Luther. He knew everything before he questioned me. And I practically begged him mentally to kiss me. Then the last time when I was so brazen with him, he could read my thoughts then also. Why? Why, would he do that to me? A terrible sadness came over me. I felt betrayed.

Satan was watching me carefully. He started to laugh again and came closer to me. And lifting my chin and looking into my eyes he said,

"I would never lie to you Becca. I have nothing to hide."

I didn't want to think about it right now. I would think about it later when I was alone and I didn't have his curious brown eyes staring at me.

I began to sulk quietly. Satan continued showing me the grandness of the castle, but my mind was in a blank state. I wasn't interested in what he was showing me and I didn't dare think about what I wanted to right now. A sadness engulfed me because I felt like I had been deceived by Rafe, and I didn't know why.

"Well that is all of the castle Becca, you don't seem to be very impressed. You seem to be preoccupied with other things."

He didn't laugh this time.

"Please have dinner with me Becca, it will take your mind off of other things."

"No, I'd rather not. Please may I go to my quarters?"

"No! You will dine with me."

I was too stunned over Rafe reading my mind to have the energy to argue with him. I just followed him into the great dining room where the servants were already setting up a feast. We sat down and one of the servant girls brought us both golden goblets filled with wine. So much of this world seemed to be centered in medieval times. Satan continued to talk through the whole meal, trying to convince me how wonderful it would be to love him, and how much he would lavish on me if I would but give him a chance. I ignored him for most of the conversation and shouted an emphatic "No" the rest of the time. I kept drinking the wine trying to numb my brain so that I wouldn't think tonight. Finally when I could scarcely keep my eyes open, I asked,

"May I please go to my room Satan, I am so tired. I can't keep my eyes open any longer."

"Only if I hear you call me Luther."

I didn't want to argue and was too tired and slightly drunk to put up much of a fuss, so I looked at him with the most disgusted look I could muster and said,

"Luther, may I go to bed?"

Chapter 9
PRISONER

I was so tipsy from drinking all that wine that I didn't even change my clothes; I immediately found my usual place on the floor and fell asleep.

Sometime during the night I felt myself being lifted onto the bed. When I started to roll on my side, strong arms turned me onto my back. When he lay across my body and took me in his arms. I thought it was Rafe. My mind was so foggy, and it was so dark in the room, that my eyes could not focus.

Finally I looked up into soft brown eyes that were so inviting that I couldn't resist his touch, but somehow in my boggled mind I knew that I had to.

His hands were moving all over my body and I weakly pushed them away from me, but his lips captured my mouth and became insistent, trying to break the last thread of my resolve.

I felt myself sinking, sinking into the oblivion that I knew would bring nothing but horror for me, and torture for Rafe. I began to fight harder, pushing against Satan, writhing underneath him, trying to shove him off of me. But he was much stronger and very experienced in knowing what a woman wants and winning her affection.

I felt myself weaken as his kiss became more persistent. It was as if my whole body was on fire, betraying me so much that even the blood in my veins felt like it was beginning to boil from his unyielding forceful embrace.

"I'll make you want me Becca. I'll make you want me and forget everyone else."

He began moving his body against mine, rising my body to a new tempo of feverish desire. Than he slowly pulled himself away from me, and with eyes full of lust he whispered huskily,

"Becca, take your clothes off for me. I want to see your beautiful body. I want to watch you undress."

Something in his words reminded me of the filth of the words of Baragio! I looked at him horrified! HE WAS SATAN, THE DEVIL! Oh my God, how could I have ever let him touch me? I shook my head as if to clear it. I bolted to my feet in disgust trying to run from him. But it was of no use! He caught me by the arm and threw me back on the bed. He was on top of me again in a second, forcing all his weight on me.

"I can do this the hard way Becca," He said, ripping at my clothes

" I wanted you to want me. It would have worked so much better that way, but I will have you one way or another. I plan for you to be mine. It is my last opposition against heaven. It's your choice, willingly or by force. It makes no difference to me. I'll take what Raphael can't."

I screamed a blood-curdling cry.

"Rafe! Rafe! Please help me."

"That's right, call him. That coward can't save you." He laughed as his mouth drowned out my scream. I bit his top lip and he slapped me so hard across my face that I actually saw stars; I could taste my blood dripping into my mouth.

In the next instant I heard a loud whooshing sound, and I looked up to see my beautiful angel pulling Satan off of me. Raphael looked furious, first at me and then at Satan. I had never seen that expression on his face before, and it scared me almost as much as Satan trying forcefully to rape me. He grabbed Satan by the throat and yelled,

"Satan, you murderous bastard! I'll send you straight to hell myself."

He threw him across the room, and Satan laughed. Raphael was on him in an instant. And then Michael the Archangel was there along with Raphael. Michael looked at me in disgust.

I had to get out of there. I didn't want Satan to get his hands on me again, and I didn't want to face the wrath of the two archangels, that had been summoned to protect me. Especially since I now knew they could read all my thoughts, I was so scared and humiliated that all I wanted to do was get out of there as fast as my feet could carry me. I jumped from the bed and ran to the door and for a change it was unlocked.

I ran and ran, running through the halls, I found a tunnel and hid in it for a while as the Swiss Guard were changing their watch. I quickly ran into a church at the end of the tunnel. I stopped and looked around me for an exit, but I didn't see one. I heard footsteps coming down the tunnel. I hid behind a large statue of the La Pieta, and then, it hit me! Oh my God, I was actually experiencing my dream. I looked up to see if I could crawl up into the ceiling, but I guess that was a part of my dream that wasn't real. I stayed behind the statue, being very quiet. It was the Swiss Guard! They came into the church and looked around. They were speaking in Italian, so I couldn't understand a word that they were saying. I was terrified. I could hear my heart pounding in my ears.

I prayed that they wouldn't catch me and return me to Satan. I didn't know whether they were the Palace Guard or Satans Guard. If only I could get to the stairs that were across from the marble altar. Maybe I could escape. At least there were windows on the second floor, or was it the ground floor. I had no idea what part of the Castle I was in.

One of the Swiss Guard went over and turned off the lights in the church, and the only light that lit the church were the large white candles glowing on the altar. I shivered. This was another part of my dream. The guard left the church and I leaned my head against the cool marble of the statue and closed my eyes in relief.

When all was quiet, I crept out from behind the statue and quietly walked up the center aisle of the church until I was in front of the marble altar. I stopped. There was a noise. Should I duck into one of the church pews? No, they would find me there. I looked at the door, and in came six Swiss Guard. As soon as they spotted me, they began running up the center and two side aisles. I ran for the stairs and got to them just in time before they had a chance to block my way. They were right behind. I ran as hard and fast as I could. It felt like the breath was being sucked from me. Finally when I realized there was no other exit, there was nothing I could do but jump through one of the stained glass windows. It was that or be returned to Satan. I just knew that I was going to die of fear. If I jumped through the window, chances were that I would be killed anyway, because I had no idea what was on the other side. The Swiss Guard was getting close, closing in on me. I shut my eyes tightly and dove through the window that was in front of me, shielding my eyes with my arms. I fell with a thud to the ground below. It turned out that it wasn't as large of a drop as I imagined it to be. Maybe one floor, two at the most. I had cut my right arm pretty badly in the process. I tore the sleeve that Satan had already ripped, from my arm and wrapped it as tight as I could around the wound, making a tourniquet to try and stop the bleeding. The material soaked up the blood as fast as I tied it there, but I knew that the tourniquet was tight enough that it wouldn't bleed much longer.

I jumped to my feet and started running again. I fell down twice before I reached the Angel Bridge. I was running across it as fast as I could. The blood was trickling down my arm and it was beginning to throb. . I looked back across the bridge to see if the Swiss Guard had followed me. Damn! They had. I began running again, passing each angel statue. This was sure nothing like the day I stopped to admire each one with Rafe. When I looked up again there was Swiss Guard coming from the other side of the bridge also. I didn't know what to do. I couldn't swim in water over my head. There was nowhere to go except in the water. Maybe I could make it. Swimming didn't look very hard. I stood on the side of the bridge, climbed up next to one of the angel statues and paused. This would kill me. I knew it would. At least I wouldn't have to worry about Satan anymore, and Rafe wouldn't have to worry about me anymore. He could get on with his life, the way it was meant to be. I looked at the statue. My eyes filled with tears. My love began on this bridge. I guess it was only fitting that it should end on this bridge. Without another thought, I closed my eyes and jumped.

Before I hit the water, strong arms caught me and with flapping wings flew me back to the bridge. I didn't open my eyes. If I was on the bridge, it had to be Satan.

"Becca, Becca, open your eyes. You are safe."

Oh, thank God! It was Rafe.

He sat me down on the bridge and I opened my eyes and looked at him. His expression was immediately one of relief and then it transferred to confused and ended at pained.

"Becca, why did you try to kill yourself? I can't believe you did that!"

His voice was taut with anger now.

"Oh Rafe, I didn't want to be Satan's prisoner, and I didn't want to be a burden to you any longer. Don't you see, with me dead Satan could never get his hands on me and you wouldn't have to be constantly saving me from something that was my own fault. Michael doesn't want you to have anything to do with me. Your life was so perfect before you met me. I want everything to be perfect for you."

"Becca is that all the more you love me? You could just throw your life away and not think of the consequences to your soul or to me?"

"I never thought of it that way Rafe. I just wanted to give you peace. I seem to be such a burden to you."

"Burden to me! Do you know what a burden it would have been if you died? I would never be able to lead an army. Promise me you will never do anything like that again Becca. I can't continue if I think you are ever going to end your life because of me! Promise me Becca!"

"Before I promise you anything Rafe, tell me why you never told me that you could read my thoughts?"

"What! Who told you that?"

"Just answer me Rafe, is it true?"

"Rebecca, I want to know who told you that!! Now!"

"I'll tell you what Rafe, you answer my question and then I will answer yours."

"Rebecca Malone, you are one stubborn woman! I cannot read your thoughts. I can't imagine why anyone would tell you such a thing. My gift is healing. Not reading thoughts."

He grabbed me by the right arm and for a minute I thought he was going to hit me, but he pressed on my wound very hard and removed the material that I had tied around it. There was noting left but a tiny pink scar.

"Michael can read minds, not me. Now! Who told you that?"

I was suddenly so ashamed, ashamed to even admit who had told me. I looked at my beautiful angel. How could I ever think he could do anything cruel to me? I lowered my head in shame and whispered.
"Satan."
"And you believed him? The father of the lie! Becca!"
I could tell he was livid.
He shook his head.
"We'll talk about this later. I have to get back to my battalion. Take her to the Papal Apartments, and don't let her leave,"
He ordered the Swiss Guard. Then looking at me again with the same anger in his expression, he said,
"You'll be my prisoner for a while now!"
He left, flew off of the bridge into the darkness. I watched him, wondering what he was thinking. It was obvious that I had wounded him deeply. Would he forgive me? Could he forgive me?
The Swiss Guard escorted me to the Papal Palace. I was surprised to see it was still
standing. I had imagined it was gone with all the buildings that succumbed to the earthquake.
I wasn't happy as we entered the Palace, as the Guard locked me in a room in the upper story of the Palace, and planted themselves outside of my door. There would be no jumping out windows here. Not that I would want to leave. I thought that being Rafes' prisoner was not a bad thing. It kept Satan away from me. And it kept me safe for Rafe. But all the same, I hated being in any room that I couldn't get out of.
I plopped myself across one of the twin beds in the room. The more I thought about the stupid things I had done, I worried about how Rafe would feel about me. How could he ever forgive me? He was so perfect and I was such a mess. It seemed as though everything he warned me not to do, I did. Now to top it all off I had willingly believed Satan without even thinking he might be lying to me.
I had no idea what time it was, but the sky was starting to get a little lighter so I knew it must be close to morning. The more I thought, the more I began to cry. All that kept going through my mind was the expression on Rafe's face when he realized that I had tried to kill

myself, and the hurt in his eyes when I had accused him of a lie. I hated myself for ever causing him pain.

By the time one of the Palace staff brought me breakfast, I was so exhausted that I could barely keep my eyes open. Still, I could not sleep. I tried to put all the facts together to help me deal with the pain I caused Rafe, but I couldn't. That was what got me in trouble in the first place. I thought Rafe would be better off without me, and now after seeing him again, I wanted to give him all my love until he had to leave. I would worry about myself when the time came. I could only hope he would forgive me for the excruciating pain I had caused him last night.

I spent the day looking out the window at the demolished city. One of the Guards informed me that many more people were dying from new strains of viruses as a result of unsanitary conditions of the city, as well as the lack of food and clean water. The day seemed to drag on.

I ate dinner alone and went to bed. If there was even a broadcast on the air, there was no television set or radio in the room. So obviously I couldn't follow any news reports. There were no books to read or magazines to leaf through. There was absolutely nothing to keep me occupied, not even a clock on the wall. There was nothing to do but sleep, and sleep didn't come easy that night either, even though I had stayed awake the night before. It seemed like a million years ago. I'd never forget it that was for sure.

It was lucky for me that Rafe showed up when he did to deal with Satan. He was only using me as a pawn to hurt Rafe, and in the process to hurt God. And then I tried to hurt both Rafe and God by jumping into the Tiber River to end my life. The same scene kept passing before me. That terrible hurt in Rafes eyes. I kept seeing it over, and over, and I prayed for sleep to come so that I wouldn't have to think about it anymore.

The next day came and went.

And then the next three days came and went.

I couldn't take it any longer. Wasn't Rafe going to ever come back? I needed someone to talk to. I went and knocked on the door. It wasn't long before I heard the key turning in the lock and one of the Swiss Guard came into the room to see what I wanted.

"Do you know when Mr. Rafe is going to come and let me out?" I asked.

"No Signore, we were only told to make sure you didn't leave."

"Well could I at least walk with an escort around the Palace to get me out of this room? I feel like I am going to lose my mind. There is no television, radio, books or anything to keep me occupied."

"I'm sorry Miss Malone, we were strictly told to keep you in this room and to not let you out for any reason. We were also instructed to make sure that you had no kind of entertainment whatsoever."

"Why?"

"That was just what Mr. Rafe directed."

"Mr. Rafe told you that?"

"Yes Signore."

"When did you see Mr. Rafe?"

"He was here the day before yesterday."

I was infuriated. I couldn't believe that Rafe told them to make sure I had no entertainment. Why hadn't he come to see me when he was here? I felt a lump in my throat, and a sick feeling in my stomach. I just couldn't envision Rafe doing anything like this to me.

"Are you finished Signore?" The Swiss Guard asked.

"Did he say when he would see me?"

"No, he just said to keep the door locked."

He closed the door behind him and I heard the familiar sound of the key turning in the lock.

I didn't understand. I really was literally Rafe's prisoner. If he was that angry with me, why didn't he just turn me loose to fend for myself? I still couldn't believe that he was here and didn't see me. I also could not believe he would leave me with absolutely nothing to do. He knew I was the type of person who had to keep busy all the time. Maybe he didn't trust me anymore. Not that I could blame him.

Well, he'd better come back soon. I had enough of this being locked up crap!

Another day went by,

And then another.

After a week of being locked up with nothing to do and no one to talk to, both anger and fear raged anew. I was beginning to get cranky and started to look for any means of escape, but the only possibility I could find were the windows and as they were covered with iron bars, and I was four stories high, that was certainly out of the question.

When one of the staff brought me breakfast that morning, I watched very carefully to see if there was any way that I could get out of the room. I couldn't figure a single avenue of escape. I spent the day brooding about it and getting angrier by the minute. How could someone love you and have you treated like this?

I knew that I had hurt Rafe, but he must also be beyond furious with me to lock me up for this long. What was he going to do with me? Well it didn't matter. I decided that I had been patient long enough. If he didn't come by this evening, he was going to be sorry that he ever locked me in this room.

I was brought lunch and than supper and still no Rafe. I had my answer. I went to bed for the first time since I'd been here happy that I had a plan to finally get Rafe's attention.

The next morning I looked around the room for anything that I could find that was breakable. There were plenty of glass objects around. I stacked everything neatly on the table. I got dressed into one of the few outfits that the Guards had brought to me the day they locked me in here. I decided to start before breakfast. I went to the door and started hollering for the Guard to open the door. He obliged me immediately.

"I'm leaving this room right now!" I said to him.

"No Signore, I'm afraid I can't allow you to do that."

"Well I don't really care whether you can or not. I'm tired of being locked up, and I am leaving, right now!"

I started to push my way past him. He and the Guard next to him crossed their swords in front of me blocking my way. I tried to knock their swords aside, but it was like hitting a brick wall. When I turned around they quickly crossed them in front of me again. I tried to duck under the crossed swords, but when I did, they both grabbed me and shoved me back in the room and locked the door without either one of them trying to harm me physically.

This was going to be fun, and I was sure that it would eventually bring Rafe!

I began to pound on the locked door again.

"Let me out of here. Damn it! I'm tired of being locked up."

I continued to pound on the door yelling and screaming the entire time.

The guard eventually let one of the palace Staff in who usually brought my breakfast. All he had was a pitcher of water, and a glass. The employee looked at me very apprehensively and said,

"Mr. Rafe said all that you can have is water for breakfast, unless you decide to settle down and stop acting like an insolent child. And the same would go for the rest of your meals for the day."

He turned and when he got to the door I threw the water glass at him, just missing his head as it crashed against the door. The door quickly opened and the Guard looked at me wide eyed as the employee scurried quickly through the door.

"Miss Malone, you had better settle down or you are going to end up in a lot of trouble."

"Trouble! Trouble! I'll show you trouble!"

I winged the other glass at him and it crashed into the door as he closed it, breaking against the door in the exact place that he had been standing.

So either Rafe was in the building, or they had already called him. It looked like he had made up his mind to ignore whatever I decided to try. I didn't understand why he wouldn't just release me and send me out on my own. I bet Michael was going to be furious with me for throwing this tantrum. But it was the only way that I knew how to try and get Rafes attention.

I continued to scream and curse and pound the door. At one point, I just lay down on my back on the floor and kicked and kicked the door. My shoes left dents and scratches all over the bottom half of the beautifully shellacked wood. I didn't care about the beauty of this place anymore. I just wanted out. Whenever anyone opened the door to say anything, I threw a glass object at them. I was getting tired of screaming, but I was enjoying making everyone's life miserable.

Finally when I realized that Rafe wasn't coming and all I had done was scratch a door and go without meals for a day, I became outraged. I picked up a large vase that was sitting on the floor and threw it through the window. It crashed against the bars breaking the window behind them with a loud noise. I heard the door open and without looking to see who it was, I picked up the pitcher full of water and threw it toward the door. It went whizzing past Rafes head. Luckily he ducked in the nick of time and the pitcher crashed to the floor outside in the hall.

Rafe was furious, his face livid. I could see the gold flecks sparkling in his eyes from clear across the room. I ran for the open door, but two things happened. The Swiss Guard closed the door before I got to it, and Rafe reached out and caught me by the arm as I tried to run past him.

"What is going on here, Becca? If you were trying to get my attention, you now have it. You might be sorry you wanted it this badly," he said, looking around at the broken glass everywhere including the broken window. He pulled me around so that I was facing him. I tried to jerk my arm out of his grasp, but he just held on that much tighter.

"Who do you think you are to lock me in this room for all this time without anything to do or occupy my time, or anyone to talk to? You let me go NOW!"

I tried to jerk from his grasp again but it was useless. The fury in his eyes and the strong hold he had on my arm confirmed that he wasn't going to let me go.

"Why did you make this mess Becca? Do you have any idea what I would have done if that pitcher of water had hit me? This is no time for playing childish games. We are in the middle of planning a war."

"Childish games! How dare you say that. I was trying to get your attention so that you would come over here and let me out of this god-awful prison that you have put me in. It isn't a game Rafe! You just went off and forgot about me locked up in here. Now, so you don't have to waste your time on my childish games, just let go of my arm, call your monkeys off, and I'll walk out of here and you won't have to waste your time on me anymore."

He momentarily had a pained expression on his face, but it quickly passed. However he did let go of my arm.

Just to show the depth of my anger, I picked up the other vase and smashed it against the wall, cursing while I did it. Then I grabbed the last piece of glass that was on the table and slammed it to the floor in front of him and it shattered around his feet.

He backed away, pulled a chair over and sat down, glaring at me the whole time. He looked like he was in deep thought for a split second, and then the anger was back in his eyes. He jumped up and grabbed me, turned me over his knee and began to spank me.

"Becca, this is your own fault. You deserve this. If you want to act like a child, you are going to be treated like a child."

He continued spanking me a few more times, and then he dumped me off his lap onto the floor.

He stood up and looking down at me said,

"Clean up this mess. I will be back in exactly one hour. You had better have yourself composed when I get here, and then we will talk. You are not rational right now, and if you make me lose my temper anymore than I already have, not only will you be sorry, but I might be sorry for what I will do to you."

He walked to the door and called for the guard to let him out, and without so much as even looking back to see my reaction, he exclaimed,

"Lock this door!"

I sat up and leaned against the wall. I refused to clean up the mess. He deserved to be treated the way that I had treated him too. He couldn't just treat me like I was some kind of animal and expect me to simply take it like some fragile little wallflower. I thought he knew me better than that. I couldn't believe that he had the nerve to turn me over his knee and spank me. My backside still hurt from where he had smacked me.

Then after everything that had taken place, he actually had the gall to ask the Guards to lock the door again. I wished I had more things to break. I'd show him a thing or two.

No I wouldn't, I thought, as I rubbed my sore bottom.

True to his word he was back in an hour. I heard the key turn in the lock and he came in the room, much calmer this time. But then I wasn't throwing anything as his head, for the moment.

He walked over to where I was still sitting on the floor, and looked around at the glass that was still spread all around me, seeing that I had refused to clean it up. He hesitated momentarily and I thought he was going to get angry again, but instead he just reached out his hand to take mine. I resisted for a minute and he just stared at me, his expression daring me to put up a fuss. I meekly took his hand. He pulled me to my feet and led me over to the sofa, where we both sat down.

"Rebecca, first you must understand why you were locked in this room with absolutely nothing to do. When you jumped into the Tiber River, you had every intention of ending your life. You never thought of the consequences to your eternal soul, or to me. Then to top that one, you actually believed that liar Satan when he said that I could read minds. I could not and cannot believe it. I actually thought you knew more than you obviously do. You were locked in this room to impress upon you what it would be like to be locked out of Gods kingdom. Only it wouldn't be for a few days, it would be forever. You would burn in eternal damnation, that is the consequences for taking ones life. We kept you from communication with anyone and nothing was given to you to help pass the time, because you would have no such luxuries in hell. You would have absolutely nothing to do but suffer.

It devastated me to leave you and not be able to come and visit you, but Michael conferred with God and it was decided that maybe if you were taught a small lesson you might think twice before endangering the precious life God has given you, and you especially had to learn that you can never, never believe anything that Satan the father of all liars would try and tell you. Like I said, suicide is immediate damnation to hell and so is believing Satan. You would have been damned if I had not been allowed to save you. I could not bare for anything like that to ever happen to you, and I'm sure you really don't want that either. I should have known, knowing you the way that I do that it would be just be a matter of time before you tried to break free. You might be able to do that here, but it would never be possible in hell. Am I making any sense to you?"

"Yes Rafe. Now it does make sense, but I couldn't imagine you not keeping in contact with me. So, of course, I thought the worst. That either Michael commanded you to forget me, or that you had stopped caring for me. I was going crazy without hearing from you, or seeing you, and I just had to get out of here before I lost my mind."

"Well, I am not going to lock you in here anymore, Becca. If I want to get on with this war, I don't need you tearing down what is left of the Vatican because you are angry with me. I'll say one thing about you! You sure have spunk for a woman! You would be formidable as a soldier if you were a man."

"Becca, I need you to promise me that you will stay on these grounds until you see our armies crossing the sky. Then you need to hurry to our little park where you will be safe.

Everything except for designated spots throughout the earth will be destroyed. I promise that I will come for you there. But stay there until I come. Do you understand? I promise you, it should take no longer than a week."

"Oh Rafe, I do promise you. I will do anything you ask me. Just please, please don't ever do to me what you did this past week. I really thought you didn't want me anymore. I am ashamed of my actions. But you see right or wrong, I was deathly afraid to be caught up in Satan's clutches again. I pray that he doesn't bother me again."

"Rafe?"

"Yes?"

"How long will you be able to stay with me this time?"

He looked at me, and I noticed that the expression in his eyes was beginning to soften.

"I will probably be able to stay with you for the rest of the evening Becca, and then I

will have to leave."

I just had to bring up the subject.

"It didn't seem like it was to difficult for you to turn me over your knee and spank me earlier Rafe."

I was curious to see how he was going to explain that act of anger to me.

"It wasn't! And if I were ever around you when you threw a tantrum like that again, I would do the same thing all over. Once in a while you have to be let known that you can't be as independent as you like Becca. That's exactly what always gets you into trouble."

I stored that in my memory as I stood up. I was still sore from his spanking. I would never admit that to him though because he would just laugh.

He suddenly had a very serious expression on his face, and he took me by the hand and pulled me back down onto the sofa. He looked in my eyes and seemed to be studying my face, which he did for quite a while. His breathing became heavy and I could see the lust beginning to take over his expression. He tilted my chin up to kiss me, but I pulled away and looked down. He took his hand and began to stroke the side of my neck. I closed my eyes, it felt so wonderful to have him touching me again and I began to feel the familiar tingle in the pit of my stomach, just from the touch of his hand.

"No Rafe! I won't be responsible for you breaking any of Gods laws. I've caused enough trouble already."

I jumped up from the couch and walked over to the window. He was right behind me. He put his hands around my waist and turned me to face him.

"Becca, I have no intention of breaking any of Gods laws."

He ran his fingers along my cheekbone to my neck and rested his hand there for a moment, staring into my eyes. His expression was soft and vulnerable. He cupped my chin in his other hand and ran his thumb slowly back and forth across my throat and said,

"Becca, I love you so much. I wish I could spend every minute with you. You are on my mind all the time. When I realized that you almost took your life because of me it tore my heart out. When Michael talked to me about teaching you a lesson, I didn't want to make you suffer anymore than you already had, but in our world you pay the price immediately for any transgressions against God. We had to make you see how horrible your life could have been for your actions. All I wanted to do was just take you in my arms forever and protect you from all the horrible things that must have been going on in your mind to cause you to even think about jumping from that bridge. Oh, if only I was just a mortal man."

He furrowed his brow for a moment, shaking his head from side to side as if it pained him terribly to think about it, but then he lowered his head and slowly brought his lips to my mouth, and lingered just barely above my lips for just the shortest moment, and then he kissed me passionately, long and hard. I wanted to cry from the sheer joy of having him kiss me once again. It was a persistent kiss, full of bittersweet love. When he finally pulled his mouth away from mine to look at me, his eyes were filled with tears.

"Becca, please stay safe for me, and always know that I love you more than anything else on this earth."

"Oh Rafe, I don't know how I am going to live without you. But I promise that I will live as long as I can so that you will be able to look down from heaven and know that I love you with every breath that I take."

We had dinner together in one of the many dining rooms in the Papal Palace then we just talked for the rest of the evening. I asked him where the Pope was staying and he told me that the Pope had fled to Jerusalem a few days before. I was glad. I sure didn't want him to have heard me throwing a temper tantrum.

I smiled to myself. It did work, though didn't it? It brought Rafe to me.

Chapter 10
DEATH

Rafe explained to me that all of the plagues had been waged against the earth and that now it was up to the angels to take their revenge against Satan and all the evil spirits and to spill God's wrath upon sinful man who he had given so many chances to lead a righteous life.

When he was telling me all these horrid things, my thoughts turned to the infamous Nicholas, I would be glad when he would never be a threat to me again. I interrupted Rafe,

"Rafe, you know when I was at the Castle of the Angels, I never saw Nicholas once. It was bad enough putting up with Satan, but I expected that he would have had Nicholas around to torment me too."

"Becca, I ran into Nicholas during one of our small battles and I took care of him once and for all, and then Michael banned him to the fiery pit forever. Believe me, it was enjoyable destroying him. I cherished every minute of the anguish that I put him through."

I cringed thinking about how that must have been. I wish that they had taken care of Satan too. That would have been one less thing I would have to worry about. It seemed like he never had any trouble finding my weak points or me. I shivered in disgust thinking about what almost took place.

"Rafe, I haven't had a chance to ask you what took place between you and Satan"

"No Becca, you couldn't have asked me. You ran out on me too fast to ask anything. Remember?"

"Ouch that hurt! Please Rafe, I feel bad enough about that as it is."

He looked at me for a minute and than quietly said,

"I'm sorry."

"Becca, just what exactly took place between you and Satan?" He never took his eyes off of me when he asked me this question.

"Why do you ask?"

"Well Satan kept goading me on trying to imply that he could have made love to you easily, if I hadn't shown up."

He continued staring at me. I could tell he really didn't want to hear the answer, but he needed to.

"Rafe, I am not going to lie to you. I had too much wine to drink with my dinner. I thought it would help me sleep. Sometime during the night he came to my room and in my alcoholic stupor, I first thought that he was you, and he was tempting me so much that I thought I was going to give in to his advances, and when I realized who it was, I tried to get away from him. Thank God it was about then that you showed up."

He looked away from my face, looking down at the table, absentmindedly tracing little circles on the white tablecloth with his forefinger.

When he looked up at me again he whispered in a soft voice,

"Did he try to, you know, to…"

I didn't let him finish the sentence.

"Yes."

The expression in his eyes was one of fiery rage. If angels had the ability to hate, I knew without a doubt, that at that moment Rafe hated Satan with his whole being.

The muscle in the side of his jaw began to twitch, and I could tell that he was clenching his teeth! His hands were knotted into fists so tightly that they were beginning to turn white.

"I wish I could be the one to destroy him." He said. "He is such a vile bastard."

"Please tell me he isn't going to bother me anymore Rafe. He knows how to bring out the weakness in people."

I was beginning to get nervous just talking about Satan. My heart started to pound wildly in fear of seeing him again when Rafe was gone. My face must have gone ashen because Rafe got up from the table and came to my end of the table and pulling me to my feet he took me into his arms, and held me tightly against his chest.

"I can't promise you that Becca, but I will have the Swiss Guard with you at all times. I promise. You know that if I had my way I would spend every minute I could protecting you."

I pulled my head away from his chest, looking up into his eyes.

"I know Rafe, I know. It just seems like no matter how hard I try, I always end up doing the exact opposite of what you want me to do. Satan found me after the earthquake. I was exhausted from helping people who were caught up in the rubble, and I was trying to find my way home. Finally I was so weary that I fell asleep on the ground, and I woke up in his arms, being flown to the castle."

"Oh Becca, you have been through so much since this ordeal started. I really should have been more considerate of you. But you sure didn't give me my other choice the way you were running away from me."

He pressed my head to his chest once more. I could feel my heart beating faster than normal, but this time it wasn't from fear. I so wished we were back at my flat and he could stay with me. I was so happy back then. I closed my eyes and held on to him tightly. I wanted to cherish this moment. I had to. I never knew when it would be the last time that he would be holding me.

There was a knock on the door, which startled the two of us. One of the Swiss Guard came in and Rafe went over to the door and the two of them spoke quietly, then the Guard left quickly. Rafe walked back over to me and I could tell by the expression on his face that it was time for him to leave.

"Michael has called me back to headquarters. We are about to begin Becca. Don't forget when you see us filling the sky; you need to run to our park. Don't stop for anything. Not to help anyone, or any other reason. It is to late for this world Becca. Just run as fast as you can away from the city until you reach the park. Do you understand?"

I nodded my head up and down, lost for words.

"I'm not going to have your door locked anymore but please don't leave the Palace and don't go far from the Swiss Guard."

"Rafe, is there anything that I should know that is about to happen that will frighten me terribly?"

"After you see us in the sky, ask God for protection. Things will only get worse than anything that has taken place so far. That is why it is so important that you go to the park. Nothing bad will take place there, but everything below the park will be destroyed. There will be fire falling from the sky. Don't wait for anything or anybody. It is most important. That you get to the park as soon as you see us, or you will be caught in the middle of the devastation and it will be a lot more complicated to find your way if you get caught in the chaos of the destruction."

"I don't know what to say to you Rafe. I'm afraid I will never see you again, and…"

"I will come to the park to take you to safety Becca. I only hope that I will be able to stay with you for a little while. But I don't know how long it will be. This is not goodbye my angel. It is only; I'll see you soon. Stay safe for me. As far as Satan is concerned, I am hoping he will be too preoccupied with us to worry about kidnapping you. However, anything he can do to hurt God, he will try. Just be on the look out and if he comes near you, call my name. I will either come to your rescue or Michael will.

Let's hope that as I said, we keep Satan too busy for him to worry about you."

He held me in his arms again, then he stared into my face like he was memorizing all my features. He leaned down and kissed me softly on the lips. Before I could respond he pulled away and turned and walked out the door.

I followed him, and when I turned the doorknob the huge door opened. The Swiss Guard was still standing outside my door, but Rafe was nowhere to be seen. I went back into the room and went and sat on the couch thinking about how much I was going to miss him.

I realized I was really drained after the ordeal of the temper tantrums I had thrown today. I didn't want to lie on the bed, so I grabbed the pillow and blanket off the bed and lay down on the couch. I fell asleep very quickly, and the next thing I knew it was morning.

After I got dressed and had breakfast I asked the guard if I could walk around the Palace with one of them coming along as chaperone of course.

It seemed strange to see the Palace as empty as it was. The only Swiss Guard left on the premises was the six that Rafe had left to protect me. In fact the only noise that you could hear throughout the corridors was the echo of your own voice and your footsteps.

One, of the two Guards that were with me asked if I would like to see the Papal apartments now that the Pope was gone. First we went to the Popes Chapel, which had been revamped since I last saw it. Everything in it was decorated in a Gothic style, even the cross on the wall. The simplicity of Pius XIII was gone. The new Pope evidently was more into decorum, because there were statues crammed everywhere in the little chapel. All in all it was pretty elaborate.

The apartments were decorated in the same manner as the chapel. I felt like I was intruding into the private part of life that was none of my business so we didn't remain very long.

We continued into the Palace courtyard. There were quite a few people milling around like they had no other place to go and the Vatican seemed to be their last hope. I was amazed how many people there were who now believed in the prophecies. I asked if St. Peters Basilica and the gardens had really been destroyed, so they took me over to witness the damage. It wasn't as bad as I had thought. I was told it was destroyed, but actually it was only minorly damaged.

As we were walking outside of St. Peters, who should be sitting on the steps next to one of the statues, but Mike. I ran to him and threw my arms around his neck. The Swiss Guard was right behind me, not sure of what I was up to. I spoke to them first.

"It's okay. I'm not trying to leave. This is a very good friend and fellow employee from the newspaper."

That seemed to satisfy them for the time being.

"Oh Mike, I am so happy to see you. Why are you here? I thought you didn't believe in God. Have you seen anyone else such as Heidi, or Mr. Bellini?"

I was so excited to see him that I started throwing my questions at him all at once.

Mike picked me up off of my feet and swung me around.

"Oh Rebecca, I never thought I was going to see you again. How did you get here?" He asked. "And how have you survived all the destruction? I lost you right away when we were leaving the building. I looked for you for about an hour and then decided I must have gone in the opposite direction that you had gone. Can you believe all this destruction?

You once asked me if I believed in God. Well, I am here to tell you that I do believe now. I actually saw an angel flying in the sky. It didn't take much more than that to convince me. So I started asking every Christian I ran into to fill me in. Now I know exactly what is going on. Do you?"

I simply nodded my head yes.

"Rebecca, we are in the end of the world! That is so frightening to me. You seem so calm about it. It surprises me that you are actually holding up better than I am."

"No Mike, no, I'm not holding up as well as you think. I feel like I am in a dream, I've felt like that for quite awhile now. Maybe I'm in a state of shock. There is absolutely nothing we can do about changing our lives now. It's too late. All we can do is hope we are one of the lucky ones that are included in the beginning of the new Earth."

"Yeah," Mike nodded, "otherwise it is hell for us I guess."

"Don't talk about it Mike, I shudder to even think about it. But I guess we will have to take whatever is coming to us."

"Okay, I'll change the subject. The last time I saw Heidi and Mr. Bellini, they were waiting at the elevator, when the rest of us went down the stairs. I don't know whether they made it or not Rebecca."

"Oh my God. I hope they did. The building starting coming apart before I even got to the bottom of the stairs."

I looked at some of the destroyed buildings around us that were now laying in a heap of rubble, parts of them still standing.

"What an awful site this beautiful ancient city is now."

"I know." Mike said. "It is really sad. I've been taking pictures with my camera, but I don't know who I think will ever publish or develop them if this is a global event. Let me show you the picture of the angel that I saw. I was able to get a photo of him."

He showed me the picture on his digital camera and there was the angel as large as life. I was surprised that he didn't recognize him. It was Rafe. I wanted to tell him, but I decided I had better not. He probably wouldn't believe me anyway. I couldn't see any point anyway since we were so close to the end.

The Swiss Guard got my attention and summoned for me to go with them back to the Papal Palace.

"Mike would you like to come and stay in the Papal Palace with us?"

"No Ma'am," one of the Swiss Guard quickly interrupted." We are not allowed to let anyone into the Papal Palace but you. Those are our orders and we have to obey them."

"Wow! Why are you so special Rebecca?"

I didn't know what to say. I really wasn't special. Only to Rafe and I supposed that this was all his doings. Before I could gather my thoughts enough to answer him, the other Swiss Guard spoke up and said,

"She knows people in high places. The Papal Palace is otherwise restricted from civilians. I am sorry sir but we cannot let you enter."

I was so embarrassed. Why did he have to put it that way? Now Mike was going to wonder who I knew. Mike wouldn't give up. He would drive me crazy with questions. I frowned, wondering what to say.

"Don't worry Rebecca, I recognized the angel in the picture. I was just waiting how long it would take you to say anything to me You knew he was an angel didn't you?"

He was being careful with his wording. I could tell he didn't want the Swiss Guard to know what we were talking about. He quietly asked,

"How much do they know?"

I didn't know how much they knew either, so I just kept my mouth shut.

"Sir, it is strictly for religious reasons that I cannot let you into the Papal Palace. I assure you that is the only reason." The same guard intervened.

Mike waved him off,

"It's perfectly okay. I understand. Besides, I have been staying in my car. I have one of the few running cars left around here and I wouldn't really want to abandon it. Will I see you tomorrow Rebecca?"

"Yes Michael, I hope so. That is if any of us are still around."

"Could we keep your meeting at the front door of the Papal Palace? We want to keep you safe in the event the end does come," number one Swiss Guard asked.

"That'll be just fine."

I looked at Mike and winked at him.

"I'll see you tomorrow partner."

"Hey Rebecca. Wouldn't it be something if you and I were two of the people chosen to start the new world together?"

"OH yeah, I could see it now! Woman keeps running from man, but he won't take no for an answer. That would be just great. UGH!!" I laughed "Friends only Mike."

He started laughing.

"A guy can hope can't he Rebecca? Who knows, you may change your mind one of these days."

"Very doubtful Mike, be satisfied being my friend." I turned and walked off with the Guard, and he hollered after me.

"See you tomorrow morning in front of the Palace."

When I got back to my room someone had sent me beautiful red roses, but there was no card. I looked at the guard who let me in my room.

"This is disconcerting not knowing who they are from."

"They are probably from Mr. Rafe, he was so concerned about how you felt when he left the last time."

I thought about it though and I didn't think Rafe would send me anything anonymously, as jumpy as I was right now.

One of the other Swiss Guard who had remained at the Palace looked at us and said.

"They came from the Castle of the Angels, delivered by one of their Guards."

Oh No, That meant that Satan knew where I was! That was his way of letting me know that he wasn't finished with me yet. My heart began to beat a little faster, and I walked over to the trashcan and dropped the flowers in it.

Now I really had something to worry about. I had hoped that Satan's altercation with Rafe had deterred him from wanting to have anything to do with me, but obviously it was still his goal to get revenge toward Rafe through me.

I went over and sat in the windowsill, looking out at the darkening sky. I wondered when the angels were going to take their flight to end all of this. I felt so anxious about it and noticed that every time I thought about it, I looked up at the sky. Surely the angels wouldn't take a flight at night or Rafe wouldn't have said to watch for them and to leave when I saw them flying across the sky. It was too dark right now to even see anything in the sky except for the dark ominous clouds that threatened rain. At least if it did there would be some fresh water that people could gather for drinking.

I began to think of all the people in Vatican Square and I felt so sorry for them, and Mike, who were sleeping on the sidewalks or in their cars with no other place to go, their homes being completely destroyed. It made me feel guilty for having a nice bed to sleep in and meals to eat.

I went to the door and asked the Guard, if they would mind getting something for Mike to eat and take it to his car for him. They reluctantly agreed. They were fearful all of the street people might expect the same help, as we didn't have enough to supply them. The cupboards in the Papal kitchen were beginning to get sparse. I didn't push the subject any further, as they were right of course. But they assured me they would take him something to eat tonight.

My thoughts soon turned to Mr. B. and Heidi, I worried about them and I hoped that they had made it to safety. I supposed we wouldn't see each other again unless we happened to run into them as Mike and I had.

Mike looked exceptionally good. I was shocked at the change in his belief. But seeing Rafe could do that to you. He was so magnificent. His wingspan was in itself was most impressive. And the armor that he wore just accentuated his muscles all the more. What a stunning man-angel he made. But then I was a bit prejudice.

The next morning Mike was waiting in front of the Papal Palace just like he said he would be.

"Rebecca, I hope you slept well. Thanks for sending me something to eat. My stomach was beginning to feel like it was touching my backbone. I have something to tell you that may not be good news, but then I don't know whether it is true or not."

"Oh no, Mike! Please tell me that nothing has happened to Rafe."

"You would think of him first wouldn't you Rebecca? No, as far as I know, he is fine. I probably couldn't find out anything about him anyway because I have been trying to find him for the last week or so because I figured you would be wherever he was. But I could never get any answers about him. Most people don't even know who he is.

No, it's not about Rafe, but it is about as bad. I found out that anyone who was waiting for the elevator at the office never made it out of the building before the floors collapsed beneath them."

"Oh no Mike! That means that Heidi and Mr. Bellini are…"

"Wait a minute now Rebecca let's not jump to any conclusions until we know more. There is no sense in getting upset about something we are not sure of."

"Oh Mike! You shouldn't have said anything to me then. You know I am going to worry about it regardless of whether it is true or not. I pray that it isn't."

He looked at me for a minute with questioning eyes.

"What Mike? I can tell you want to ask me something. Go ahead, we're friends, I'll answer anything you ask."

He lowered his eyes for what seemed forever and as I was about to say something, he looked at me again and said:

"Rebecca what happens now that we know your Rafe is an angel? Surely that would change my idea that the two of you might be in a relationship. There can't actually be anything romantic going on between the two of you can there?"

"Whoa Mike. You are getting too personal now. I can tell you this much. He can't stay on earth with us humans, that's all I want to say about it."

"Do you love him Rebecca?"

My eyes started to burn; it was going to be hard to keep from crying. Now it was me that looked down.

Mike must have had second thoughts about asking me, because he took me into his arms and hugged me, trying to comfort me and apologizing for interfering in my business, when a voice out of no where said

"Well, well isn't this just cozy. She has yet another man chasing her. I thought two was enough and now it's three? Becca you should be ashamed of yourself. Everyone is going to think you are a loose woman."

I looked up to see Satan standing just inches from us.

Mike immediately confronted Satan face to face before I had a chance to say anything.

"I think you owe this lady an apology, sir! What a terrible way to speak to a lady!"

Satan began to laugh.

Mike then took both of his hands and shoved Satan, who didn't move an inch.

"I said apologize to the lady."

"Mike please don't goad him on." I said. "You don't know what you are getting yourself into."

I tugged on his arm.

"Come on let's leave!"

Satan laughed once again. "He isn't going anywhere. I'll take care of him and then you are coming with me, and we will take up where we left off."

My heart started pounding again. Mike wasn't going to back down and Satan wasn't going to be happy until he took me to hell with him. Maybe that is what my fate was supposed to be and I just wasn't accepting it. I couldn't accept it.

I hollered for the Swiss Guard.

"Help! Help! Someone please get out here and help us." I noticed the Swiss Guard running toward us but when I looked back at Satan, Mike had taken a swing at him and Satan caught him by the arm and picked him up by the throat, twisted his neck and threw him as hard as he could against the building.

"No, no." I said, running to where his now crumpled body lay. I sat down and took his head in my arms, but it was too late. He was dead.

"No! No! No!" I screamed. I sat rocking Mike back and forth, crying hard.

The Swiss Guard was fighting against Satan, but obviously he was much too strong for any of them to be more than a nagging thought. He threw them two at a time across the courtyard until there were only two left. I couldn't pull myself away from Mike to try to escape.

When I looked up he was coming right toward me.

"Why did you have to kill him you bastard? He was so good. He wasn't a vile creature like you. Why did you kill him?"

He grabbed me by the arm and yanked me away from Mike. I was so furious when I saw Mike's head hit the ground that I began kicking and biting and doing anything I could to hurt him.

"You'll pay for this Rebecca." He started laughing. "You must have been really infatuated with this guy to throw this much of a fuss over him."

He grabbed my other arm and twisted both my arms behind my back.

The words came quickly for me.

"Rafe, Rafe, Please help me. I NEED YOU NOW!!! Please, please hurry. He is going to take me away again."

Suddenly I heard the strong flapping of wings. As soon as the angel landed on the ground I recognized him. It was Michael the Archangel. Satan looked horrified and let go of me and quickly took two steps backward.

"Do you want me to send you to hell now, or do you want to try and fight with your demons? Because I can be quick to oblige."

There must have been something special about Michael's sword because Satan couldn't take his eyes off of it. It was most obvious that Satan was very afraid of Michael.

"Becca, go inside the palace! Have the guards who are left lock the door. Don't let anyone in and do not go outside again! Do you understand me?" Asked Michael.

I could tell by the tone of his voice that he was pretty well irritated with me. I always needed help. I didn't want this angel upset with me.

"What about Mike?" I asked, crying.

"I'll take care of him. Now get inside the Palace walls. Now!!"

I didn't utter another word. I hurried inside the Papal Palace. I found the two remaining Swiss Guard and told them to lock the doors, and that we were not to let anyone in.

"I need desperately to go to my room."

I ran up the stairs to the room and went in and slammed the door. The Guard knocked on the door.

"Are you alright, Miss Malone?"

"I'll be fine, I just need to be alone for awhile."

There was silence from behind the door. I lay across the bed and sobbed and sobbed. I still could not believe that Satan had killed Mike. Oh my God. All Mike ever wanted was for me to love him, and I couldn't reciprocate. He had always been so good to me.

I remember the first day that I came to the newspaper. Mike was the first one to greet me and offered to show me around. I was so nervous that day. It was my first time out of the United States for any length of time, and my first time living in a foreign country. It was fortunate that the first person I should meet was an American like me. Mike and I had formed a bond from that day forward. I felt like he was my big brother. And he somehow fell in love with me. He didn't deserve this. He died trying to protect me. I started crying again. In fact, I cried so much that I thought I was going to be sick.

The door to my room opened and when I turned to see who it was, I was surprised to see Michael the Archangel standing in the doorway. He was beautiful, not as beautiful as my Raphael, but his was a regal beauty.

"I am sorry about your friend Rebecca. I have sent him to be buried. I am now going to ask you, no, I'm going to demand from you. Don't call Raphael again. He has too much on his mind to deal with you right now. I would not let him come. This is the last time that you'll see me also. I want you to be sure you understand that I have forbid Raphael to return to the Palace. Don't worry; Satan will not bother you anymore. He is going to be much too busy trying to beat me in this war, and as you could plainly see, he is clearly afraid of me. Becca can I trust you to listen to me until this is all over? That's all I ask of you."

"Michael, you have my word. I am sorry that I had to call Rafe, and that you had to come. I really didn't know what else to do. I panicked when he got his hands on Mike and then he told me that he was going to take me away. I just knew he was going to kill Mike, and Mike, poor Mike, didn't even know who he was."

I started crying again. My heart was broken. Not only had I lost Mike, my friend, but I may have lost my new friend Heidi and my boss Mr. Bellini. I put my head into my cupped hands and the tears poured from my eyes.

Michael stood for the longest time staring at me. It was almost as if he didn't know what to do. I doubted that he knew how to comfort a real person. He probably comforted people every day spiritually, but when it came to flesh and blood, he had not been around humans like Rafe had. He probably looked on us like we were vile creatures, just like I did Satan.

"Are you done with me now, Michael"

"Yes, I am. Watch the sky Becca." He said softly.

He turned to leave.

"Oh! And Michael?"

"Yes."

"Thank you for saving me."

Chapter 11
ARMAGEDDON

The rest of the day was a blur. I was given a sedative because I couldn't stop crying. I think it was a combination of everything. Watching Mike be killed. Perhaps the loss of Mr. Bellini and Heidi, Satan almost capturing me again, plus I knew the time was drawing close that I would lose Rafe and before it was all over, I could possibly lose my life as well. I slept the night through and woke the next morning filled with dread.

I was afraid to go outside because I knew that Satan would be waiting for me now that he knew where I was staying.

I went and sat in the same windowsill that I always seemed to gravitate towards. Normally the view from the Papal Palace was beautiful, but the view certainly didn't have an appeal anymore. I yawned as I looked up at the sky. The sedative had left me pretty drowsy. I had to look at the sky again. Was that a flock of geese that I saw in the sky, or was it something else I couldn't recognize. I shielded my eyes because the sun was shining directly into them. Oh my God! It was the army of angels! I kept staring and staring until my eyes were burning from squinting against the suns' rays. Then suddenly I saw them; the whole sky was full of angels. I felt a cold chill go through my body. It was the most beautiful sight I had ever seen.

I knew that the supernatural battle was about to take place between the angels of God and the fallen angels of Satan. I began to panic remembering that Rafe told me to go to our park as soon as I saw them filling the sky. I opened the door to my room and was about to ask one of the Guards if he would go with me when I noticed that they not only were nowhere in sight, but when I screamed for them there was no answer.

I headed for the stairs, running as fast as I could down and through the door out into the street. Just as I reached the door I heard a loud bugle blow. It was Rafe blowing his horn for battle. People in the square were pointing and staring up at the sky. Some stood frozen in their footsteps, not knowing what to do or where to go. Others were running in all different directions. It was utter chaos. I was soon running, fighting my way through the crowd, trying to get out of the square as fast as I could, I knew that if I had to remain there much longer I would be trampled to the ground by the throng of hysterical screaming Roman citizens.

When I reached the gates of Vatican City and ran out into the city, most of the people had stopped and were just staring up at the sky in disbelief. I wondered for a split second how the unbelievers were trying to explain this away. I never stopped running even when demons and angels alike would fall to the ground next to me still fighting as if they had never left the air. It was horrible I could hear the clinking of their swords behind me. As I heard their screams, I knew that one of the winged warriors had killed the other, a cold chill went up my spine as I remembered that Raphael had told me that this would be the first time since creation that the angels and demons would be able to kill one another in battle. My eyes filled with tears thinking that Raphael could be killed in this as well. I kept running and running, the tears running down my face causing my vision to blur. I wiped at my eyes without missing a step. My heart was beginning to pound wildly and my lungs were beginning to hurt from a combination of running and crying.

If anything happened to Raphael it would be hard for me to go on living. Oh my God, I prayed, please keep Raphael safe from harm. I couldn't think of killing myself again. It got me into too much trouble. I didn't want this war to be in vain. The angels were fighting because of our sins. This was not the time to think about piling any more shame on the mess we had created.

I took a moment to stop and catch my breath then began running again. I heard a loud crash and looked behind me where I had just been standing to see a huge fireball hit the spot. I looked up. The whole sky was on fire. More fireballs began to hit the earth like hail and began to destroy everything that remained from the earthquakes and plagues that had already destroyed so much. I had to dodge big chunks of hot ash that was falling, and the heat from the buildings that had caught fire was beginning to lash out so that I had to run in the middle of what was left of the road. The few people I did see now seemed to be in so much fear that they didn't even notice each other and most of them were running in the opposite direction.

The temperature must have risen twenty degrees. It was so hot that I was beginning to feel faint.

It took me several hours to get to the park. There had been children wide-eyed and frightened, holding on to their parents' hands that were just as frightened as they were. I saw many people who had either been burned or killed by the fireballs, or the flames from the burning buildings that whipped out of control. It was difficult for me not to stop and help people, but Rafe told me not to stop for anything, so I ran and ran.

At last, I was climbing up the side of the hill that would take me to the place where the park was located. I could hear the horrible sounds of screaming and battle cries echoing up from below me. When I finally reached the summit, I was so happy that I had listened to Rafe and done exactly what he had told me to do. It got me here in one piece just as Rafe said it would. He told me I would be safe here so I relaxed a little and walked over and sat down on a tree stump that was just a few feet from me. I needed to catch my breath and rest for awhile. I thought I would never forget how beautiful this park was, but my memories didn't do it justice.

I looked around to see beautiful meadows and abundant fruit trees, and cedars with birds flying to and fro pulling worms out of the rich earth to feed their nestlings. There were pretty fragrant flowers blooming everywhere. Than I spotted the weeping willow tree hanging over into the creek that ran through the park. It's leafy fingers reaching toward the water. This was the very same tree that we had spent so much time sitting under, basking in its' shade while we enjoyed our picnic. I hoped this place would not be destroyed.

I reached down and touched the angel pendant that Rafe had given me when we were here. We had such a beautiful time together that day. It was like time stood still for both of us. He had brought me here to let me know that we would be in this place again and that he would soon be leaving for heaven. I stood up and walked across the meadow. I didn't want to think about that right now.

I walked over to the side of the hill that faced the Tiber River and looked out over the valley below. Everything was on fire. There was terrible lightening and thunder. I watched as a large bolt hit the ground below. I realized that there was no fire, no thunder and no lightening or any damage for that matter here and I was thankful for that.

Surprisingly, even though there was not another human being up here, I was not frightened in the least. I felt as though I was wrapped in the safety of arms upon this quiet hill. Everything I saw below me seemed as though it was happening in slow motion. It was almost like I was the audience in a theater watching a war movie, except the actors were angels and demons instead of different countries fighting against one another.

It was difficult for me to tell whether it was daylight or night, as neither the sun nor moon were able to shine through the smoke and devastation that was taking place in the air.

I was totally exhausted so I went and lay down in the lush tall grass under one of the willow trees. I don't know how long I was there, but I must have fallen asleep because I woke up hearing voices coming up from the side of the hill. I quickly hid behind a large boulder. What if it was Satan or some of his demons? I didn't realize at the time that the evil spirits wouldn't dare venture onto this ground.

I peeked from behind the boulder to see eight people climbing onto the summit. I was afraid to come out from behind the rock because I didn't recognize anyone.

Then I saw her; she was pushing her matted hair off of her forehead. It wasn't in the usual bun I was used to seeing it in, and that's probably why I didn't recognize her right away. I was overfilled with joy as I ran to meet her.

"Heidi! Oh my God Heidi, I thought you were dead. How did you find this place? I have been up here all by myself for hours. Thank God, now you are safe."

She hugged me and started crying, and then I started crying also. She didn't know the other seven people who she had followed up the hill.

"Oh Becca! Thank goodness you are here. I have been looking everywhere for someone that I knew. I lost both of my parents and then Carlo was killed just a few hours ago by one of those huge fireballs that were falling to earth. This has to be the end of the world."

It wasn't my place to explain anything to her. That would have to be up to Rafe or someone else that was more educated in the Bible and Prophecy than I was. But I did say to her,

"I think you are right Heidi. I don't know what else it could be."

She was shaking all over. Her clothes were torn and covered with ashes just like mine. I walked her over to the willow tree and we sat down next to each other in the grass. She cried and cried. She began crying uncontrollably between long sobs.

I thought she was never going to catch her breath. I continued to console her until she started to calm down. I felt so sorry for her. We had been through so much, I was surprised that we were even still sane.

"Oh Becca, I have no one left in this world but you. Please promise that you will stay with me. I don't even know what happened to Mr. Bellini. I haven't seen him since we all tried to leave the newspaper building. Carlo was worried sick about him. Now my Carlo is gone." She began to cry again.

"Heidi, how did you get out of the building? I was told that everyone who was waiting for the elevator was lost when the building collapsed. I thought maybe you and Mr. Bellini had perished when that happened. The last time I saw the two of you, you were both running toward the elevator."

"Oh, we were Becca, but when I saw you running toward the stairs I decided that might be a little safer. I tried to talk Mr. Bellini into going with me, but you know how stubborn he can be at times. He just said he would meet me outside and stayed at the elevator. By the time I got to the bottom of the stairs where those last two steps were broken off from the earthquake, it took me a few minutes to get brave enough to jump down. I looked all around for you, but you were long gone. You must have been running. Thank goodness…"

and here she began to cry again,

"…Carlo was waiting for me in the parking lot. We never saw Mr. Bellini exit the building. I have to admit that I really felt safe as long as Carlo was by my side. When the fireball hit him, I wanted to die with him, and I have been afraid ever since."

"Oh Heidi, I won't leave you. I promise. You are safe here. We just need to make sure that we stay here and don't go down the hill again."

"Becca, where is Rafe? Nothing has happened to him has it?"

"Oh, I hope not!" I said "he is supposed to meet me here."

"I knew it. I just knew that you two were becoming involved. You should have seen the way you two looked at each other. I tried so many times to tease you about me wanting him, just to see if you would admit to me that you were seeing him. But I could never get you to admit it. I will tell you this. I do think he is one of the best looking men I have ever seen."

I decided we really needed to find out who all these other people were, and it was a good way to change the subject.

"I wonder where those men come from Heidi, did they tell you?"

"No, they just invited me to follow them up here, where they thought we might be safe."

After Heidi finally fell asleep, I walked over to where the others were to introduce myself. I learned their names were, James, Paul, Antonio, Roberto, David, Ramon and Eduardo,

They were all young priests just out of the seminary who had been ordained at the Vatican by Pope Pius XIII, prior to his death. They were working in the Vatican until the last earthquake when everything became too chaotic. They had come here often to study and to pray and were hoping that it was still intact. They were amazed that everything up here was in perfect order, considering everything else was destroyed in the city. There was no sign that the earthquake had destroyed anything up here.

Paul said he felt that God must have kept this place safe for a special reason. Antonio asked me if I minded if they remained up here for the duration. It was obvious that I knew the girl who had come with them, and they knew it could be awkward for two women to be amongst a bunch of men.

I looked at all of them and said,

"You must have been sent here for a reason. We are probably safer here than anywhere else. Of course you are welcome to stay."

"We won't bother you, I promise, and we probably could be some help with anything that comes up and needs a mans muscle." Antonio said.

They had seen the angels in the sky also. Paul felt sure that this was the end of the world, and only hoped that all of us wouldn't have to suffer to horrible before our lives were ended. They said that they had run past dead corpses of both people and animals on their way here. Eduardo commented that he would hate to be one of those elected to clean up the city after this was all over. He said it was a destructive mess.

"It definitely is a most horrid mass destruction is the correct phrase." Said Paul.

"We are all so hungry. We haven't had any substantial amount of food for the last several days, just some crackers we found, some unblessed communion wafers and a few bottles of wine. At least there is a stream here that seems to be untouched and maybe if there are any fish in it we can catch some for a nice meal for a change. I'm sure you ladies are famished as well," Paul said, looking over at Heidi who was still deep in slumber and then back at me.

I felt guilty knowing that I had meals brought to me everyday when I was at the Papal residence while these people and many worse off than they, had very little, if anything, to eat. I looked over at Heidi. She did look as though she had lost some weight and she had big circles under her eyes.

Paul was watching me intently and I could tell he was waiting for me to say something, anything. I'm sure they felt odd, as priests stuck with two women. I tried to continue the conversation where he left off.

"Paul, or should I say Father Paul?"

"No Becca, Paul is just fine."

"Okay then, Paul. There are fruit trees up here also. So fruit and fish would not only be good for our health but good to eat too."

"Good for our health!" repeated Antonio, and we all started laughing.

Ramon added, as if to stop the laughing.

"Tomorrow, maybe the men could try and find something to build some kind of a shelter. For the ladies first of course."

We all sat around on the grass and talked and got to know a little bit more about each other. They were surprised that Heidi and I knew each other since I was already up here and she had followed them up the hill. They had felt so bad for her because she just seemed like she was totally lost, and so they told her she was welcome to follow them up to this park if she would like. They felt it might be a safe haven away from the city and at least she wouldn't be alone.

It seemed like we had talked for hours and soon realized how very tired we were. I bid them good night and walked over to where Heidi was asleep and laid down next to her. I lay there for a long time thinking about Rafe and hoping he was safe and that I wouldn't have to wait too long before he came to find me. But I dreaded the thought that he would be leaving soon afterwards and that I would never see him again. I hoped that Michael would let him spend a little bit of time with me. But I sincerely doubted it. I really felt that despite the fact that Michael was here to protect us, we humans were an annoyance to him due to his strong love for God and our ignorance and ungratefulness when it came to our understanding of God. I knew he couldn't fathom how Raphael, one of the angels who stood before the throne of God, could possibly have fallen in love with a mortal. I suppose if I took the whole scenario in from his point of view I certainly couldn't blame him.

What was I going to do when Rafe left me for good? I couldn't even imagine life without him. I vowed to never love anyone again, provided of course that I even made it out alive.

Sleep was a long time coming that night in our beautiful park; first of all strangers had invaded it. Secondly, when Rafe finally did get here, would he let them know he was an angel? What would the priests think? It would be hard for me to hide my emotions from them. And Heidi, it would definitely be a complete shock to her.

Then I started thinking about Mike and how he had died, and my eyes filled with tears and I started to cry silently for him all over again. I tossed and turned in the lush grass unsure what the future had in store for me.

The next day I woke to the smell of fish frying. It smelled wonderful. I hadn't realized that in one day without food I could feel like I was starving to death.

"Well, good morning sleepy head. I thought you were going to sleep all day."

Heidi was cutting up some kind of sweet smelling fruit she had found growing on one of the trees, and when the priests assured her that it was safe to eat she went about collecting enough for breakfast and was using one of their pocket knives to cut it up.

I stood up and stretched and looked around to see the priests busily fishing, scaling the fish and frying them on an old piece of tin they had found which they laid over the fire they had started. They were also cooking what looked like some scrambled eggs.

"Heidi, are those eggs they are cooking over there? Where on earth did they find any eggs?"

"Yes, isn't it great? They found a swan's nest and took two of the eggs out of the nest for all of us. I would never have thought of cooking swans eggs. Would you?"

I shook my head no, and then thought of the two swans that Rafe and I had compared to us as being mated for life. My heart skipped a little beat, as my thoughts returned once again to that unforgettable day.

"Heidi, I'm going to go down to the stream and wash my face. I'll be right back."

She turned and smiled at me nodding her head as I turned to leave.

I didn't even have a toothbrush, let alone a clean change of clothes. I squatted down next to the stream; looking back at me was my disheveled refection. My hair was all-scraggly and I had soot on my face and hands. I scrubbed them as best I could with the cool water, then I took some water and smoothed my hair. I wished I had a rubber band so that I could at least put my hair in a ponytail or braid. I guess I would have to be satisfied with it being unkept and hanging down my back.

Before I went back to Heidi, I walked over to the ledge of the hill and looked over the side. The wreckage below was unbelievable. All that was left was black charred lumps where buildings had once stood and black toothpick like stumps sticking out of the ground where I thought the Vatican once stood. But I couldn't figure out directions now, so I wasn't sure. I just knew that anywhere I looked, everything was completely in ruin. I wondered how many of us were left. I also wondered how many charred bodies were lying amongst the ashes. I sighed deeply, turned and walked back to where Heidi stood looking sadly in my direction.

"It looks horrible doesn't it, Becca? What do you think is going to happen to us now?"

"I don't know, but if we stay here we are going to have a lot of work ahead of us. That is unless someone doesn't track us down and kill us."

Of course I was thinking of Satan.

Her eyes grew wide with horror.

"Why would you say that?" She said.

"Oh, I don't know Heidi. Don't listen to me. I'm just as confused as you are right now."

We all ate our breakfast in silence. I think it was the best meal I had ever had in my entire life. Maybe it was because I felt so lucky to have any food at all right now. When we were finished eating, Paul spoke up.

"Don't worry too much ladies. I think we will be safe now."

I looked at him. There seemed to be something so innocent and caring about him. In fact, all of the priests had that same aura about them. It was comforting, but strange.

"Do you think the war is over?" I said continuing to look at him.

"I doubt it. I think we would in some way sense if it had come to an end, or for that matter surely someone would come to tell us. This is a global event and Rome is only one tiny little speck in this huge world. I would imagine it would take a few days or even a few years before it has ended. Gods' time is not the same as ours, so it really is hard to say."

After breakfast the men went to look for fallen trees that they could use for the frame of a shelter. Heidi and I found some thick grass reeds that we began weaving together to try and make some kind of mats that we could sleep on to get us off the damp ground at night.

We did sleep on the ground for the next few nights until our shelter was finally finished and ready for us to move into. It was great. We had a roof over our heads and nice mats to lie on at night. The men had fashioned a circle of stones to contain a fire that we could light at night to keep us warm. It was situated right outside the shelter. There were no walls on the shelter, just huge logs that held up a sturdy roof. We were so thankful for these men who were kind enough to help us in anyway they could to ensure our comfort.

They didn't seem to mind sleeping on the ground and didn't seem to worry about hurrying to make themselves a shelter, and every time Heidi and I would say something about it, they would tell us that they weren't in any hurry. They seemed happy to sleep out amongst the stars and huddle under the trees when it rained.

"Aren't they typical of most men Becca? Always putting off what they need to get done."

She was laughing and wrinkling her nose, as she usually did when she had just said something she thought was clever.

One night while we were sitting next to the warm fire, Heidi looked at me calmly and said,

"I wonder what ever happened to Mike? Do you think he is around somewhere? I really liked him. He is such a nice guy. I think he also had a crush on you, Becca. Just how do you attract all these men? Besides your obvious beauty?"

"Heidi, I don't want to talk about this right now. I will tell you this much though. I watched Mike die, and it was the most horrible experience I have been through in my life. That's all I can say about it for now. Later, when it is not such a fresh wound in my mind and heart, I'll explain to you what happened."

Her mouth flew open, but nothing came out. She stared at me and then she began to cry, which in turn brought on my own tears.

Father Ramon came over to the shelter and asked both of us if we were okay, and if there was anything he could do for us.

I answered him with tears still streaming down my face.

"Thank you Father. We will be fine. We just realized that a mutual friend of ours had died and we are both very upset about it."

"I'm sorry, ladies. After this war ends, we won't have to worry about losing any of the people that we love ever again. It will be a world ruled with everything in perfect harmony."

He winked at us and walked back over to where the other priests were sitting around the fire.

The nights were beginning to be quite chilly, and with no blankets I became cold pretty easily. It didn't seem to bother Heidi at all. I woke up one morning with a slight cold and everyone worried about me and doted on me like I was a little child. Father Paul made me juice from some kind of fruit that he made me drink religiously every morning after breakfast. When I spoke up and insisted that I wasn't coughing anymore, he reluctantly gave up his daily vigil.

Heidi was just as smart out in nature as she was in the office. She spent a lot of time studying the different vegetation growing in the park, trying to find different ways that we could use it. One day she took some thin twigs and with one of the priests' knives she sharpened the ends until they were very pointed and then carved an eye in them and fashioned sewing needles for us to sew the tall grass that she had found to create makeshift blankets to cover ourselves at night and to lay atop our mats, making our beds a little softer and warmer. We made some for the priests and they were amazed and appreciative that we had made some for them as well.

We also began drying some of the abundant fruit that grew everywhere. There was such a large variety to choose from that we would have plenty to get us through the winter when the food would be more difficult to come by.

The priests took chunks of fallen trees and carved large holes in them to make buckets so that we would have devices to carry water from the river to camp. They also insured that there was always firewood stacked for us whether to cook with or to heat our camp at night.

All in all, we were becoming an organized although busy little group.

Still none of us left the safety of the mountain. We only felt safe looking over the side to the valley below. We did feel protected here and didn't know what we'd find if we ventured down the hill. I was especially afraid of being recaptured by Satan, assuming he happened to still be around. But I never mentioned my fear of Satan to Heidi or to any of the priests.

One night, falling asleep after a long and busy day, my dreams returned. It was more terrifying than I remembered. I was carrying Boots in my arms as I ran. Satan was chasing me and gaining on me. He finally caught up to me and started ripping my skin off of my face and laughing at me while he threw pieces of my flesh to the ground. I woke screaming so loudly that I woke everyone else on the mountain. I was sweating profusely.

Father Paul and Heidi crouched down next to me and Heidi asked me what I was dreaming about. Since I didn't want to tell them I said I couldn't remember. Father Paul felt my head.

"Oh my goodness Heidi, she is burning up with fever again. We need to get her down to the river and put her into the water and see if we can break this fever."

When they put me in the river, I became so cold that my teeth were clattering and my lips were trembling but I didn't want to get out. It felt so much better than being as hot as I had been. After they took me from the river, Heidi dressed me, and of course my clothes just clung to my wet body because we didn't have anything that resembled a towel in our new living environment.

All I wanted to do was sleep. I didn't want to eat, and they had to practically force me to drink water. Heidi was fretting, but Father Paul said the best thing for me to do was rest and sleep. He said that would help me get well faster than anything else, which was fine with me as that was exactly what I wanted to do. They both were concerned about my lack of drinking and every day my cough worsened. I finally told them that I felt like I could barely breathe and my chest was beginning to rattle.

One morning I woke to see Heidi sitting next to me crying.

"Heidi, why are you crying?" I said. She seemed like she was very far away from me at the end of a tunnel

"Oh Becca, you just have to get better. Try to stay awake for a while. Father Paul has made you some hot broth out of some kind of fruit. I need you to drink it. We have to get something down you. You're beginning to lose weight. You can't keep doing this. I know you feel truly awful and don't want to drink anything, but you have to try."

Father Paul brought some warm broth he wanted me to sip, and as soon as I smelled it I began to gag. They made me drink it anyway. It was awful, and as soon as it hit my stomach, it came right back up.

That was the last thing I remembered. Heidi told me later that after everyone went to sleep that night, that I got up and went down to the river and took off my clothes and they found me on the bank of the river the next morning with my lips all blue and trembling, because I was freezing to death. She told me that from the looks of my hair, I had either been sweating all night or spent my night in the river. She got me dressed and took me back to the shelter. Father Paul told her he didn't think there was too much that they could do for me anymore, because I wasn't responding. The only thing they could do now was try to keep as much fluid as possible down me and take turns at night staying up and watching that I didn't go to the river. He felt that I was delirious and might wander off again.

Heidi said that one morning I opened my eyes and looked right at her and said,

"Heidi, where is Rafe?"

"Becca, I don't know where Rafe is."

"But he promised he would come for me! Why hasn't he come? Is he gone for good?"

She said she could hear the panic in my voice and see the fear in my fevered eyes.

"Becca, keep talking. Anything you can do to help you gain strength will help. Here drink some water for me."

I weakly kept pushing her hand away and turning my head from side to side to keep from drinking any water.

"Father Paul, come and help me. Becca is awake!" She hollered at the gentle priest.

Father Paul held my head while Heidi spooned water down my mouth with me fighting against them the whole time. She said they got some water down me, but as much of it as I could let spill out of the side of my mouth I did.

She said I looked at Father Paul and said,

"Father Paul, did Rafe go to heaven without coming for me?"

He looked at Heidi and at me and she said she was shocked when he said,

"Becca, I'm sure he will come for you. But you have to get better. You don't want him to come for you and find that you have already died. Think how terrible that would be for him."

Heidi said she had to ask Gods' help to keep her from slapping him across the face. She saw a tear slide slowly down my cheek and she looked at him and said,

"That was totally uncalled for Father!"

His retort was,

"I don't know Heidi, this Rafe seems to be the only thing she is holding on to . Maybe we can scare her into getting better."

"Becca!"

I opened my eyes,

"It's Heidi. Rafe loves you honey, but you have to get better so you will look good for him when he comes for you. You have lost so much weight."

She told me that all I would say after that was,

"I'm never going to see Rafe again. If I can't see him, I want to die."

She said that they finally came to the conclusion that they had lost me and it was just a matter of time before I wouldn't wake up anymore. She tried everything to snap me out of it, but I was just too sick.

Then when I was finally lost in oblivion and didn't care whether I was alive or dead, someone began annoying me by shaking me.

"Open your eyes Becca, come on, and open your eyes. Someone wants to see you."

Heidi was trying so hard to get me to open my eyes. She pinched me, shook me, slapped me. Trying anything that would wake me up. I vaguely remember the slap. I think it brought me around just enough that I remember feeling someone lifting me and the next thing I knew, I was being dipped in cool water. I could hear the others and especially Heidi, screaming.

"No, Stop! You are going to kill her."

I began to shiver and I felt something dry being wrapped around me. I was carried back to the shelter and then I remember being rocked in warm arms.

"Becca, Becca, darling. It's me Rafe. You're going to get better now. I'm here. Do you hear me? It's Rafe."

He kept rocking me and rocking me until I fell asleep in his arms.

At last, I remember waking up. I was terribly hot and I wanted to go down to the river and cool off. I struggled to get up, but he held me tight in his arms.

"No Becca, you have to stay here. I know you are hot. My body heat will make your fever break. Don't struggle. You know I can help you darling. I've helped you before, but you have to quit struggling. You're wasting too much energy."

I think I spent the rest of the day or night, I don't know which it was, struggling to get away from him. I laugh now when I think about it. Could anyone ever imagine me trying to get away from Rafe? But all I could remember was that I was so hot and I was sweating and getting nauseated. I guess I vomited several times. And Heidi said I became very angry with Rafe because he was keeping me from getting away from him to go to the river. I was much too weak to fight him so I began to curse at him.

I woke up on my mat and when I went to turn over, someone was holding me around the waist. It frightened me.

"Where are you going sweetheart?"

I recognized the voice immediately. I turned in his arms to face him.

"Oh my God Rafe, you are finally here."

I put my arms around his neck and held him as tight as I could and began crying. He tilted my head up to look at his face.

"It's about time you decided to put your arms around me. You haven't been very happy about me holding you."

I looked at him confused.

"What on earth are you talking about?" I asked.

"Welcome back my angel, we thought we were going to lose you for good, there for a while. But you are on the mend now. It will take a while for you to gain your strength back, but I'll be here to help you."

Heidi had seen me crying and of course she began to cry also. I couldn't believe it when they told me that Rafe had been here for three days, and this was the first day that I was completely coherent. I remember bits and pieces, but today was the first time in quite a few days that my mind was back to normal and my fever was gone.

Rafe looked at me lovingly, and then he winked at Heidi.

"Thank you Heidi for taking such good care of Becca until I got here. I don't know what I would have done without your help."

"No Rafe, it is really thanks to you that she is alive and doing so well. We had given up on her. We couldn't do anything else for her.. She was so sick and she seemed to finally become so weak that I think she finally gave up the will to live. All we were doing was keeping her comfortable."

Heidi had the guiltiest expression on her face as she answered Rafe.

"Stop it both of you! Heidi, you and the Fathers did all you could for me. I am thankful to all of you for taking care of me, and Rafe, Thank God for your getting here when you did. I love all of you. Now is there anything to eat, because I am famished."

They looked at each other and started laughing at the same time.

"Rafe, that's the best thing I've heard her say in weeks!"

Rafe stood up and bowing to both of us said:

"I'm going to go and see if I can find something for you to eat."

He kissed me on the forehead and smiled.

"I'll see you ladies in a little while. I have to find some food to help my girl build up some strength and of course to grant her wishes."

After he left Heidi looked at me wide eyed and said:

"I just can't believe that you are better. I really thought you were gone. It is thanks to Rafe showing up that you are alive."

"I know Heidi, he has a way of doing that."

She now looked at me strangely and asked,

"Can I ask you a question Becca, or are you too tired now to talk?"

"Are you kidding, how long have I been sick? Believe me I'm ready for anything. Well, maybe I better not go that far, but I am ready and happy to carry on a conversation."

"Becca, did you know that Rafe is an angel?"

I looked at her a bit surprised by her question.

"Did he tell you that?"

"He didn't have to, when he flew into camp, I realized it with my own eyes. He is a most magnificent angel."

"Yes, he is, isn't he?"

She looked a little shocked again.

"Then you did know!"

"Yes Heidi. Did he tell you who he was?"

"No, he said he would let you tell me later.

"Who is he?"

"Oh Heidi, I'd rather talk to Rafe first before I even try to explain any of this to you because it boggles even my mind. I can assure you when I answer your question you are going to have a zillion more."

"Darn, Becca, you are being so mysterious. I guess I'll just have to wait a little longer."

When Rafe came back he had killed a deer. He also found some wild asparagus and some watercress growing in one of the many cold streams that ran through the park. We had a feast for dinner that night. None of the others had ever tasted watercress before and were surprised at its peppery taste. I couldn't get enough of it as I hadn't eaten it since I enjoyed it as a little child. It grew in the streams of the Sierra Nevada Mountains where I was raised in the nearby tourist town of Lone Pine, California before my family moved to Arizona.

We all sat around the fire that evening spending the time reminiscing about the different places that we had lived and the variety of foods that we had experienced in our lifetime. The world would never be the same, as we knew it again, making us realize that we needed to treasure the memories that we had from the earth before this war. We grew quiet and I know each of us was growing a little sad as a result of our great loss. Rafe tried to cheer us up by telling us that what we had in store for us would be more wonderful than all the memories that we had from our earlier life. But for now, it was difficult for any of us mortals to visualize.

Rafe wouldn't let me stay up too late that night; which was fine, as I was anxious to be alone with him. But I soon found I was just to exhausted to do anything but fall asleep. The one enjoyable thing about going to bed early this time was that he lay down next to me and put his arms around me to keep me warm. I didn't complain about not having any blankets as long as I had him near me and could feel the warmth of his granite hard body. He kissed me on the cheek and rocked me in his arms until I fell asleep.

This wonderful arrangement went on for about a week, and then finally I began to look like my old self again. I was full of energy. My cheeks were pink and I had a healthy glow. I was happy. I didn't think once about Rafe leaving. I didn't want to.

The last night that he slept with his arms around me, I woke from my sleep and I was kissing Rafe lightly on his mouth. He pinned me under him. Holding my hands against the mat and he kissed me so passionately that I thought I was going to faint from the sheer pleasure and the fluttering sensation that I felt in the pit of my stomach. Suddenly he pulled away. But while still pinning my arms to the mat, he looked at me through tear filled eyes and said:

"Remember me. Oh my precious angel, please remember me."

Before I had a chance to reply, he quickly released me, jumped to his feet and without turning and looking at me said:

"Don't follow me! Stay here!"

"Oh Rafe!" I cried. "You aren't leaving are you?"

"Not just yet! Please stay here Becca. I need to be by myself for a while."

I watched him walk down to the river and lean against the willow tree where we had sat the first time we came here and professed our love to each other. The memory of it brought tears to my eyes and I looked away. I wanted to run to him, but I knew that I had to let him have his private time so that he could sort out his wounded feelings.

I didn't see him for several hours, but when he did come back he was his old self again. It was as though this morning had never happened. He never mentioned it again, but at least he didn't seem like he felt guilty. And he shouldn't! He had done nothing to feel guilty about.

He was exceptionally quiet though, and finally he gently took my hand in his and said,

"Becca, this will be our last day together. Michael will be here tomorrow and I will have to leave with him. I am leaving you here; because this is a place that God wants this part of civilization to begin from. All together, there will be about ten of you here in the park. Five men and five women, and of course the priests will stay here until they are assigned somewhere else."

"Rafe, please don't send anyone for me. I can never be with another man."

"Rebecca, that is not my choice to make that decision. It is strictly in Gods' hands what becomes of each one of us."

"Please Rafe, could you ask him to not put that burden on me. I know I couldn't love another as I love you. I beg you, plead with him not to do this to me."

He just looked at me and pretended like I never said anything. I began to tremble with fear. How could I obey a command to love another? My heart and soul belonged to Rafe."

Chapter 12
GOODBYE

The next morning the Archangel Michael entered the park and brought Blake Yardley with him. Michael was not trying to hide his identity anymore. There was no need to.

He entered the clearing from the woods in his entire angel splendor. When he introduced himself, Heidi began to cry and the priests immediately fell to their knees. I stood back and my eyes filled with tears, not because of his splendor, as I had witnessed it before, but because I knew that the time had come that I was going to lose Rafe forever.

Michael immediately told the priests to rise, and to only show that kind of respect to Our Heavenly Father. Nonetheless, everyone was in complete awe of him.

He then introduced Blake to the group. He was a good-looking man, who I estimated to be in his late twenties or early thirties. He had blonde wavy hair, blue eyes and look like he spent a lot of time in a tanning booth. He was tall and muscular, not nearly as muscular as Rafe, but ample enough. I thought to myself, so this was going to be the man who was to be in charge of our new group.

Michael walked up to me and asked where Rafe was. I told him I hadn't seen him since he left with two of the priests earlier in the morning to hunt for the day's food.

"Today he needs to leave with me and return to heaven, Rebecca. His job here is finished."

He might as well have just stabbed me with a knife. The words dug deep, even though I knew he would be here today. The actual words shocked me and my heart felt like it was going to break in two. How could it possibly continue to beat with my love gone forever?

Father Paul had overheard the conversation and seeing the shock on my face came over and put his arm around my shoulder.

"St. Michael. Rebecca has been very ill, and we almost lost her. Is it possible that you could let Rafe stay just a little longer with us? I am afraid the shock will send her into a relapse and after all, it was Rafe that brought her around. He gave her the will to live."

"I know that," Michael said.

"Then you know that he was responsible for saving her life, that is how close to death she was before he arrived."

"I know that too."

He looked at me, and than back to Father Paul.

"Becca is strong, She will be fine. She knew this day was coming. You see Father, she and Raphael the Archangel, that is Rafes' real name, fell in love with each other. They knew the consequences and how this would end all along."

Father Paul whirled around and looked at me in shock.

"Rebecca, if I didn't know you better, I would consider this a sacrilege. You have some explaining to do to all of us."

Michel raised his hands to stop him, shaking his head no.

"No Father, there is no need for that. They did nothing wrong except for fall in love with each other. Their conduct was impeccable. But they did know that the day was coming when they would be separated from each other."

I stared at Michael, wondering if he really needed to go into so much detail. I wasn't ashamed of my love. Heidi had now joined our group and was looking just as confused as Father Paul.

I couldn't stand there and cry in front of them so I excused myself and walked down to the bank of the river. I couldn't think of anything else except for, what was I going to do now? I knew that I had to be strong until Rafe left. I didn't want him to see me totally break down. I was staring into the water when I heard someone approaching from behind me. I wiped the tears from my eyes, just in case it was Rafe. I turned to see Michael standing a few feet away. He was such a magnificent creature. It was difficult not to kneel down in his presence, especially since I knew that he was mainly responsible for the banning of Satan to hell.

"Becca, I know how badly you feel. But please, you need to think of one thing. Raphael is not a man. He is an Archangel. You know him as a man. If he had come to you all along as an angel, do you think you would have felt the same way about Him?"

"Michael, I never had the chance to find out. God sent him to me disguised as a man. I can't help it if I fell in love with the man. Maybe I would have felt different if he came to me as an angel, and maybe it wouldn't have made a difference at all. I don't know."

"Becca, all I can say to you is I am so sorry that this has happened to you. Raphael will be fine as soon as he gets to his heavenly home. It's you I worry about. Give yourself some time and be open minded about a relationship with a real man. You will get over Raphael, I promise you. There is a saying on earth that actually is true, and that is 'Time heals all wounds.'"

"Oh Michael, you don't understand. I will never get over Rafe, I mean Raphael. I love him too much. He is my soul mate. I just don't know how I could ever fall in love with another man; I doubt that another human could ever replace Rafe. Now please if you don't mind, I need some time to myself to sort out how I am going to handle the loneliness after he leaves. I promise you this though; I will be brave for him. I don't want Rafe to have any regrets about something that he has no control over."

He stood and stared at me for a moment seeming at a loss for words, and then he lowered his head, turned and walked away. I knew he had no idea what else he could say to soothe my sorrow. I was resolved to the fact that Rafe was leaving. That was the main reason that our relationship had never evolved any further than it had. But now so many thoughts were going around in my mind that I felt like I was on the brink of panicking .

I had no future to ever think of with Rafe, and I knew that. From the day he told me who he was and where he belonged. We fell in love, and we both knew how dangerous these feelings were and now the day had arrived for us to suffer the consequences of a love that should have never been. I paused on this last thought when I heard him call my name.

"Becca, what on earth are you doing down here by yourself?"

It was my beautiful angel.

I turned to see him standing several yards away in all his glory as Raphael the Archangel. It always took my breath away when I saw him this way. He was so magnificent with his wings spread out fluttering softly back and forth. I could not take my eyes off of him.

I started to walk toward him, but he held up his hands to stop me.

"Becca, you can come to me. But please don't touch me. I am going to my Father now. I have been purified. That is a requirement before we can return to heaven.

And human hands from this moment on cannot touch me.

Michael thought this would be a more gentle goodbye, and possibly, if you remembered me as an Archangel it would be easier for you to forget me in the future."

I didn't utter a word. I simply stood and stared at him. What did he mean I

couldn't touch him? Oh, my god, I hadn't figured his departure to be anything like this. I had at least imagined one last embrace with possibly at least a kiss on the forehead. I didn't care if he appeared to me as an angel, anymore than I cared if he appeared to me as a man. I loved him either way. There was no separating the man from the angel anymore. It was too late for that. I wanted him to be mine and he never would be, and now I was being cheated out of a proper goodbye to the only man I would ever love.

He must have known exactly what I was thinking, because he looked at me with a concerned expression and began walking toward me. When he was right in front of me, he stopped, and stared at me. His eyes were full of love and hurt. I knew this was as difficult for him as it was for me. I had to remind myself. Remember Rebecca; you promised not to upset him anymore than he already is. My eyes were burning from holding back the tears. In fact they were burning so badly that I felt like my eyes would pop out of my head, but still I held them back and said to him,

"So this is goodbye?"

He lowered his eyes to the ground and said,

"Yes."

"How soon Rafe?"

"Now!"

My heart began to beat erratically, and I felt like I was going to faint. My hands began to tremble, and I quickly clasped them behind my back, hoping that he hadn't noticed.

"Rafe, please don't say anything, because you don't need to. Just listen to me. You have been the most beautiful thing that has ever come into my life. I love you more than life itself. Don't feel badly for me my darling. I knew this day was coming eventually and you know as well as I, that no matter how much I could have prepared myself for it I would have never been ready. You know that! I don't regret one second of the time we have spent together. You have always kept your loyalty to your Father and you should be proud of the way you conducted yourself. Most other men would never have been as strong as you. Remember this one thing for me. My love goes with you. It will never belong to another man for as long as I live. It is yours, forever and ever."

When I looked into his eyes I noticed that they were filled with tears and my first inclination was to wipe them away. But of course I didn't touch him.

With a whisper he looked at me with a pained expression and said,

"Becca. My angel. I will love you through all eternity. Remember that always."

With those final words, he lifted himself into the air, flapping his powerful wings; I could feel the wind from their thrust whipping my hair. We kept our eyes locked on each other, until Michael joined him and they flew away. I watched them until they grew smaller and smaller in the sky. Finally all I could see were two tiny little specks that disappeared from sight.

I must have stood there for hours looking up into the sky, because the next thing I knew I was looking up at stars, and still I hadn't shed a tear.

Heidi walked down to the riverbank where I was standing.

"Rebecca, I cannot believe you have been standing in this same place for so long." She put her arm around me.

"Please come and eat dinner with us. You can't stand down here all night. They are gone, honey."

"Heidi, I can't eat, and I won't eat right now. I have no feelings left to do anything right now. Please go. I'll walk up to camp in a little while. Thank you for checking on me though."

I finally lost my battle, right there on the bank of the river. I fell to my knees and started sobbing and sobbing until I thought I was going to be sick. I couldn't stop. The tears kept flowing. I looked up at the night sky one more time and I screamed and screamed as loud as I could. As if that was going to give me any relief.

Evidentially they heard me in camp because everyone came running down to the river and stood staring at me in disbelief.

Father Paul came to my side and reaching down, he took hold of my elbows and pulled me to my feet.

"Rebecca, come with me please! You cannot stay down here all night crying and screaming. We don't need you getting sick again. Please come with me now. Tomorrow is another day. You have mourned enough for one day."

I let him lead me up the hill to our shelter. He left me with the thankful Heidi. Her eyes were filled with tears.

"Please Becca. You need to get some rest. If you aren't going to eat, at least lie down and rest. You have had a horrible day, and you have been standing almost the entire day on the bank of that river. I know you have to be exhausted."

I lay down on the mat and thought to myself. Father Paul is right about one thing that he said tonight. I am mourning.

I don't know whether I slept or not that night. It seemed like I was awake the whole time with tears running from my eyes.

I know at one point I dreamed though, because I can remember seeing beautiful cobalt blue eyes staring into mine. It woke me, and I thought of every little characteristic of Rafes. His hair, the way he laughed, the way his eyes sparked specks of gold when he was angry, the way he kissed me, his firm yet gentle embrace. I tried to burn them into my memory, praying that they would never fade from my mind. Then the tears came again and I sobbed silently, trying to keep from disturbing Heidi.

The next day went pretty much the same as the day before. I had no appetite, my eyes felt like two black holes in my head. I cried more. I wanted to scream to heaven again, but I didn't. Only because I knew I would upset everyone in camp again. I didn't comb my hair, or even get dressed. In fact I never left the shelter. I sat that day staring out at our beautiful park, thinking to myself that the park even seemed to be mourning by crying with me, because it rained all day long.

Heidi tried several times to start a conversation with me, but to no avail. I had nothing that I wanted to talk about with anyone. Between the tears that seemed to constantly fall from my eyes, the only other thing I did was stare off into space.

At the moment I felt like my life was over, and in all reality life, as I had known it with Rafe was over. As a matter of fact, life that I had known since the day of my birth was over as well. Thank God Rafe was here to get me through the worst of it, or I may not even be here now, which at the present time didn't seem like such a bad idea. I really wished that I could just disappear into nothingness.

Father Paul came to see me again later in the evening. He sat down beside me and held my hand and stroked my hair, telling me that everything was going to be all right.

"You are young Rebecca. You have a whole life ahead of you in a brand new world. As soon as you get through this terrible ordeal, you'll see, you will be able to go on with your life. I'm not saying it will be easy. It's always hard to lose someone that you love. This is almost like a death because Rafe left this earth. He didn't leave you. He left to be in heaven. Isn't that the real goal for all of us? One day we will do the same thing. Life goes on, and you will eventually go on with yours as well. It will take time, but you will see that what I am saying is true. It's a matter of survival. Don't mourn yourself into ill health. This is exactly what you are going to do if you keep refusing to eat, and I will spoon feed you if I have to. I could always have Father Anthony hold you down." He patted my hand and laughed. But I wouldn't have been surprised if that is exactly what they would have done.

The next morning I was dressed and ready before Heidi even opened her eyes. Not because I felt any better, and not because I was in a hurry to go to breakfast. It was because I had not slept all night. My heart felt like it had a huge hole in it. I had decided to go to breakfast just to keep from drawing attention to myself. I had to learn to mourn in silence. I was thankful that everyone had been concerned about me and wanted me to be fine. But I wasn't fine, and I didn't plan on being fine any time soon I didn't want them to worry about me anymore. It would just disrupt their lives, so I had to start acting normally, even though I had no idea how to do that anymore. When Heidi woke up she was surprised to see me up and dressed already. But at least I could tell it eased her mind some. After she got dressed, we both walked over to have breakfast with the others. This morning they had cooked squirrel and cut up fresh fruit. I picked at my food and pretended to eat, because Father Paul was watching me intently. Whenever he looked away to talk to someone else I would stick the food in my pocket. When there was very little left on my plate, I excused myself. But Blake asked all of us to stay for a few minutes because he wanted to talk to us.

"I just would like to make sure that you all realize that at the present time I don't know how long we will be asked to remain here. We will have to venture off this hill eventually. I'm sure you all have noticed that the earth is now lush and green. Probably like it was in the beginning. There is no destruction anywhere. No smog, no smell of pollution in the air, and thank God no exhaust fumes from automobiles. The Angels of heaven have done a miraculous job cleaning the earth and it is up to us to keep it this way. Our Heavenly Father has given us a paradise to live in, so let's not mess it up this time. We saw what the end result was the last time he let us do things on our own. That's all I really wanted to tell you for now, because we don't have any orders as of yet. Rebecca, I hope I get to know you a little better when you feel more like yourself."

"Thank you Blake, but if you will excuse me, I'm just not good company right now."

All the men stood up as I rose to leave. Heidi followed me a few feet and said,

"Becca, you don't mind if I stay here a while and talk to the others do you? Will you be alright?"

"I'll be fine, Heidi. I really want to be alone for a while. I just can't get involved in any conversations right now. I know you understand. I just hope that everyone else does too. I'm going to take a little walk."

"Okay, then, if you are sure you will be okay."

I just nodded yes as I walked away. I knew that I would never be okay again. How could I be? My sunshine, my healer, my protector, my love, my best friend, and my life were gone.

I walked to the spot where Rafe and I had our picnic on that special beautiful day, the first day that we came here together. I reached down and held the angel pendent in my hand. Besides my memories, it was all that I had left of him now. Was he happy? Now that he was back in his real home, had all his memories of me been erased? In some ways I hoped so. I couldn't bear the thought of him feeling the way that I was feeling. It would break my heart to see him this sad.

I spent several hours that day lost in my thoughts, and brooding over my dilemma. I knew that I could not continue to go without food indefinitely and Rafe would not be happy if I mourned over him to the point of becoming sick. I promised myself that I would find something to keep me busy to pass the time. I just had to keep my mind occupied or I was going to go absolutely insane.

I looked up toward the heavens and said out loud.

"You win Rafe, I will go on with my life, just like you are going on with yours. You have always known your destiny, while I on the other hand have no idea what is in store for me in the future. But this much I do know, and I vow to you. I will never fall in love with anyone again. If I can't have you, I don't want anyone."

It was late afternoon before I walked back to the shelter. Heidi was nervously pacing, but she smiled when she saw me approaching.

"I was just trying to decide if I should ask Father Paul to go and bring you back. I'm happy that you came on your own. It shows a little progress on your part. I really hope you are going to be okay. I know how sad you feel. I felt the same way when I lost Carlo. I never thought I would be happy again, but then along came Blake, and I really think I could fall in love again."

"Heidi, that is just great, but then all of us aren't the same. I don't want to ever fall in love again. No one could ever live up to a man like Rafe!"

"Don't you mean an angel like Rafe? I hadn't talked to you about that yet because you have been too upset. But what was that like?"

I put my hands up in protest.

"Please Heidi, I don't want to talk about it! I just spent the last several hours trying to hash this out in my mind, and I really don't want to go over it again. At least not right now while the wounds are so fresh."

I spent the next several days on the bank of the river collecting rocks and building a shrine at the spot where Rafe gave me the pendant. It seemed silly in a way, but at least it kept me busy. I went down to the river and found some flat stones to make a sitting area under one of the willow trees where I spent a lot of time sitting and staring into the water or up at the sky.

As time went on I cried less and less, but the hurt and the loss, the hole in my heart, never left. Heidi and I took on the job of cooking and cleaning. The priests protested, but we felt that they had enough to do with hunting and fishing for our daily meals. We began to eat more fruit and vegetables. The men found wild potatoes, onions, squash and a variety of other vegetables and fruit growing down at the bottom of the hill. We ate less game since everything was beginning over in our new world there were less of the animal species, just like there were less of us and we didn't want to cause what was left to become extinct.

The world was a beautiful place now. There was nothing to clutter it up. It was filled with all kinds of vegetation and beautiful species of flowers growing everywhere. There were no cars, skyscrapers, bridges; nothing of our former existence, and most important there was no evil. Yet we still didn't have a clue as to what kind of society we were supposed to build.

I looked at Blake one night after dinner when we were all sitting around the fire talking about the beauty and vast changes we were so thankful to be a part of and I asked him,

"Blake, I thought your job was to give us a plan of how we are supposed to live in this new society. Isn't that why you were sent here?"

"No, not really Becca. That's not what I was told. There are orders in the making right now that someone else will be sent to us with the instructions of what we are supposed to do, and then I am the one who is elected to make sure that those instructions are carried out."

"I see." I said. "Well I wonder when this person will be coming?"

"Well Becca with the way transportation is right now I'm sure it will take a while for someone to get here, unless it is someone local, and since we haven't heard anything I am assuming it is someone from another area of the Earth. We'll get a message when the time is right. You'll see."

I watched as Heidi moved a little closer to him as if giving him moral support. Blake and her were becoming very friendly and were spending more time together. She had blossomed. I was so happy to see that my friend was finding happiness again. She certainly deserved it. To me, they seemed they would make the perfect couple.

Of course the more time Heidi spent with Blake, the less I spent with her, which gave me more time to brood. Not because I didn't have anyone, but because I didn't have and never would have the one I loved.

A few more people were sent to join our little group and we accepted each of them as the brother or sister they were meant to be.

We now had a total of twenty citizens in the park, seven women, six men, and seven priests. Since Heidi already had a partner, and I wasn't interested in one that left five women and six men. That could prove to be an interesting arrangement. I mentioned that to Heidi when we were getting ready to retire for the evening and were back in out private shelter. She just looked at me for a few minutes and said,

"You know Rebecca, if you could bring yourself to realize it, that means six men and six women besides Blake and I. If you would show some interest in one of these men there would be an equal paring of men and women. Maybe that is the plan from above."

I looked at her incredulously.

"You have got to be kidding Heidi! I...I can't even believe you would say such a thing. I'll never belong to another man. Never! Do you hear me?"

"Well what if that happens to be God's plan for you Rebecca? What are you going to do? Go against Gods' wishes?"

First, she called me Rebecca, which she hadn't done since before we had become good friends, or when she was really worried about me. Which didn't seem like the case right now. Second, this wasn't the Heidi I knew. This was cruel and Heidi wasn't cruel.

"Becca." She said softly. "I'm only trying to get into your stubborn mind that God may have other plans for you than what you want. I'm not trying to hurt you. I want you to live in the real world, which is exactly what David Rafe, or more importantly, Raphael in his spiritual realm would expect of you. Think about it. Don't close it out of your mind."

I put my hands over my ears.

"Stop! I don't want to hear anymore of this nonsense. It will never happen. God didn't give me these feelings for no reason. There will never be another. If I was meant to be with another man, I would have been interested in one. God would be a cruel God if he made me have a relationship that I didn't want. In that case he should have let me remain as Satan's prisoner, it would be the same kind of torture."

She came over to me pulling my hands away from my ears. She looked at me wide eyed and confused.

"Becca, what on earth are you babbling about? What do you mean Satan's prisoner?"

Father Paul had come to see what all of the arguing was about. It was something that seldom took place in our new world.

"Girls, girls, what on earth are you arguing about? Everyone in camp can hear you.

This isn't the way we are to conduct ourselves anymore. I have never heard the two of you get into an argument before. I would have never expected this from either one of you. No, I am not leaving here until you tell me what brought this all on, and Becca, I heard that last comment you made. What is going on?"

Why had I lost my temper? Now I was going to have to explain everything to them.

"Father Paul, remember when Michael the Archangel was here, and he made a comment about Rafe being an Archangel like himself? You told me I had some explaining to do. Will I guess this is as good a time as any."

"No Becca, St. Michael explained the situation and made it plain to me that you needn't explain anything. We don't need to go there."

Heidi looked like she was fuming.

"Yes, Father, yes we do! I can't help Becca if she only sticks to her own stubborn ways with no concern for the rest of us who love her, and she is babbling on things about Satan's prisoner. I don't know whether to think she is losing her mind, or there is something we need to know that has taken place in her life so we can help her."

'Heidi, can't you get it through your thick skull that I don't want any help?"

"Me? Me? You think I have a thick skull? You are the most stubborn person I know in this camp, Rebecca Malone."

"Stop it! Both of you! Let us sit down and talk about this calmly, right now, before either of you says something that truly ruins your friendship, and our chances of a blissful life on this planet!"

We sat down. Heidi and I could not even look at each other. Father Paul said a prayer asking Our Father above to guide us and help us put this argument to rest.

I told them the whole story, from the kidnapping of Pope Pius the XIII to my capture by Satan. I didn't miss a single thing that had taken place, except for the very personal things that went on between Rafe and I. But they both knew by the end of my explanation that Rafe and I did truly love each other and how Satan and his evil spirits had come to destroy this earth and I just happened to get caught up in the middle of it.

Father Paul was the first to speak.

"Oh Becca, I knew you had been through a lot, but I had no idea just how very much you had gone through not only personally, but on behalf of Our Holy Father. I am so glad that you explained it to us. It makes it so much easier to understand your love and devotion to Raphael, and I am sure God above knows exactly what is going on inside of you.

Time heals, and God will heal you to be the person he wants you to be. I don't think it will be with much effort on your part. If He thought of you as such a precious jewel that he saved you from the clutches of Satan once, I'm sure he doesn't have any bad plans in store for you now. Just pray my child. Trust God and the answers will come to you.

Heidi, it is not up to us to judge Becca. That is for God to do, and while I know that you honestly have her best interests at heart, I think this is something she needs to work out between herself and God. She has had enough trials and tribulations as it is, and all we can do is love her, and let her heal on her own. And above all girls, we cannot do anything to jeopardize our lives here. Which includes name-calling. You know we still have the judgment to look forward to. Now I want you to apologize to each other."

Heidi was staring at her feet

"Heidi, I am so sorry that I called you thick skulled. I am also sorry that I cannot see my life with anyone but Rafe, but that is where I stand. If it damns me to Hell, it will be God's will, though I hope I never have to see that day."

"Oh Becca, I am the one who should be apologizing. I had no idea. I wish you could have told me when it was all happening. I knew there were some times that I thought you acted frightened, or aloof, and I never could understand why. Now everything is so clear and I can understand why you feel the way you do. I will pray for you my special friend, and I promise to never interfere in your feelings again. I can't imagine what must be taking place in your mind after all that has transpired. Do you forgive me?"

I walked over and gave her a big hug.

"There is nothing to forgive Heidi. You made me realize one thing, that you did deserve an explanation. Even though it wounds me deeply to have repeated all of those wonderful and some horrible events.

Father Paul, I couldn't live with the thought of you thinking that I was a horrible person and even though I knew I had to one day explain all of this to you, I'm sure I would have put it off for as long as I could have just to keep from having it so fresh in my mind again. If the two of you will excuse me now, I need to take a walk and be alone for a while. I'll be back soon."

I returned to my favorite spot and of course I spent the time there crying all over again.

It seemed like all of the time I spent with Rafe was just now coming to an end and he was leaving me all over again. The pain was incredible, but I had to go on. I had no choice in the matter. I wished I could call him back to me. I would experience every bad moment that I had gone through all over again, just to relive once more the time that I had spent with him. I didn't stay in our special place very long. Just long enough to look up into the night sky and wonder just where my precious angel was, and if he even remembered my name anymore. I sighed. I would never know.

When I returned to the shelter Heidi was already sound asleep, and I quietly crawled onto my mat and tried to sleep. I dreamed all night of angels and demons and wars, and running away as fast as I could. I woke the next morning feeling like I was lost in another world. But then in reality, that is exactly where I was. Lost in another world and time with no idea what was going to become of me.

Heidi had already left for the kitchen to help prepare breakfast. I wondered why she didn't wake me.

I hurried and got dressed and ran to the men's shelter where the kitchen was located. I was out of breath by the time I opened the kitchen door.

"Goodness sake, Heidi. Why didn't you wake me? Now breakfast is going to be late."

I turned to look at her after I had closed the door. One of the newer girls was helping her by busily paring potatoes.

"Becca, don't get excited we have everything under control. You slept so fitfully last night that I felt like you needed to sleep in this morning. Now relax. Could you put this fruit in that big bowl and take it out to the table?"

I calmed down, once I realized that Heidi, as usual, had everything under control.

As I placed the bowl of fruit on the table Blake, who was sitting at the table with another gentleman, looked up and smiled at me.

"Ahh, Becca, just the person I wanted to see. I'd like you to meet Larry Penacho, he was sent here to help us with our gardens. He was the horticulturist for the Smithsonian before the war from Heaven.

Larry Penacho came to his feet and reached out one short muscular hand to shake my hand.

"How do you do Becca, it's nice to meet you and nice to be invited to be a part of your group."

I smiled, nodded my head in acknowledgement and said,

"Pleased to meet you Mr. Penacho. I hope you enjoy it here. It is such a beautiful place to live. This has always been my favorite place in Rome. I really think you'll feel welcome here, we accept each new person as a part of our family. The Lord knows we certainly need someone to help us with our fruit and vegetable garden. Well Larry, it was nice to talk to you, but I really need to get back to work or the girls are going to kill me."

"We certainly wouldn't want them to do that now would we." Larry laughed. "Oh and please call me Larry."

We had breakfast and everyone went about his or her work for the day. I cleaned up our shelter and then walked back down to my little shrine to sit and be lost in my memories.

At dinner that evening Larry sat next to me. And we had a pleasant time talking about the United States. He was born here in Rome, but went to college at Notre Dame and after he received his Masters Degree, was hired by the Smithsonian Institute and had remained in the U.S. ever since. He only returned to Rome after the Battle of Armageddon. He was with a small group of Americans, when he was asked to come here, and since it was here that he began his life, it seemed only obvious that this is where he should return.

Larry was a good-looking man. He was just a little taller than me. Not on the muscular side, but solid. He had beautiful soft brown eyes, and the olive complexion of most Italians. What stood out the most about him was his beautiful white-toothed grin and his sun bleached blonde hair. He reminded me of a California Surfer.

It became a nightly ritual that he always sat down to dinner next to me, and I really enjoyed his company.

One evening after dinner, I left the group and walked to my shrine for my usual evening vigil. I didn't know that Larry had followed me. When I reached the shrine, which I always considered my private little spot in the park, a voice from behind me suddenly said,

"Who made this spectacular little structure?"

I must have jumped, because he quickly apologized for startling me.

The shrine by now had beautiful flowers growing around it where I had planted them and a nice variety of ivy was slowly winding it's way up and around the shrine. It really looked beautiful.

I didn't answer his question, I just said,

"I didn't know anyone followed me."

"I'm sorry Rebecca. I hope you don't mind. You just seem to be by yourself most of the time and I thought maybe you wouldn't mind some company. I'm not interfering with anything, am I?"

I wanted to tell him yes, but instead I just said,

"No, I'm just kind of a loner and enjoy spending time by myself."

I was being rude and I quickly added,

"I'm sorry Larry. I don't mean to sound so rude, of course I would enjoy the company."

He reached out his hand and took a hold of my elbow because I was just about ready to slip on a rock. I jerked away, shocked by his familiarity, and I fell flat on my bottom.

When I looked up at him he just shrugged his shoulders and sported a crooked little grin that reminded me of Mike.

The sheepish grin never left his face as he said,

"You should have let me help you and maybe you wouldn't have slipped."

He stifled a laugh looking at me sprawled on the ground. And then we both began to laugh.

"Friends, then?" He said.

"Friends." I repeated. It felt good to laugh and I needed someone to be my friend. Someone I could laugh with.

After that he spent the next several evenings walking with me down to the bank of the river. I purposely stayed away from the shrine.

We would talk about the old world and what we thought this new world would have in store for us. We shared stories of our childhoods and I told him as much about my life in America as I could remember. He told me many things about Rome that Rafe had not had time to share with me.

We would sit on the bank of the river dangling our feet in the water, laughing and splashing each other as we talked. I finally felt human again.

I never told him anything about my relationship with Rafe.

Finally I couldn't stand it any longer. I had been away from the shrine for too long. So when I got up from the dinner table one evening to walk and Larry stood to go with me. I turned and looked at him and said,

"Larry, please. I don't want to hurt your feelings, but I would really like to walk by myself this evening. I need to be alone."

I looked down at the ground, scooting my foot back and forth in the sand making a half circular pattern. I knew I had hurt his feelings, but he quickly sat back down and said,

"Sure, Rebecca, I understand."

I practically ran out of the dining area without looking back. I didn't mean to hurt Larry's' feelings, but I really needed to be alone with my thoughts of Rafe with no interference from anyone.

When I got to the shrine, I pulled all the weeds that were growing amongst the flowers and promised to never neglect this place again. I looked up to the heavens and said,

"Rafe, forgive me darling for not coming to our special place for the last few weeks. I have made a new friend. His name is Larry Penacho and he makes me laugh once again. I don't think I have laughed since you left. I cannot bring him here, because this is our special place and I will never share it with anyone."

I was fondling my angel pendant all the while that I was talking. My eyes filled with tears. Even when I laughed and had a good time in this beautiful park, I knew that nothing could ever repair the gouge that had ripped through my heart the day that Rafe left my life for good.

The next day Larry asked me if I would like to go fishing with him. I started to make up an excuse of why I shouldn't, and Heidi looked at me rolling her eyes.

"Oh go on Becca, it will be good for you. You always laugh when you are with Larry. Go and have some fun."

Blake, who was sitting next to her, looked at me and winked and nodded his head in agreement.

"All right. You all will get your way. But I guarantee you Larry; I won't take a fish off the hook. Ew, that makes me sick to think about it."

Everyone began to laugh.

Larry looked at me still laughing.

"Is that the only reason you didn't want to go? I'll take the fish off the hook if you are lucky enough to catch one."

"I'll catch one." I laughed, punching him in the arm.

We fished, and of course I didn't get one bite on my fishing line. Larry caught enough fish for lunch. While he was cleaning them, I lay down in the grass, folded my arms behind my head and looked up at the sky. The next thing I knew Larry was beside me. He leaned over me and taking my head in his hands said,

"Poor Rebecca, Blake told me your story. I want you to know that I will always be here for you as your friend for as long as it takes, I hope to one day be more than just your friend. He bent down to kiss me.

I pushed against his chest.

"No, Larry, please don't spoil our friendship."

"Oh sweet Rebecca. I just want you to know what it feels like to kiss a real man."

Before I could say a word, his lips captured mine; he crushed me to his chest, and all I could think of was that I was being untrue to Rafe and myself. I pushed against him again, trying to get him off of me. He immediately released me when he noticed the fear in my eyes and said,

"Oh Rebecca, I am so sorry. I had no intention of frightening you. I just care so much for you that I had to kiss you."

I got up from the ground, glaring at him. I couldn't speak. I just turned and ran as fast as I could back to the shelter. He didn't follow me. I could not believe this. Why did he have to spoil the beautiful friendship we were building?

As soon as I ran into the shelter, out of breath, Heidi looked at me wide eyed.

"Becca, what on earth is wrong. Your face is as red as a beet. Sit down and try to catch your breath."

I sat down, and gradually my breathing returned to normal. I began to cry.

"Oh Heidi, he spoiled it all. He kissed me."

She started to laugh.

"Becca, didn't you expect that? Blake and I were beginning to wonder what was taking him so long. I guess he is just an honorable man."

"Heidi, you know I can't do this. My love belongs elsewhere. Please don't lecture me about this again. I just can't do this. I thought we could be friends like Mike and I were. I guess I was fooling myself. I certainly had no intentions of leading him on if that is how it looked to all of you. I truly like Larry, but I only like him. It will never be anything more than that."

I started to cry.

Heidi put her arms around me.

"Oh Becca, you really need to talk to him about this."

"Tomorrow, Heidi. Tomorrow."

The next day at breakfast Larry was very quiet all through the meal. When we had finished eating I asked if I could talk to him alone.

We walked to the river in silence. When we finally arrived. He bent down and picked up a handful of stones and began throwing them one by one into the river; he reminded me so much of Mike, but then, he wasn't Mike, and I knew now I should have never made the comparison.

"Larry, could you stop for a minute and look at me. I have some things I want to share with you."

"Rebecca, before you say anything, I want you too know that I am so very embarrassed about yesterday. I should not have been so hasty with you. Especially knowing your past. But I know that you like me, and I just couldn't help myself. I'm so sorry."

"Larry, listen to me. This is just as much my fault as yours. I should know that a woman usually cannot be just a friend with a single man. I never meant to lead you on."

"Rebecca, you didn't lead me o…"

"Oh Larry, please don't interrupt me. Let me get this out and over with. My love, my life belongs to another. And if you know the story, you also know that nothing can ever materialize from that relationship. But my love forever belongs to him. The bond between us is unbreakable. I'll never want another man. From this day forward, our friendship is over. I will speak to you, and I hope you speak to me. But I will never spend another moment alone with you. It isn't fair to you. Please concentrate on someone else. I never meant to hurt you. And if I have I am sorry. My mind is made up. Thank you for trying to be a friend, but I should have realized that it would have evolved into something more. I'm sorry, but for my part it never can."

I turned to walk back to the camp and he said,

"Rebecca, wait. We can make this work. We can be friends…"

"Larry the answer is no, a profound no. Please you have to accept it."

He turned me to face him, and my body immediately stiffened. He released me, and looking straight into my eyes, said,

"If you ever, ever change your mind Rebecca, I will be there for you. But I will honor your wishes, and I promise to never bother you again unless you ask me too."

"Thank you Larry, that's all I can ask of you. Please don't wait for me. You need to find someone to care for you, and someone you can care for."

"I thought I had Rebecca."

I looked at him and I could see the hurt in his eyes. I didn't say anything else. There was nothing else to say. I just walked back to the shelter and spent the day there alone.

The days dragged on. I had gotten so used to spending time with Larry that now, that I was alone again time seemed to stand still.

The one nice habit that I observed was that all the people in our group seemed to be aware of each others feelings and no one ever tried to upset any of the other residents of our community. I wondered if it was like that everywhere. Tempers very seldom flared, and when they did, Blake or one of the priests always rectified the situation immediately.

We all kept ourselves busy searching for food, hauling water and just generally keeping ourselves fed and clean. We didn't want to make any changes to the environment until we had orders to do so.

Heidi and I worked almost every day getting reeds from the bank of the river to weave into baskets and platters and any kind of utensils for the kitchen. The newer women were in charge of the clean up and setting tables and making of eating implements, which we really didn't need a lot of because almost anything that we ate could be eaten with our fingers.

We also helped the men by pulling weeds from the vegetable gardens and bringing water for the plants if there wasn't enough rain for a while. This very seldom happened because nature like us cooperated with Gods' every wish. We seemed to have an abundance of anything we needed from nature. God had made everything in this new world absolutely perfect.

Larry Penacho turned out to be quite the farmer and had a green thumb for almost anything that he grew. Blake put him in charge of the gardens and harvest and he always made any of the work that we had to do in the gardens an interesting and joyful experience by explaining the different plant species or cracking some joke. It was an absolute joy to be told it was your turn to work in the gardens. He never brought up anything about our friendship again, and always treated me with the utmost respect.

One day as I was returning to the shelter from working in the gardens all day, I overheard one of the other women ask Heidi why I didn't seem to be interested in any of the men. I stopped and stood behind a tree as I heard Heidi begin to tell her the story of Rafe and I. I didn't want to embarrass her by walking in during the middle of her explanation. So I walked down to the river and sat down on the stone by my shrine. I took the pendant from around my neck and looked at the beautiful angel. Rafe surely must have realized when he gave it to me just how important it would be to me one day, when he was no longer around. I read the inscription on the back over, and over. I had rubbed my fingers across it so many times that I was surprised that the words had not begun to fade. They were always there though as a reminder to me. I thought about him. His features were beginning to fade from my memory a little more with each passing month, which upset me badly, but not his cobalt blue eyes. They would never fade from my memory.

I suddenly remembered Satan telling me that it was cruel of Rafe to fall in love with me. But I would not ever want to change one single moment of the time we spent together, not for anything in this world. The days he was with me were precious to me, even if I was in pain now. I always had the memory of his love to carry with me for the rest of my life.

I was just getting used to the idea of having the newcomers in our midst when Blake called a meeting of the whole community. We were all anxious to see what was so important that he actually called us all together at once.

We were all gathered and sitting on the ground on the lush green carpet of grass. After we finally quieted down from our speculating about what this sudden meeting could mean. Blake finally stood up and shushed all of us.

"First of all, I want you all to know just how very thankful I am that you all seem to try your hardest to make sure you always get along so well with each other. Secondly I think we all need to thank Mr. Larry Penacho for his horticulture expertise and his knowledge of which fruits and vegetables are edible and which are poisonous. Otherwise I'm sure some of us would be sick or worse, by now."

We all applauded Larry. He was very good at his job and we all were thankful for his being sent to us.

Blake continued, "Now, I am sure you are all wondering why I have gathered you together this evening. I have some exciting news that I would like to share with you. Sometime tomorrow there will be another twenty people joining our little group…"

Despite myself, I moaned aloud. I couldn't bare the idea of more people being sent to this beautiful park. Everyone looked over at me and began to laugh.

Father Paul shot us a warning glance and shook his finger at me.

Blake cleared his throat and everyone quieted down.

"...Now, if I may continue! What is especially exciting about this arrival is that our leader will be amongst them. Finally, it will now be possible for us to get on with the task of forming our society in the manner that God has planned for us. I knew this would be good news for all of you. Those of you who are curious are invited to share a fruit dessert with us tomorrow evening to greet the new arrivals and our new leader. Otherwise you are free to meet them on your own over the next few days.

At least now we will know where our future is going and what is in store for us."

Blake sat back down and the whole group was alive with questions.

I just sat their quietly thinking it all over.

Father Paul came over and sat down beside me.

"Becca, I know you aren't looking forward to more people coming to the park, and I understand why this place is so special to you. Try not to be selfish. This place belongs to Our Heavenly Father and he makes the rules. He has wonderful things in store for you, Becca."

I wondered what on earth made him say that, maybe because that is what we were to look forward to. I lowered my head in embarrassment and shame for my earlier outburst.

He tilted my chin and smiled as he lifted my face to look in his eyes.

"Becca, you are always going to be a little on the unpredictable side and someone is going to have to always keep you under control, and I guess right now I am elected to do that job. You need to know that things cannot always go the way we would like them to."

I looked at him and sighed.

"How well I know that, Father. I really think I've learned that lesson well. It if will make you feel any better all I have to say about the whole new resident episode now is: To the Future!"

He put his arm around my shoulder and pulled me against his side and I could feel his whole body shaking with laughter. He winked at me and said,

"That's my girl."

Then he walked me back to our shelter. I thanked him for getting me away from the crowd for the evening. I stood for a few moments staring down towards the river. At least I felt comfortable here, away from everyone.

Chapter 13
THE LETTER

    The next morning Heidi got up early, dressed and left the shelter to help Blake prepare for the arrival of the newcomers. When she asked me if I'd like to come along, I turned over on my mat with my back to her and grumbled half asleep, because as usual I had a bad night and hadn't slept.

    "Becca, do you want me to come back and get you later so that you can meet everyone?"

    I told her I would just meet them all individually over the next few days. I wasn't really interested in conversation right now. I spend most of my time quietly living in my own world. I didn't need any distractions from the way of life I had chosen for myself. When I tried being friendly, it always got me in trouble. If I was aloof, I always came across as a little on the grumpy side. I couldn't win.

    I don't know when they began to arrive, but I could hear them all laughing every now and then and I was happy that everyone seemed to be having such a good time. Heidi must really be enjoying herself because she usually came back to check on me once in a while, but today was the exception.

    I used the comb that one of the priests had made for us out of a large bone, and combed through my long hair. It must have grown a good three inches since we arrived here. I combed until it was silky soft, and as I pulled it forward to comb it I noticed that it had a nice sheen to it today. Maybe one of these days we would figure out how to make a brush. That would be nice. It wouldn't take as long to brush through our hair as it did to comb. I sat for a minute thinking of all the things that we took for granted in our old world. I missed those conveniences now.

For a lack of things to do, I cleaned the shelter from one end to the other. Stacked some wood by the fire pit for later in the evening, and then I walked down to the river. I walked past the shrine and sat down on the rock table I had made after Rafe first left. It seemed like a long, long time ago now. But I still had the huge hole in my heart that I knew would never heal. I still thought about him every single day of my life. I was thinking about this when Heidi came running up behind me and startled me. I brought my hand up to my chest

" Oh my goodness Heidi, you just scared me half to death. My heart is still pounding. How did you sneak up on me so quietly?"

"I didn't sneak up on you. I ran all the way. You must have been preoccupied. First I went to the shelter and when I didn't find you there I figured you would be down here, so I came as fast as I could."

She grabbed me by the hand, yanking me to my feet, and said, "Becca, quick! You need to come with me and meet some of these new people. Father Paul sent me to get you. He didn't want you being miserable here all by yourself. He said if you didn't come with me that he would be down to get you; if he had to carry you back to camp. I am so excited. We really were sent a nice group of people. They are all so nice and seem to fit right in with all of us. Come on let's go, they are all looking forward to meeting you."

She was so excited. I knew she must have run all the way because she was so out of breath and so excited that at first it was hard for me to understand her and I had to calm her down.

"Gosh Heidi, they must really be something. I don't think I've ever seen you so excited over newcomers as you are now. In fact, the only other time I remember seeing you this excited was when you finally figured out that Blake was as much in love with you as you were with him."

I let go of her hand and took a step back.

"Oh Heidi, I would really rather not. I can meet everyone over the next few days. You know it is so hard for me to talk to anyone anymore. I don't have anything to say. I think I'll just stay here if you don't mind."

"Becca, please! I don't ask you to do a lot of things for me. But I really want you to come with me this evening. I also want you to meet the new man that has been sent to us as our new leader. He is so nice."

Her eyes were so full of excitement that I almost felt guilty not wanting to go with her, but I persisted.

"I'm sure he is, but I can meet him at another time, or when he calls a meeting. I'm sure he is tired and a little overwhelmed by everyone anyway. He won't even miss that I'm not there."

"Oh Becca, I think you will see that you would really enjoy yourself, I have never heard all of us laugh as much as we have tonight and it would be nice to see you laugh too. It's been a long time. You know you might even enjoy yourself. Won't you do just this one thing for me?"

How could I keep telling her no? She had done so much for me since we came to this park. She was such a giving soul and never asked for anything in return.

I looked at her for a moment longer, and then I finally smiled.

"Heidi, I really don't want to, but…"

She jumped up and down like a little child screaming and hollering, before I could even finish my sentence.

"Oh, I knew you would. I just can't wait for you to go over there and meet everyone."

I looked at her in disbelief she really truly was excited.

"Heidi, settle down. I said I would go. Let me go and wash my face and then we'll go together."

I didn't know what could be so exciting about a bunch more people coming here. I like it just fine when there were just a few of us here. But I splashed my face with the water and decided to go and get the meeting over with. I supposed I wouldn't have to stay for long.

When we were almost to the campsite Heidi looked over at me and said,

"I just can't wait for you to meet this man. I am so excited about it."

I stopped in my tracks, and looking at her with a furrowed brow, and a look of distrust on my face, said,

"Heidi, is that the only reason you want me to come down here? To meet a man? How many times do I have to tell all of you that I am not in the least interested? I'm not interested nor will I ever be. There just can't be anyone for me anymore. I'm sorry. You are wasting your time."

I turned to leave, when Father Paul ran out and grabbed my arm to stop me.

Come on Rebecca, you've walked this far. You might as well meet these people and our new leader and get it over with. Heidi was so excited that I let her come and get you instead of me. Is it going to kill you to sit with these new people for a little while?"

I looked over at Heidi who looked like she might burst out crying at any moment. I looked at Father Paul with an expression that said I really didn't want to do this. But finally I gave in and said,

"Okay, you two. Heidi, I'll go along and on one condition. Promise that you aren't going to push any man on me."

She ran up and hugged me. "Okay! I'll promise you anything as long as you come and be a little sociable for a while. I know you won't be sorry."

We walked over to the fire that everyone was sitting around, people were busy chatting and laughing with each other but they stopped and looked up at me when we entered the circle. I felt more than a little conspicuous, but I smiled.

Father Paul had to embarrass me more, saying,

"Everyone, can I please have your attention. This is our girl we talked about earlier."

Oh no, what did he tell all these people about me?

"Her name is Rebecca Malone, but her friends call her Becca. She is our camp sweetheart."

Sweetheart! I raised my eyebrows when I turned to look at him and uttered in a whisper, so no one else could hear I said,

"Oh father, you are trying to butter me up to stay here aren't you? Wait till these poor people get to know me. They aren't going to think sweetheart. They'll probably come up with a much more colorful curse word for me, don't you think?"

He just gave me a look that indicated I should stop talking. Before I had a chance to whisper anything else to him, he started introducing me to all the newcomers. There were nine women and ten men in this group. I thought that there were twenty. Oh well, maybe Blake misunderstood when he was told, or maybe one of them didn't come for some reason or another.

I pretended to be excited to meet everyone, but in reality, I wished I were back at our shelter by myself. I was talking to one of the women, when Heidi came up behind me and said,

"Becca, I would like you to meet the man God sent to be our leader. We just found out that he has been right under our noses on the other side of the park building a house for the past several weeks. The girl who marries him is going to be one lucky woman."

I couldn't believe my ears, what was she doing? I felt my face turn red, and I rolled my eyes at the woman I had been talking to and turned to give her a nasty look. There was a tall man coming from out of the darkness toward us.

"Heidi you better hope he didn't hear you just say that, or you are going to have hell to pay from me when we get back to the shelter. What's wrong with you? Don't say things like that. Maybe this man doesn't want to get married, did you ever think of that? If he's been on the other side of the park for a few weeks without us meeting him, it sounds like he might be anti-social like me."

Father Paul called to me softly and I turned to look at him.

"Becca", he whispered. "Now be nice. To Heidi and our leader. Don't let him get the wrong idea about you right away."

Now I was beginning to get livid. Why did I let them talk me into staying here? All Father Paul and Heidi were going to do was embarrass me all night. I had never seen either one of them act like this before.

Heidi touched my shoulder and I whirled around to look at her, but when I looked up, there standing a few feet from me was Rafe.

I didn't know what to do for a few seconds. I began to tremble and then I started crying. Some of the newer people looked at me like I was crazy, and I could hear them whispering amongst themselves.

I looked up again just to make sure I wasn't seeing things. No, it was Rafe and he was walking toward me. When he got close enough for me to actually touch I ran to him and threw my arms around him, sobbing.

"Oh My God, is it really you? How long do you get to stay? Oh, never mind, I'm just so very happy to see you."

He leaned down and in front of God and everyone; he kissed me square on the mouth. The same feelings I always felt when he kissed me immediately washed over me. Neither one of us was embarrassed by the presence of the crowd. We were so happy to see each other that it didn't matter how many people were there.

When we finally broke our embrace, everyone who knew us began to applaud. The others who had never seen us before looked at everyone, and even though they had no idea what was going on, began to applaud also.

Rafe looked at the group of people, and then back to me and he said,

"If you would now excuse Becca and I, we have some unfinished business to attend to"

He put his arm around my waist and started leading me off toward the bank of the river where we had our picnic.

When we got about halfway there, I suddenly became frightened. What if he had to leave again? I don't think I could live through another goodbye.

"Becca? What's wrong, aren't you glad to see me?"

I looked at him frowning. "Rafe, when do you have to go back? I can't stand another goodbye to you. I won't live through this one. I won't want to. It will kill me, I know it will." I started crying again.

He continued to lead me the rest of the way to the willow tree in silence. When we got there he turned me to face him, and pulling a hankie out of his pocket he wiped the tears from my eyes.

"Becca, I never have to leave you again. God was so impressed with the way that you and I love each other so unselfishly that he gave me the choice of remaining in heaven as his archangel or coming to you as a man, and so I made the ultimate choice and he sent me back as a man. You are my choice. We will be together for eternity. I will never have to leave you again."

"Rafe, are you serious? Oh my God, are you serious?"

I started crying again. he cupped my chin in his hand, and bending once more to kiss me, he paused for a few seconds, his blue eyes were ablaze with passion, and then he kissed me a kiss I thought would never end. It was so passionate that my legs began to tremble and buckle beneath me. He slowly broke our embrace and looking at me said,

"It's not my loyalty to God that is stopping me this time Becca. I want to take you to our home that I've been building. There's something I've been wanting to do for a long time, and we don't need any interruptions from anyone this time. Especially not from me."

We walked to the other side of the park and there in the middle of a group of pine trees, stood the most beautiful little house I had ever seen. It was simple, but it fit our new way of life in every way, with its rustic look on the outside. Rafe lifted me into his arms and carried me through the door. The inside of the cabin was open and lovely. He had little bouquets of flowers in little nooks all over the house. He put me down in the middle of the floor.

"Oh Rafe, this is absolutely beautiful. I just can't believe that you have been here for a while and I never heard any noise coming from this side of the park."

"I had some help. Michael came and helped me with it and so it went very fast. He couldn't understand how I could leave heaven. But he wanted you and I happy, so he came and helped. If you only knew how hard it was for me to not let you know I was here. But I wanted everything to be just right for you. I did come over a couple of nights and watched you sleep fitfully though. I hope now that I am here those kind of nights will be behind you. Come here Becca, and let me look at you."

I walked over to him and he looked at me with so much love in his eyes that my heart felt like it was beginning to heal. I wanted to pinch myself and see if this was real or a dream. But I knew it was real from the way he had kissed me.

"It looks like you have lost a little weight Becca, but all in all you look as beautiful as I remember you. Blake and Heidi have told me what a difficult time you have had. I am so sorry my beautiful Becca. I promise to make your life happy from this moment and forever."

He put his arms around me staring into my face, and I reached up and wrapped my arms around his neck.

"Oh Rafe, I thought I would never feel myself in your arms again."

He continued staring at me, and then he leaned over to kiss me, and pulled me close to him, and it felt so good to feel his body against mine. I pressed myself against him, and he walked me backwards, kissing me until my back was against the wall. He pushed his body tightly against mine and began trailing kisses down my neck and across my collarbone, and then he stopped at the side of my throat and kissed me there. I could feel my pulse beating wildly. His mouth left my neck and he stared into my eyes one more time, silently letting me know that he had no intention of stopping this time. Suddenly his mouth was on mine again, and his kiss was urgent and demanding. His arms unwrapped from around me but he never quit kissing me as he slowly began to slip my homemade dress from my body. The next thing I knew his hands were exploring my body, I leaned my head back against the wall and moaned with pleasure. Then suddenly, before I knew what happened, we were both on the floor. I reached for him to pull him close to me again, but he captured both of my hands in his massive hand and held mine against the floor above my head. When he spoke his voice was raspy and came out in slow short gasps.

"No Becca, please, don't touch me just yet. I am enjoying exploring you at the present moment and I want this to be a lasting memory for both of us."

He was slowly kissing my whole body, exploring me with his tongue in all the right places. I was moaning wildly in pleasure. In a passionate frenzy I pulled my hands free from his grasp and rolled on top of him. I cupped his chin in my hands and kissed him, forcing his mouth open to kiss him more deeply. I pressed my body against his and began slowly moving against him with a slow writhing motion. He began to breath heavily, and when he started to moan, I knew that I was doing something right. But before he lost all control, he was suddenly towering over the top of me once more. He took some time to regain his composure by looking over the entire length of my body with pleasure and a hungry look in his eyes. Normally, I would have been embarrassed if someone would look at me the way he was, but I wasn't. I wanted him and I wanted him now. I wrapped my arms around his waist pulling him closer to me, but he resisted, he wanted to enjoy this moment as long as possible. He began to kiss and tease me until I reached a tempo where I was begging him to make love to me. Finally when I thought I was going to go insane. His eyes looked into mine as he lingered above me. His next kiss was one of passion and need, we became one. Our bodies were in perfect rhythm with each other and we reached heights we had never been before. We both cried out in contentment, and his mouth covered mine once more to drown out the echo of my screams. It was beautiful, one of the most beautiful experiences of my new life and well worth the wait. We made love to each other all night, into the wee hours of the morning till we fell asleep in each others arms, perfectly content and more in love with each other than we had ever been before.

The next morning I slept in and when I woke, my first thought was that I had a beautiful dream, until I realized I was in our house. I got up and wrapped a blanket around me and walked into the main room. Rafe had breakfast waiting for me.

"Good morning, my beautiful angel." He looked at me and teasingly said,

"I am going to ravish you over and over until you beg me to stop. You don't know how long last night has been on my mind. I thank God for sending me back to you. You are exactly where I belong."

I ran over to him and flung my arms around his neck. The blanket fell from around my shoulders.

"I will never grow tired of you Rafe. You are my dream come true. I want to grow old with you and have lots of children together. We'll be like the two beautiful swans whose song graces this park, bonded for life in an everlasting love."

Of course with me standing there completely naked, breakfast didn't last long and we made love once again and as passionately as we did the night before.

When we were finally dressed we walked outside next to the stream that ran through the forest. Rafe had made sure that he built the house where there would be a stream nearby, with willow trees, basking on its bank. It was a warm sunny day and the birds were singing. We sat in the grass under the tree. I sat between Rafes' legs with my head leaning against his chest and we watched the squirrels currying up and down the trees, chattering and playing with each other. There were two rabbits nearby eating grass, and a turtle was sitting on a rock in the stream basking in the sun. Rafe had his eyes closed and was nuzzling my hair. When I looked over and saw the two swans floating effortlessly down the stream, swimming very close to each other. Their two necks entwined every once and a while, in a loving embrace. I nudged Rafe. He looked over and when he saw the beautiful black swans, he squeezed my shoulders in acknowledgement. I looked up into his face and excitedly said,

"This is the first time I have seen these swans since we had our last picnic on the other side of the park, the first time you brought me here."

He reached down and played with the pendant that was hanging around my neck and then took my face in his hands and kissed me a kiss filled with love.

A doe and her baby fawn came out of the woods and walked right up to us and let us pet them. None of the animals seemed to be afraid of us, and in fact they treated us as though we were one of them.

I looked lovingly at Rafe.

"This is going to be a beautiful place to live. Long ago this was one of the happiest places I ever remembered being, and I never changed my view about it. But now, that you are here with me, not only is it beautiful, but it is absolutely perfect."

After a while we stood up and walked to the edge of the park and looked out over the valley below. It was luscious and green, with no pollution anywhere.

Rafe turned and looked at me. He put his arms around me and pulling me close, he looked into my eyes and said,

"Becca, I have a letter for us that was sent to us by Our Lord. He asked me not to open it until you and I were together. This seems like the perfect spot to read it."

I looked at him completely surprised. What could the Lord have to say to me after all the selfish ways that I acted?

Rafe took a folded piece of linen paper from his pocket, unfolded it and read it to me. All it said was:

Rafe & Becca
"Welcome to Eden, where the angels have
guarded the entrance since the fall of man
I have saved it just for you two lovers.
I leave it to you Rafe and to you Rebecca
to go forth and multiply, and fill the world
with the seed of your loins
and to become the New Adam & The New Eve."
I smiled at Rafe and said,
"With pleasure my darling."

We looked out over the valley below us once more. Rafe had his arm around me, and we both felt proud to be a part of this new world. We would live here filled with a love that would last for generations to come and our seed would fill the earth.

The Beginning!

Would you like to see your manuscript become a book?

If you are interested in becoming a PublishAmerica author, please submit your manuscript for possible publication to us at:

acquisitions@publishamerica.com

You may also mail in your manuscript to:

PublishAmerica
PO Box 151
Frederick, MD 21705

www.publishamerica.com